I0638295

FAR FROM OUR HILLS

A STORY FROM THE AMERICAN WAR IN VIETNAM

RV BARTLETT

FAR FROM OUR HILLS
A STORY FROM THE AMERICAN WAR IN VIETNAM
by
RV Bartlett

Copyright 2023 by RV Bartlett

All rights reserved

Title: Far From Our Hills: A Story From the War in Vietnam

Subjects: Vietnam War, 1968-1969| United States Air Force| Tactical intelligence| McNamara's Electronic Wall| Thailand, 1968-1969|Men in war-fiction|Psychology-destruction of values|Social conditions, 20th century.

LCCN: 2024903425
ISBN: 979-8-9883159-0-2 (paperback)
ISBN: 979-8-9883159-1-9 (ebook)
ISBN: 979-8-9883159-2-6 (hardcover)
ISBN: 979-8-9883159-4-0 (audio)

This is a work of fiction. Names, characters, places and incidents either are products of the author's imagination or are used fictitiously.

To Marylen, who
has been patient
And to Marcus and Andrew
With thanks to Van and to Claus

There is no resting place between the naïve and the ironic; and the nemesis of irony is absurdity.

Iris Murdoch, *The Sea, the Sea*

Between the intention and the act, life was often a tale told to the deaf.

Martin Cruz Smith, *The Girl from Venice*

What triumph can an ultimate chameleon claim if he gains not even the world, but only his basic continuity, at the price of his soul?
Stephen Jay Gould, *The Hedgehog, the Fox, and the Magister's Pox*

1

L et's just say that it began on Cape Cod. That's where the recon wing formed, and that's where Luke joined them for the war of Vietnam—a year out of college, a month out of intelligence school, a week out of survival school. Summer, nineteen sixty-seven. Hot and dry; pale, flat skies; hurt your eyes bright, with listless high cirrus that promised but never brought rain. And soon, not long after crossing the Bourne Bridge, like smoke from distant fires, the tang of pine cooking in the heat, and the dank of mudflats at low tide.

We *could* say that it began in tiny Mount Brookville, from whence he hailed. Population a hundred and fifty, give or take, depending, where barbed wire fences traced the hillsides like elevation lines on a topo map, sugar maples dotted the hills and the putt-putt of tractors filled the hollows from early spring to late fall. Where oncoming drivers still stopped in the middle of the road to catch up on the news, and late each afternoon the Holsteins, mixed with a few Jerseys and Guernseys, loped slowly and instinctively along well-worn paths of their own making towards the

barns for milking. And where a hand-painted plaque with
the names of all those who had served in World War Two
was tacked beside the front door of the white clapboard
community hall for all to see. In Mount Brookville the
houses were old and musty with the smell of history, and
history was the day before yesterday. Luke's closest friend
was Fergie Gunn, and in Fergie's parent's bedroom a Springfield rifle collected dust in a corner under the eaves, left
there a hundred years before by Fergie's great grandfather,
returned from the war to free the slaves. Luke's understanding of home included things like this, like mis-
matched wood chairs at white enamel kitchen tables and
doors in living rooms that opened on narrow stairways
leading to unheated second floor bedrooms. In the black
leather ammunition belt that hung from the Springfield
were seven small paper packages of gunpowder, the kind
soldiers tore open with their teeth to pour the powder down
the barrel. The cartridges were labeled "Richmond
Armory," and Luke wondered the chain of events where
Confederate ammunition wound up in a Union soldier's
pouch and then in the palm of his hand, and if, should he
tear one open, the gunpowder would still fire.

Or you could go back to the only photo on his mother's
bedroom dresser—her brother Tom—Uncle Tom—smiling
in the cockpit of his World War Two pilot trainer, white silk
scarf, lamb's wool collar on his leather flying jacket pulled
up to his ears. He flew B-17s and died in early nineteen forty-
five, two months after his twentieth birthday, and the photo
remained on the dresser until the late fifties, when finally
his mother turned her attention elsewhere.

If you were so inclined you could go back to nearly every
war, including the revolution. Tuttles served. So we'll just
say that for Luke it began on a base on Cape Cod, Patty Page

singing "Old Cape Cod," on his car radio as he drove over the Bourne Bridge.

The base was vast and pretty much empty, a mere shadow of its World War Two self. Once past the pines and onto the base proper it was mainly vacant fields, and Luke wondered what would grow there—tomatoes maybe, or corn, that liked good drainage, but not much else, not enough to make a decent living. Mount Brookville was rich loam, and he knew not a land so sterile and impermanent, sand blowing across the fields and through the pines and onto the roadways, covering the shoulders like a way of life.

He was billeted along with the other junior officers in three old barracks of peeling paint and curled linoleum, in a broad field where once had stood dozens more, populated now by quartets of concrete foundation blocks that looked like stubby tombstones. Their headquarters was in the abandoned Strategic Air Command building, two-story brick buried in the pines near the flight line where not so very long before KC-97 Stratotankers had waited on alert for the call to refuel the bombers on their way to Moscow. The recon wing used only the second floor, and the ready room on the first floor, once the beating heart of the SAC wing, was vacant and musty, filled with broken-down stuffed chairs and a couch that sat in the corner of the room like a sway-backed old horse in an over-grazed field. Whore's dust accumulated in the corners, and in the faded photos on the walls, nameless crewmembers still took a knee in front of their now-obsolete aircraft.

They flew Lockheed Super Constellations—Connies—the aircraft of three tails, the first long-range, intercontinental airplane to enter passenger service after World War Two. Four engines, propeller driven, a graceful body shaped like a porpoise. A third of a football field long, once carrying

90 passengers, now a crew of 17. Dragged out of storage in the Mojave and reconditioned. Engines rebuilt, tip tanks added so they could fly twenty-four hours at a time if need be, and filled with electronics for listening to North Vietnamese trucks moving supplies down the Ho Chi Minh trail to South Vietnam.

Soon the Connies were a presence on the flight line, camouflage green and brown with white underbellies next to the dull grey early warning radome Connies and the air defense fighter interceptors permanently stationed at the air base. The camouflage made the recon Connies look like serious weapons of war, which they were not, not directly, anyway. By late August they were nearly all there, men and machines, and the runway was busy with the great lumbering Connies taking off and landing, fledglings taking wing, flying training missions out past Nantucket over the grey, corrugated North Atlantic.

For practice they tracked National Guard trucks grinding through the woods of the nearby Army camp, their mission so secret the Guardsmen didn't even know what they were doing. Then it was all there in the *Boston Globe,* about the Connies and the sensors they listened to on the ground, some for picking up vibrations, some for picking up sound, all part of McNamara's electronic wall that was supposed to stop the endless stream of trucks moving down the Trail, and even that they called themselves Batcats and wore polka-dot ascots like Wonder Bread wrapping with their flight suits, and patches on their breasts depicting mythological black panthers with wings, and that they were going to be flying out of Thailand, which even they hadn't known.

When they weren't flying—weekdays, anyway—they were in the officer's club bar or watching television in the lounge of their quarters. The Red Sox were hot that summer, and they sprawled on the chairs and sofas and lay on the worn linoleum floor to watch, and the aluminum chains made from the snap tabs of their beer cans festooned the walls like garland. Weekends they joined the vacationers in the Falmouth bars, the women in their seersucker blouses and matching shorts, the men in rumpled chinos and button-down Gant shirts and Weejuns without socks. Vee-neck sweaters tossed over their shoulders for the evening chill. The music was changing, Jefferson Airplane and the Doors supplanting Frankie Valli and Petula Clark, while Sergeant Pepper announced the second coming of the Beatles, and the purifying smell of pot wafted through the air like incense from a swinging censer.

For Luke it was like college all over again, only now with money in his pocket. When he wasn't training he drove the Cape—Hyannis and Sandwich and Wellfleet and Truro and the seashore, once taking the ferry out to Martha's Vineyard to see the machine gun emplacements at Gay Head, his new car small and English, with a proper sound to it, and he loved gearing down through the rotaries, taking the corners hard. And yes there were rumblings in the cities and on the campuses, days of challenge to the time-honored way of thinking, but most of that was about Martin Luther King and civil rights, and there was none of it on the Cape, not around Falmouth, anyway. Vietnam wasn't a war, not yet, not really. Sure there had been the Tonkin Gulf incident, and Operation Rolling Thunder was dropping bombs on North Vietnam, and yes the Marines were in Da Nang, but nothing much was happening and everyone still believed what they were told, no questions asked, least of all about how the war was being fought, and why.

Then on a cold and rainy day late in November they

deployed to Thailand, to the flatlands of the Khorat Plateau, where at first they lived in tents while construction of their quarters and barracks proceeded apace, but it was the dry season and it didn't matter much. Nights were cool but not cold, and they knew that their quarters would soon be finished. They began flying over the Trail, tracking the mechanical spoor of trucks, and before long they were in their groove, flying 24/7, two hours to station, two hours back, eight hours flying circles over the jungle, and already monotony was setting in.

2

This day over Laos, dawn creeping over the jungle, soft shadows slowly emerging, revealing ravines and ridges, undulating to the horizon like a vast, empty, rolling sea. The Connie turning in its orbit; the sun's first rays sliding slowly around the cockpit; the doppler thrum of the engines pervading like a heartbeat.

Mists seeped up through the jungle canopy like wisps of smoke from smoldering fires. Luke imagined a scene below: A band waking. Women breathing life into smoldering ashes. He put faces on them: Tribal? Pathet Lao? North Vietnamese? This last thought brought a feeling of unease, and he pushed it out of his mind. *Innocents.* Yes, innocents. Better. Wearing hand-me-down western clothes pulled from missionary barrels like the ones he helped fill in his church back home in central New York, back in Mount Brookville, raggedy pants with patched knees, tee shirts with faded and incongruous names written across their chests: a car repair shop in Skokie, Illinois, maybe, or maybe the faded orange of the Baltimore Orioles. Letters barely legible, logos unintelligible. More women appear, carrying bundles of sticks, hems of their worn house dresses, tents on their small bodies, soaked with morning dew. They're followed by men, and the men—unease intruded into his overactive imagination—the men carry Kalashnikovs, the ubiquitous Soviet bloc automatic rifle, and there, shining dully in the open doorway of a thatched roof hut, the launch tube of a shoulder-fired missile.

He wondered the lay of the land, places to camp and build a fire. Reminded himself of the topo map stowed in his briefcase back in the intelligence center. But the map had blank spaces, white spots marked "unexplored" that were like holes through to prehistory. Where would one build a fire? Fetch water. Take a dump. The irony didn't escape him—super-sophisticated equipment, the best, and yes, it was clever, but still their maps said, *we don't know*.

His roommate, Alan Gropper, the co-pilot, sat in the left seat. "Over here, Lucas," he said. Gropper pronounced like Groper, he said, but with two 'p's. Spoken slowly, choosing his few words carefully. When he started a sentence he sometimes paused while he considered the best way to say something, then proceeded, building an idea, as if he were a speaker of great truths, which, much of the time, he was. Lucas instead of Luke. He was their airplane incarnate— ponderous, dependable—and the plane was his second skin. He sensed everything, knew instinctively what to do, situations far beyond those in a flight manual, or what he'd learned from instructors. The accepted wisdom was clear— don't trust your gut, rely on your instruments. For Gropper it was different. Flight instruments only confirmed what he already sensed, much of it hands-on and taught by Major Woodrum, their aircraft commander, much of it his own sixth sense about things mechanical and how they moved through space and time.

Gropper motioned outside the cockpit. His olive drab baseball hat was perched far over on the left side of his head, blocking out the morning sun and reminding Luke of the dairy farmers back home, so many of whom wore their hats on the sides of their heads to keep fabric between their scalps and the cow's flanks when they were milking, fending off ringworm. In a sort of reverse Proustian moment, Gropper's hat brought the treacly smell of ringworm salve to mind, and then thought of Fergie Gunn sitting in the pew in front of him in church, the left side of his neck slathered in salve, and then the smell. He smiled to himself, and then remembered that Fergie was now in Pleiku. Seven now from Mount Brookville. He counted them off in his mind. Too many. Too many for their small hamlet.

"There's a search and rescue going on down there," Gropper said. "A Sandy went in." A low and slow attack plane. He pushed back in his seat to make room for Luke to lean in front of him.

Luke stood and looked out Gropper's side of the cockpit. Helicopter blades flashed in the sun, so close to the jungle they could have been the shiny leaves of an exotic tree.

"Who is it?" Luke said.

Gropper shrugged. "I think. I think. Isn't that...isn't that, you know, isn't that your area?" he said. He reached overhead and cycled through his radio to the search and rescue frequency. Fiddled for a moment, then settled back to listen to the chopper pilot. The response of the downed pilot was only static:

"We're gonna get you out, buddy, hold on."

Static.

"Pop your smoke."

In a moment, pink smoke drifted up through the canopy, connecting what Luke was seeing to what he was hearing.

He recalled the phrase from survival school about which end of the flare to pull: Smoke in daylight, flame at night. "The smooth end produces pink smoke," the sergeant said, speaking to the group of them gathered deep in the Rocky Mountains near Spokane. "The other end, the one circled by a row of nipples, is for darkness and produces a white-hot flare visible for miles. And what do you do at night, gentlemen? You feel titties." Luke knew he'd never get it confused.

"We're taking fire," the chopper said.

Static.

"Roger, Sandy, we've got you covered, we're lowering the collar."

Static.

"We're not leaving without you...got you covered..."

Luke imagined the horse collar dropping through the canopy, appearing like a mechanical ghost, hard yellow edges obvious in the soft lush foliage. The bad guys closing in, dark shadows moving through the brush, materializing into human form. Bullets whirring through the leaves.

They crept over the green canopy; Gropper scanned his instruments.

Captain Bronfmann appeared in the cockpit. One of the two navigators. Short, given to pudge. Flat top haircut broken by a cowlick on his forehead. Pockmarked complexion. Not a pleasant sight. "Bronfmann with two n's," he said whenever he introduced himself, always adding, "I'm not Jewish."

Yeah, but you are an asshole, Luke always said to himself whenever he heard Bronfmann clarify the spelling of his name.

"Lieutenant Tuttle," Bronfmann announced with false heartiness. "Changeover. Vacate! Your men are calling you."

"I doubt it," Luke answered. "I want to hear this," he added, but he stood and slipped out of the way. "Here you go, Bronfmann."

Bronfmann slid into the right seat. "*Captain* Bronfmann to you, Lieutenant."

"Right. Captain Bronfmann. *Sir.*" He watched Bronfmann to see if he recognized sarcasm, if he would rise to the bait, slight as it was. He never knew for sure, not with Bronfmann, the only officer he knew below the rank of major who insisted—now and then, for no apparent reason—that junior officers address him by rank. Sometimes resentment showed in his eyes. This day, nothing.

He slipped behind the co-pilot's seat, squeezing in next to Sergeant Stevenson, the flight engineer, who was scanning his instruments, rotely assessing the mechanical health of the airplane.

Major Woodward, their aircraft commander, came onto the flight deck, nearly bumping into Luke. "Lieutenant Tuttle," he said. "Que pasa?"

"Nada, nada limonada, sir," Luke answered. Their ritual greeting. He couldn't remember when or how it had started. Woody was odd, quick to laugh at little things, mouth open, head thrown back, tongue sort of humped out. A great pilot but a terrible officer, his uniform always wrinkled, as if he had slept in it, his hair messy. Old for a major, having entered the service as a sergeant pilot in the last months of World War Two. Stories abounded about him, how someone at squadron had to rewrite his officer efficiency reports, how he never showed respect for superior officers. But then one day a general from 7th Air Force in Saigon came to Khorat for a look-see, and the first person he asked for was Woody. How Colonel Crawford, their squadron commander, had steamed, especially after all the time he had spent preparing his dog-and-pony show for the general. Gropper laughed when he told Luke about it. "The general flew RB-66s with Woody way back when." A twin-engined jet bomber. "Woody taught him everything he knows about flying, same as me. He thinks Woody's the best pilot in the Air Force."

"Is he?" Luke had asked.

"Maybe," Gropper said. "Probably. One time...one flight, they lost both engines and the general was getting ready to eject, but Woody stopped him. Said no, he could bring it in, and he did. They slid off the end of the runway and lost their landing gear, dug a groove through the grass to the fence, but he did it, he brought it in."

And this day. "What's happening?" Woody asked.

"Search and rescue," Gropper said, getting up from his chair.

Woody nodded. "And you, Tuttle? Whataya seein?" he said.

Luke shook his head. Nothing, or close to nothing. He hated admitting it. They'd been on station since three in the morning, and while they'd logged some convoys, mostly threes and fours, nearly all had gotten through. These days Task Force Alpha, TFA, was in charge, the command center at Nakhon Phanom. NKP. TFA at NKP. Their computers were finally up and running, most of the time anyway, collecting the data and reporting the convoys, but for whatever reason, response time had slowed, and now it seemed like most of the convoys were slipping through. It hadn't been that way in the beginning. In those first months after they'd arrived in Southeast Asia, the crews from the Fifty-third were the ones calling the shots, radioing targets to the airborne command center, and it had been but a few short minutes from when they first spotted a convoy until a fighter jet laid ordnance on the target. Not so much anymore. Since TFA had taken over Luke's crew continued to track the convoys, for practice and in case TFA's computers failed, and they would log in the trucks, red circle the convoys, and then sit back and watch the flashes of the fighters dropping their ordnance, incredulous at how long it had taken from when they'd first seen the convoys and the ordnance went in. Not a long time, but enough. By the time the ordnance went in the convoys were long gone. They'd wait to see if the convoys showed up farther down the Trail, and sure enough they did, time and again. It was frustrating at so many levels, and not what Luke had thought it would be, way back when. On the Cape. No one had said that within months they'd be flying back up to a computer, nor that the computers wouldn't be all that effective. It left him with a gnawing, vacant feeling that he couldn't shake.

He left the flight deck and headed aft to his domain, the intelligence center, past the flight crew's bunks and the galley airline passenger seats, stopping to pour himself a cup of coffee. For a moment sat at the galley table, looking out the porthole. Cloudless sky, his view that of the two port engines churning relentlessly. Ten, fifteen minutes staring into empty sky, his mind mostly vacant. He lit a cigarette, then continued aft, past the navigators' table on his left, unoccupied as it almost always was throughout their flights, and the radio operator on his right. Sergeant Goodin. Frank. He nodded, but Goodin ignored him, ever a cipher, isolated within his earphones, listening, rarely speaking, for some quirk of personality preferring to separate himself from the rest of the crew on the ground as well, fitting neither with the flight crew nor with the intelligence crew. This morning eating a baloney sandwich, crumbs scattered on his desk and piling up on the floor all around. Luke silently cursed.

Sweeping up at the end of the flight was his men's job, and Goodin's position was always a mess. They'd even been dinged on an evaluation flight for Goodin's mess, and Luke's protests that they'd swept it once, and that Goodin had torn into yet another sandwich just before landing fell on deaf ears, and he and his crew resented the hell out of him.

Then on the left the electronic warfare officer's position, reserved for those times when they had to fly near where radar-controlled antiaircraft batteries, 57 millimeter, that could easily reach their altitude, had been spotted. On those missions an ewo flew along just in case, to jam the 57's radar. Not so this mission.

The aircraft's electronics, a bank of shelves of communication receivers and transmitters and the receivers for their sensors, sat just beyond the ewo's position, and across from that the two in-flight electronics technician's seats, at the moment empty, the technicians, Sergeant Brooks, the only Black man on the crew, and Airman Lopez, napping in the aft bunks, awaiting a call to fix equipment.

He came to the intelligence section, separated fore and aft from the rest of the plane by blackout curtains. Three rows of seats, one on each side of the aisle, all facing aft, his own first, on the right, facing the command console. The intelligence analysts sat beyond, each at their own console, where the numbered lights flashed on a screen when the sensors activated.

Just past the intelligence section was a second galley table, across from the five bunks for the intelligence crew and in-fight techs. And on the right, the main aircraft door. Just past that the electronic techs' cabinets and workbench. The latrine took up the rear of the plane, tucked into the shrinking cone of the fuselage, with a curtain for privacy, which was seldom pulled shut.

He drew back the curtain behind his position, casting light onto Sergeant Tolliver, his assistant, who was manning the command console. Tolliver looked up. "Lieutenant," he said. He made to vacate Luke's seat, but Luke shook his head. Instead he visited each of the analysts, checking their activity—Sergeant Jubal McAuley, Airmen Hugo Tanaka and John Rolphe—the fourth analyst's seat empty for lack of sensor strings to monitor that mission.

"Lieutenant," McAuley said as Luke looked over his shoulder. He touched the bill of his baseball cap with his forefinger in an informal salute. Earlier in the mission it had been moderately busy, and the top of his log bristled with check marks, many of them convoys circled in red. Now his sheet was nearly blank, a few random activations, nothing even slightly resembling a diagonal pattern, as if the light of the morning sun had chased the trucks, like cockroaches, back into the shadows.

Across from him, Hugo Tanaka. "Lieutenant Tuttle!" he said enthusiastically, which was how he greeted everyone, as if it were the first time every time, happy to meet you. A tall man, broad cheeks and a quick smile. From Honolulu, the grandson of Nisei. His father had worked at Pearl during the war, he said, whenever the subject of the Japanese internment camps came up, proving that the need to move the Japanese Americans out because they were supposedly untrustworthy was all bullshit bigotry. Played tight end for Punahou. He watched Luke look over his empty log and shrugged. "What you see is what you get," he said.

And John Constance, leaning back in his chair, eating while he watched his screens, digging into a ration cup of peanut butter with his finger, a plastic knife taped to his ruler so that he could reach his screen and flip the toggle switch to reset it without sitting up. He dipped his finger into the cup and held it up and offered Luke a taste.

"You're all heart," Luke said.

The older enlisted men on Luke's crew—Tolliver, McAuley, Frank Molino, who was sleeping in one of the aft bunks—were all sergeants of one rank or another, smart and easy to work with. Over the months since the Fifty-third's role had diminished, they had toned down their expectations, refusing to let the fruitless missions eat into their attitudes. The well-honed survival techniques of careerists. His junior enlisted, his airmen one stripe, John Constance, (Don't ask why they picked John Constance to be the one called by his full name, to distinguish him from John Rolfe, but they did. It was something that had just happened, and seemed to fit.), Tanaka, Saint Lawrence and John Rolfe, were much the same. They joined the Air Force to beat the draft, and had no intention of staying in for more than their original commitment. They were Luke's cultural peers, the product of the same life experiences, all in college when Luke was, tuned to the same culture—music, sports, sex. Beer blasts. Hopes and dreams. They could have been fraternity brothers. John Constance had been working on his Ph.D., and when he dropped out, quickly joined the Air Force before the draft could get him. To a man they were all marking time until they could get out.

Luke returned to his position.

"Anything?" he asked Sergeant Tolliver.

Tolliver shook his head.

"Task Force Alpha?"

"Not a word."

Luke took his seat. Put on his headset, adjusted his microphone. Took a cigarette out of his left arm pocket, lit up, took a long inhale. Scanned his screens. A sensor light flashed. He turned a knob, rotating through all the screens to see what was happening. Nothing.

"*So Lieutenant,*" Tanaka said on the intercom. "*Whatta you know about the Sandy?*"

"*No idea.*"

"*You mean they don't tell you?*" McAuley said, and snickered. Of the three sergeants, McAuley was the least comfortable to be around, often making cryptic comments alluding to Luke's youth and naiveté, besides his disappointment with their mission. Luke found it easiest to ignore him.

Still, Luke was curious, and he wondered if Task Force Alpha knew. He pressed his floor switch with his foot, and was greeted first by the familiar rush of white noise as the encoding scrambler kicked in. "*Igloo,*" he said, "*this is Batcat Two-four. How copy?*"

"*Got you fivers, Two-four. Whattaya have? Over.*"

"*Nothing. We were just wondering. Do you know anything about the Sandy that went in on our orbit this morning? Over.*"

"*Nope.*"

"*You know what he was doing there? Over.*"

"*Dunno. Over.*"

Luke sensed disinterest. "*Could you find out, maybe? Over.*"

Silence. Luke tried to imagine what was going on, who he was talking to, if his request had caused the man to move across a room to talk to someone, or maybe just stay where he was and holler. He had no idea what TFA looked like. Their voices came to him out of the ether, disembodied, unknown. Some spoke with authority, some not. There were missions when he felt like he was talking to the *Sanctum Santorum*, sensed it in TFA's tone of voice and choice of words. This was someone who knew, he would think, if only he could get him to talk. But no, never. No one ever seemed to know what was going on near their orbits, not in their entirety. Typically his radio remained silent. But this day, later, after he had practically forgotten, and for no apparent reason, Igloo got back to him. *"Two-four, this is Igloo. So sorry. About your question. No one has any idea, not here, anyway. Nothing."*

"And the search and rescue? Do you know anything about that? Did they get the pilot out? Over."

"Oh, that we know. That's a roger, Two-four. I do know that. They got him. Igloo out."

Luke picked at his thoughts, his feeling that since TFA's computers had come on line, they had become an ill-informed sideshow. He was struggling to come to grips with it, though he wasn't sure anyone gave a shit. It wasn't just the disconnect, it was the attitude, the men who didn't seem to care, who didn't seem engaged. He thought of them as bureaucrats, paper pushers who cared little about what was happening beyond their personal walls. He recalled an incident that had stuck in his craw since mid-February, during the early days, when otherwise things had seemed to be going so well. They had been flying support for Khe Sanh, calling in the movements of the North Vietnamese to the Marine Corps.

Tanaka had called him on the intercom. *"Lieutenant! I've got something. Listen to my acoustic!"*

Luke dialed in. At first there was nothing, then the acoustic came on, and he could hear the ambient noise of jungle. Ordinarily background noise wasn't enough to activate an acoustic, and he wondered what had turned it on. Then he heard the unmistakable clank of a tracked vehicle.

"You hear that?" Tanaka asked, excited.

"I do," Luke answered. *"How long's it been going on?"*

"Not long. A few minutes. Are you thinking it's what I'm thinking?"

"I think so."

"It's a tank. We've caught a damn tank!"

Luke heard multiple clanks, some on top of each other. *"More than one," he said.*

"I think so," Tanaka said. *"I can't tell how many, but there's several,"* he added.

Luke was excited. He radioed his contact at the command post. *"I've got tracked vehicles,"* he said, careful not to say 'tank,' knowing not to jump to conclusions, sliding into intelligence speak. *"Possible tank."* Not probable. Possible.

The disembodied voice to which he was reporting, an unknown person in an unknown post, presumably somewhere in the middle of Khe Sanh, said, *"I don't think so."*

"Whattaya mean, you don't think so? Over."

"I mean there's no evidence of tracked vehicles in your area. None. Zip. I don't know what you think you're hearing, but you're not hearing tracked vehicles. The jungle's too thick."

"This is the evidence," Luke said. He wanted to add 'asshole,' but refrained. *"We've got a clanking noise. We've got clanks."*

Ground responded. *"I'm sure you've got something that sounds like tracked vehicles, but I've got my photo intel map right here, and you're looking at jungle, impenetrable jungle, and you don't have tracked vehicles. I don't know what it is you have, but it's not a tracked vehicle."*

Luke argued, but to no avail. It was beyond frustrating, sliding into incompetent. When they landed he reported to Colonel Reilly, the chief of intelligence, and debriefed him on what they had heard. And that they had been unable to convince ground control. He wasn't sure it would do any good to tell Reilly; at that point he didn't know about him. Easy to talk to, never pulling rank, often encouraging Luke

to be frank and open. Still, he wasn't sure how much
Costello was engaged, how well tuned in he was to what was
happening, or if anybody in the hierarchy even listened to
him. He wondered. Then, a week later, Reilly called him in.
He shook his head. "I reported it up the chain, everything
you said. Like you, I didn't say tanks, I said tracked vehicles.
I couldn't tell if they were taking me seriously. I mean, yessir,
nosir, thank you sir. And now I know. They were tanks. Five
of 'em. Night before last they overran the Special Forces
base at Lang Vei. They couldn't stop 'em. The Army. South
Vietnamese. Montagnards. Some Lao. They didn't have a
chance, not a snowball's chance in hell."

Luke looked at Reilly in disbelief.

"I know," Reilly said. "I know."

"Did anyone acknowledge that we warned them?"

"Are you kidding? Apologies? In this man's Air Force?
Admissions of error?" He shook his head.

Luke wondered what it would have taken for him to
have gotten through. Could he have? Was it his fault? Was it
all his fault? Could someone else have pushed through,
made the man on the ground, at control, listen? Men had
died. A position had been taken. Because of that moment,
because he failed to get the man to listen, Khe Sanh had
become more vulnerable. At that moment, way back then,
when Costello called him in, his blood had run cold. There
was no avoiding it. It _was_ him. It was _his_ mistake. He wanted
to push the thought out of his mind, but he couldn't. He was
afraid he was becoming like the others, the other bureaucrats in this bureaucrat's war where victories were claimed
just on body counts. He wondered whether someone else,
like one of the men he had gone through intelligence officer's school with, back in Texas, that had come with him to
the Fifty-third, have gotten through? He feared maybe some

one of them could have. Pitched a fit. Made the man listen. Not given up. The whole incident had left him with a sick feeling of inadequacy that lingered like a sore throat. When the chips were down, for all his self-confidence, he had failed.

This night he reimagined the scene at Lang Vei. A small outpost, maybe atop a hill. Jungle vegetation cleared for open fields of fire. Barbed wire all around. He imagined the tanks moving inexorably through the barbed wire, breaking through the steel strands like they were cobwebs. He shuddered. Imagined the gunfire, the shouts, the screams of men hit and dying. Couldn't imagine what it had been like to be caught in such a hopeless situation.

His screens came into focus; the drone of the Connie's engines reasserted itself. He stared at his panel. Lit another cigarette. Frustration edged with despair floated through his mind. How had it happened that they could have gone from useful to useless? How had he become useless? And now they were just an airborne link. He was afraid to admit it, but he knew there would not be another chance, there would be no moment when he could vindicate himself, no moment when he and his crew could prove useful—to help the grunts on the ground trying to hold back the incoming tide. This was the way things were going to be from now on, and he just had to learn to live with it.

3

His pilot's intercom light flashed, and he toggled up to listen. Woody. *"Tuttle, we're goin' to Blue, replacing Four-eight. They've got engine trouble. Two–five launched early an'll be here in half an hour to take our place."*

Luke radioed Four-eight, who briefed him on their activity, which was pretty much the same as his own, damn near nothing. When Two-five arrived they left for their new orbit: the engines surged, the Connie's wings dipped, they pulled out of orbit and headed north.

Blue was like where they'd been, dense jungle to the horizon except for the northern part of the orbit, where jungle gave way to the vast undulating moonscape of Khe Sanh, still smoldering in the distance. A few weeks before the joint Army and Marine task force had finally broken through the siege, and now only a token force of Marines remained, soon to be withdrawn, and there was but scant evidence of habitation and the months' long fight for survival, leaving one to wonder if anyone in the higher command had ever spoken to the French or heard of Dien

Bien Phu, or how it had happened that first class shock troops, men trained to attack, had wound up manning a garrison in the first place.

Towards noon Tolliver took over and he crawled into one of the aft bunks. He slept until mid-afternoon, when he rolled out and went forward. The galley passenger seats were full of sleeping men—O'Keefe, the other flight engineer, Brooks and Perez, the electronic techs. Brooks with his barracks cap draped across his eyes to block the western sun when it poured through the starboard galley porthole each time they headed south on their orbit.

Luke drew himself yet another cup of coffee and went aft to relieve Tolliver. Outside the sky was clear and the sun was beating down and the still, quiet air inside the aircraft had the feeling of a lazy summer afternoon. Nothing stirred. He took his seat, settled in. Drank his coffee, smoked another cigarette. The chatter on the intercom was sparse; the drone of engines had been with them now for hours.

The pilot's intercom flashed. Gropper. "*Lucas, we've been extended. Our relief aborted halfway to orbit. We're gonna be here for a while longer.*"

Luke groaned. "*Shit! How long?*"

"*Probably 'til dark. If it's a problem, we'll put into Da Nang to refuel.*"

A brief thrill. Da Nang, a chance to see the real war. He passed the news to the analysts.

Later, much later, they left orbit. Shortly they landed at Da Nang, engines roaring as the propellers reversed pitch. They rolled down the runway, slowed and turned, turned again. The lights in the plane were low. Of a sudden there was a rush of fresh, tropic air—someone had popped the aft door. Relief. It had never smelled so good—humid, rich. Luke reveled in it. He stood at his position. Looked aft.

Lawrence and Tanaka and John Constance were gathered at the open door. He joined them.

They rolled along the flight line. Their eyes adjusted to the darkness. Shapes resolved into aircraft. Fighter planes— F-4 Phantoms, F-100s. Sandies. Helicopters large and small. C-130 and C-119 transports. The Forward Air Controllers' Cessnas. Others they didn't recognize. Dozens of aircraft, rows upon rows, conveying a sense of overwhelming power. He felt like the country boy he was, come to the big city, his mouth open in wonder at the tall buildings. So many! They seemed to be taxiing forever and *still* there were aircraft along the way, until finally they pulled into a refueling area where a tank truck waited. Crewmen jumped out of the cab at their arrival. They craned their heads outside the open door and watched one of the crewman set a ladder against the port wing and climb up to fit the refueling hose.

Stevenson stepped through the over-wing porthole and onto the wing, a wooden stick in hand for measuring fuel in the tank. He stood by the refueling crewman, silhouetted against the night sky. Gropper joined Luke and the others at the open door. Random flashes on the near horizon caught their attention. A moment later they heard a *whumpf!* "Shit," Gropper muttered. Though none of them had ever heard the sound before, they knew at once it was mortar fire.

"How long is this going to take?" Luke asked.

"Not long. We're just going to pump enough to get us home. We don't need to top off. Not unless...Maybe we should go to Singapore. Wanna go to Singapore? That'll take longer. We can fill up for Singapore."

"Not if it means we sit here like sitting ducks while you top off. Maybe next time," Luke said. The others laughed.

Another flash, another *whumpf*, then another. Closer. The mortars were heading toward them. As ridiculous as they knew it was, they felt like the mortars were meant for them, that the VC were tracking their way to the refueling area.

The ground crewman pulled the hose out, stood by while Stevens dropped to his knees and inserted his measuring stick into the tank.

"Whattaya got?" Gropper called.

"Enough," Stevens called.

"Modern technology," Gropper said, nodding at Stevens and his measuring stick. He headed forward. "Close it up," he said as he left. "We're getting out of here. Next stop, Khorat. Next flight, Singapore."

Luke took his seat, put on his headset and tuned to the chatter between the cockpit and the ground, "I've got one two three four blades" *whit whit whit whit* in the background as the number one engine turned over, slowly, painfully slowly, and didn't catch. He thought he could hear the mortar fire in the background moving closer; he thought maybe there was tension now in the ground crewman's voice *"I've got one two three four five six blades"* whit *whit whit whit whit whit ti ti ti ti ti* like a monstrous mechanical creature of the tropical night waking but not becoming alert until finally, finally the Connie's number one engine sprang to life. Luke pictured the cloud of oily exhaust blowing aft. *"Pull the cart,"* Gropper said, and one by one the other three engines started and revved. The Connie began moving slowly, ponderously, much too ponderously to suit Luke. They turned and bounced and Luke figured they were heading for the runway. He wished he had a porthole so he could see what was happening. Then decided he'd rather not know, not if he couldn't do anything about it. Ignorance was truly bliss. They bumped along, turned again and stopped. No, don't stop, he thought to himself, don't stop. Not tonight. Just keep going.

The power surged, the engines roared and Luke pictured blue flames shooting like comet tails out of the engine stacks, flashing brilliantly in the darkness. Then they were on takeoff roll and the aft of the Connie was swaying back and forth like it always did on takeoff and then they were airborne and heading home and finally Luke breathed a sigh of relief. Finally, he thought. Finally.

4

They got to the station in time to catch the midnight train to Bangkok. Gropper and Luke and, unfortunately, at least from Luke's point of view, Bronfmann. Not Luke's druthers, but he and Gropper hadn't seen a choice. They'd been talking about going to Bangkok on the crew bus while they rode from the aircraft back to Wing, and Bronfmann had overheard them and invited himself along. "That's great," he'd said. "The midnight special? I've been itchin' to take that one." Gropper had shrugged. Done deal. This was their first trip to Bangkok by train, and Bronfmann had made the trip many times, mainly by himself. He was a train nut, and was bound and begot to get on every train he could. He'd even managed to get to Chiang Mai, which had required changing trains at a remote station where no one spoke English. This was his element. He wandered the rail yards of Khorat like an industrial anthropologist, photographing rolling stock, diesels and steam engines—especially the steam engines—exploring their provenance. Photos of Thai steam engines lined his room, ancient coal-driven beasts the Japanese had left behind, unintelligible Thai writing painted like graffiti on the sides of the tenders, atop the shadows of painted-out Japanese ideograms. Riding in the taxi to the station, he couldn't stop talking about the trip to come, how many cars there would likely be and what kind of locomotive would pull them.

The station was old and colonial, thick white walls mottled with mildew, high ceilings, teak-trimmed archways and windows. Palm trees and white-painted rocks lined the semi-circular drive leading to the entrance. Inside, walls stained with age, floor tiles cracked like spider-webs. Ceiling fans churned slowly and precariously, rocking back and forth as if held in place by just one last bolt, worn out from years of having to move heavy tropic air.

Their footsteps echoed off the floor. The stationmaster appeared from nowhere, clad in the ubiquitous khaki of the Thai petite bureaucrat. He bowed his head. "*Khrup, khrup,*" Sir, sir. He brought his hands together in a wai of respectful greeting. "You go Bangkok?" he asked, still bowing. Too much, Luke thought, too much, much too much, but good nonetheless; this man would take care of them.

"Bangkok," Bronfmann said. "Midnight train. First class."

At the ticket window the stationmaster awakened a young man sleeping with his head on his arms behind the grate, and in but a moment they walked away with tickets in hand.

The stationmaster led them to the first-class waiting room. Enlisted a scrawny, ancient man leaning against a pillar, half asleep, to take their bags. The man was barefoot and wore a faded Thai sarong pulled through his legs and tucked into his waist, and a tattered sleeveless tee-shirt with more holes than fabric. He was skin and bones and looked like he could barely carry himself, let alone baggage, yet he hefted their three bags easily. "No probrem," the station-master said. "No probrem. Number one gee-eye. You wait here, first-class. Is very nice."

"There is dining car?" Bronfmann asked, speaking slowly and loudly, and in his own pidgin, being of the type who believed that volume and clarity of a word unknown to a non-English speaker would help him be understood. The stationmaster nodded his head. "Ah, yes, *khrup*, number one dining car, you rike, you rike *mag mag*. Number one. Is very nice."

They sat on worn cushions on pew-like benches midst a forest of potted ferns that dipped lightly in the air from the fans. They were alone. Luke expected Humphrey Bogart or Sydney Greenstreet to slip through the ferns at any moment, white linen suits and Panama hats. He basked in the feeling of a thirties' black and white movie, a bygone and simple time, easy, unhurried travel and obsequious servants. A long way from Mount Brookville, he said to himself. Five days of leave stretched before him. If the midnight train was late he didn't care. If it broke down on the way to Bangkok, he didn't care. If it happened in some small village along the way, so much the better. He would get off the train and wander the streets and if he got hungry he would buy food from sidewalk vendors. When another train came through, whenever, he would take it, go wherever it went. He needed a break from too many hours trapped in a Connie flying a useless mission, and he craved a feeling of nothing.

Noises erupted in the entrance hall, American voices

and the sing-song of the stationmaster. Luke was disappointed: He wanted this moment all to himself and his
feeling of relief to continue unbothered and to not have to
contend with making conversation with another human
being. But he brightened as the voices drew nearer, recog-
nizing the voices of Tanaka and Lawrence, the tall Tanaka,
with his wry sense of humor, who missed nothing, and was
always watching if not always commenting, and Lawrence,
shorter, but one of those short people whose presence
makes them seem larger than they are. Devilishly hand-
some, cleft chin, slightly hooded eyes that made him seem
almost malevolent, which he wasn't. Instead, except for
when he was concentrating on something, like the sensor
activations on his position, he was always smiling, everybody's friend, ever ready with a quick greeting. Between
them they brought a cohesive warmth to the backend crew,
and, Luke noticed, to many of the flight crew, at least to
those open to égalité and fraternité. Luke treasured them.
"Lieutenants," Lawrence said. "Captain Bronfmann. You
officers going to Bangkok?"

The train whistled in the distance. "You cut this one
close," Bronfmann said. Tanaka and Lawrence laughed. "If
you only knew," Tanaka said. "We didn't decide to go until
an hour ago."

"Lucky us," Bronfmann said.

The train pulled into the station. "RSR number 756, 4, 6,
O," Bronfmann said, looking at the locomotive.

"You know this shit?" Lawrence said. "That is so cool."
Bronfmann nodded, pleased to have someone acknowledge
his expertise.

They stood on the platform as the slowing cars, for the
most part stainless steel and modern, slipped by like frames

in a slide show. A car in the middle, and the last car, at the end of the platform, were older, painted metal with wood-trim windows. "First class," Bronfmann announced, nodding at the last car. "There'll be sconces with flowers. The old-fashioned way."

The old man hefted their bags into the vestibule of the nearest car, a second-class sleeper. They followed, hastily tipping. Ten *baht*. Fifty cents. The old man wai-ed in response, bowing deeply. Luke wondered if they'd over-tipped. Word was that the Americans with their full wallets had destroyed the local economy, inflating expectations beyond the common man's means, and he was thinking that this was maybe where it started. They picked up their bags and headed down the aisle towards the rear, trying not to bump into the drawn curtains of the second-class bunks. A night light at the end of the car guided their way. Heads poked through the curtains as they walked by.

The conductor came up the aisle towards them, counting heads. He pointed towards empty bunks.

"No," Bronfmann said. "First class." He waved his ticket at the conductor and tried to slip past him.

The conductor shook his head, holding out his arm to stop Bronfmann. "*Mai mee* first crass. No have. First crass awr gone. You sreep here."

"We paid first class." Bronfmann said. He held up his ticket again and tried to push past.

"No first crass. Second crass. You look." He pointed out Thai words on the ticket. "Second crass," he repeated.

"We paid first class," Bronfmann repeated.

"This ticket second crass," the conductor said.

"Shit!" Bronfmann exclaimed. "That little fucker!" He tried a different tack. "You have first class, I pay."

"*Mai mee,*" the conductor said. "You sreep here. *Mai mee* first crass." He pointed again to open bunks. More heads poked out of the curtains, all Thai. They watched for a moment, and then ducked back in, as if, having discovered that the noise came from the American *farung,* the big noses, it was to be expected. And that there was nothing they could do about it.

All except Bronfmann put their bags in open bunks. "Dining car?" Gropper asked.

The conductor nodded towards the front of the train, pointing with his chin in the Thai manner. "You coming?" Gropper asked Bronfmann.

Bronfmann scowled and reluctantly put his bag on a bunk, glaring at the conductor as he followed the others forward.

THE GALLEY WAS CLOSED, chairs stacked on tables, a forest of legs pointing upward like barren tree trunks that swayed back and forth with the increasing speed of the train. The car was old and worn and the faded walls seemed to absorb the meagre light coming from low-wattage sconces. A shaft of brighter light fell through the open door of the now-empty galley, onto two tables shoved together where the train's waiters and kitchen workers were gathered, playing some sort of tile game. They had shed their work jackets and wore only sleeveless white undershirts and olive-drab pants. While they talked they passed a bottle of Mekong whiskey back and forth that they poured neat. One of them, who seemed to be the head man, nodded at the entering Americans and toasted them with his glass. He smiled, as if to welcome the *farung* to his world. Thai music filled the car, high-pitched sing-song, relentless tempo, from a transistor radio sitting on the end of the car. Luke confessed to himself that after months of listening to the hootch girls' radio, he'd taken a liking to it.

Gropper looked around the table, scanning the faces. "Food?" he said to the man who had greeted them. He shoveled empty fingers towards mouth. "*Khow pod*?" Fried-rice.

"*Mai mee*," the man said. "Crosed," he added, nodding towards the empty galley.

Bronfmann's eyes widened. "I'm going to find the conductor," he said. "This is ridiculous. They can open the galley."

"Rotsa Ruck," Tanaka said.

Bronfmann shot him a look as if to say that he was out of line. "There's no first class," he said, "and now there's nothing in the dining car."

"Sorry 'bout that, Veetnam!" Gropper said, pronouncing Vietnam in the manner of LBJ.

The Thai head man went into the galley and returned with opened cans of orange Fanta, glasses and a bucket of ice. The officers sat at the end of the two tables; Tanaka and Lawrence cleared a table next to an open window, dropping the stacked chairs to the floor. The head man handed out the glasses and Fanta and offered ice. Luke held up his glass.

"I wouldn't," Gropper said.

"Geez, on a train?" Luke said.

"I wouldn't take the chance, that's all. It's not worth it." he added.

Luke smiled at the man and shook his head. He felt embarrassed, as if he had insulted him. The head man put the bucket down in front of the officers and offered up their communal bottle of Mekong. Gropper and Bronfmann shook their heads. "What the fuck," Luke said and held up his glass. The man nodded and poured, smiled, as if to say he was honored.

"I hear they brew that stuff with formaldehyde," Tanaka said, watching. "It'll pickle your brain." As he said this he poured his Fanta into his glass. "Fan-<u>tah</u>!" he said, and toasted Luke.

"Fan-tah!" Lawrence repeated, holding up his glass and grinning. "Fan-<u>tah</u>!" he said, kicking the 't'.

"What's that all about?" Gropper asked.

"Inside joke," Luke said. "In the back-end. We were talking about Thai television one mission, and someone started mimicking the Fanta ads. They're all the same. You watch, you'll see it. Some brawny Thai holds his can of Fanta up to the camera and exuberantly says 'Fan-*tah*!' That's it. They don't say another word. Just 'Fan-<u>tah</u>!' Standing in front of a Ferrari or something like that. Steering a motorboat across the Gulf of Siam, a gorgeous female on each arm. "Fan-*tah*!"

"Fan-*tah*!" Gropper responded, lifting his glass. Luke lifted his Mekong, downed his whiskey in a gulp. Sputtered. "Gawd!" he said. "It's awful."

"Me-kong!" Tanaka said, and laughed.

"You don't have to drink it." Gropper said.

Luke shrugged, held his glass up again and the Thai boss filled it. Luke nodded and took another long swallow. Smiled at the man while he quietly announced, "This stuff is really raunch!"

"Fer chrissakes, don't drink it," Bronfmann said.

Luke shrugged again and finished his glass, the warmth sweeping through his body and soothing his head. "Fan-<u>tah</u>!" he said. The Thai was confused; Tanaka and Lawrence laughed.

All the while they were watching the Thai tile game.

They didn't have the slightest idea what was going on, but they shared the players' enthusiasm. When the Thai laughed, they laughed. When someone seemed to win—a trick, perhaps the game—and expressed glee, they laughed. When the boss man won they toasted him. "Fan-*tah*!" Luke exclaimed. "Fan-*tah*!" Each time he emptied his glass it was refilled; he lost track of how many times.

One of the Thai, a smallish man of diminutive features, sat at the opposite end of the table, not playing, only drinking. He was solemn and lost within himself, immersed in the music, rhythmically weaving his head from side to side, eyes closed. The music seemed to have taken over his body, engaging first his head, then his shoulders, then his upper torso. He stepped away from the table and began to dance, dropping down into a crouch, legs bent and splayed wide, mimicking the graceful steps of Thai classical dance, or so it seemed to Luke. He stepped high first with one foot, then the other, and slowly swept his arms up and down, posing his hands and fingers in graceful arcs. He stepped from side to side, dipping his head and shoulders. Luke decided that this was something he could do, and that it would be fun, and joined the Thai. He relished the idea of being in a train racing south across the Khorat plateau in the middle of the night, drinking Thai whiskey, listening to Thai music. Thinking of Alan Bates in *Zorba the Greek*. Teach me to dance!

The Thai's steps were like a fencer's advance and retreat, and Luke decided to imitate him, moving back and forth in front of him, lunging and parrying, advancing when the man retreated, retreating when he advanced. He smiled and bowed his head respectfully, drink in hand. The man acknowledged Luke, but his look was odd, appraising, not at all appropriate to Luke's mood.

"I'd be careful," Bronfmann said.

Luke was surprised that Bronfmann was even watching, or that he could have something to say worth listening to. Then he realized that Gropper was watching, too. He grinned. "Not too bad, eh?" he said.

"I think he's doing the Monkey God dance, Lucas," Gropper said. "And I think the next part of the story is where you get your ass kicked."

"Come on, really? I think he's okay," Luke said. But Gropper's comment got him thinking.

The Thai moved slowly towards him, this time not looking at him at all. Luke stepped back, smiling, and the Thai suddenly gave Luke a look of anger. Luke didn't understand. He couldn't take the look seriously, he thought it theatrical and artificial. He laughed. When the Thai stepped back he moved with him, extending his arm, still wielding his imaginary fencing foil.

"Hey, lieutenant asshole," Bronfmann said. "I think you'd better be careful."

Now Luke wondered. He didn't want it to be true, he wanted this to be a carefree night that he would tell folks about back in Mount Brookville when he got home. He wanted a picture of this; he wanted a movie. He loved the moment, hands across the sea, all that. He felt like he was connecting with the Thai, with the real Thai culture. Bronfmann couldn't do this if he wanted, he said to himself, he didn't have the wherewithal to be this loose or respectful of the Thai.

Luke led again. The Thai turned and again looked stone-faced at him, backing Luke down the aisle. Luke glanced at Bronfmann to check his reaction and was put off by his eyes—they seemed disconnected, almost afloat in Bronfmann's face, as if they belonged to an alien that had taken over Bronfmann's body. Bronfmann returned his stare and didn't say a word. Meanwhile, the Thai backed away. Luke stumbled, realized he was dizzy, and that he'd had far too much to drink. Then in a quick flurry the Thai attacked, but more in pantomime, moving faster than anything Luke could muster, least of all in his Mekong fog. The Thai punched at Luke in a contrived and near judo-like action. He reared back and raised his thigh towards Luke, coming down in an exaggerated step, and finally Luke realized he was not dancing at all, not exactly, he was Thai boxing, he had finished his warmup routine and now he was going to kick his ass.

Luke went back to his chair. The Thai moved away as if he had never been with him at all.

"So what do you think now?" Bronfmann asked.

Much as it bothered him, much as he hated it, Luke had to acknowledge that maybe Bronfmann and Gropper were right.

THE TILE GAME ended and the Thai left, up and down the aisle to other cars, two into the galley where they pulled thin bedrolls down from a shelf and rolled them out on the floor. Two took chairs down from tables and pulled the tables together and climbed atop, begging the question of whether they would roll off on a curve. The head man turned off the radio and bowed and wai-ed to the Americans as he left. The day was over; it was time to turn in, like a Disney cartoon, animated creatures lowering shades, locking doors. Birds crawling into nests, yawning, stretching. The Americans stood, preparatory to heading back to the second-class sleeper. Lawrence remained at his table by the open window.

"Is everyone leaving?" he asked.

Luke, on second thought, wondered. I should sleep it off, he said to himself, but he liked the idea of sitting at the open window watching the Thai night slip by.

Saint saw him hesitate. "Lieutenant?" he asked.

Luke sat down at the table. Closed his eyes to secure his balance, and basked in the night air rushing through the open window. The smells of Thailand. Tuttle in the tropics, he said to himself. Title of a book.

"You going to be all right?" Saint asked.

Luke nodded. Yes, he thought. He was relieved, suspended in time and responsibility.

"I just don't feel like calling it a day," Saint said. "This is too great." He was wearing a blue oxford shirt with yellow pin stripes. Bright and fresh, Luke thought. "Like the shirt," he said.

"Bangkok Tailor."

"I go there; I never saw that fabric. I would've had one made."

"I got the last of it."

"Whattaya want for it?"

Saint laughed. "Forget it, Lieutenant." He took his cigarettes out, shook the pack and offered one to Luke. Luke took one. Saint struck a match and cupped his hands around Luke's cigarette, then his own. Inhaled deeply and blew his smoke toward the open window, savoring it. The smoke floated listlessly until it entered the slipstream, then was sucked out and disappeared, pulled like a floating leaf out of an eddy. He leaned back in his chair. Unconscious ritual filled the moment, dragging, exhaling, looking at the cigarette, flicking the glowing end over an empty Fanta can to drop the ash. When Saint saw that Luke's ash had grown, he held the can towards him. Tea ceremony sensitive, with meaning in each movement.

Outside the window, forest fell away and a vista opened. The land was dark, with a soft horizon that gave way to a clear night sky.

"I don't see any clouds," Luke said. "What's the weather supposed to be in Bangkok?"

Saint shook his head.

After a moment, Luke said, "Whattaya think? Was he about to tear into me?"

"Who?"

Luke laughed. "The guy I was sort of dancing with. Was he about to tear me a new one?"

"The little Thai guy? I dunno. I wasn't watching."

Luke laughed to himself. Saint's reaction was a gentle dose of humility. He realized he was sobering up, if only a little, bobbing to the surface of reality. The moment of the Thai dancer—or boxer, whichever—seemed long ago. "I've really had too much to drink. God, that Mekong is some wild shit. What a ride. It's not like being stoned. Did you ever drink the stuff?"

"God, no."

"You really didn't see? And you didn't hear Bronfmann?"

"Lieutenant...Captain Bronfmann? Are you kidding? We all tune him out."

He remembered Bronfmann's look, the creepy feeling he got that his eyes belonged to some being that had taken over his body. The more he thought about it, the more convinced he became that it was true.

The train snaked up a long curve. The windows of the cars far ahead shone softly in the darkness. The air cooled. With it came the rich smell of moist earth. He was transported back to a moment in junior high, sitting next to an open window on the bus heading home from the central school in Sangerville, turning at Mason's Corners, heading up the hill towards Mount Brookville. Gunn's knob in view. The last of the winter's snow lingered in the deep gullies, the skin of the land was soft and raw and soaked with snowmelt, and the fresh smell of earth pervaded the bus. And now a Proustian repeat. He breathed deeply. Had they gone over a stream? Were there fields nearby? Terraced, perhaps? Paddies? Or was it none of those things? He was curious—at home he knew, he knew the bird song, the cycle of the land, the clouds and the on-coming weather. Here. He wandered through Thailand in an ignorant daze, rootless.

After a moment, apropos of nothing, he said, "How did you come to be called Saint?"

Lawrence laughed. "I wondered how long it would take for you to ask. Everyone does. My mother has a sense of humor. Sometimes I almost think she married my old man just so it would make some sense for her to name me Saint." He looked out the open window. "You know, I've never taken a train before. Not here, not anywhere. I always go to Bangkok by car. Same for anywhere else."

"Where else have you been?"

"Ayutthaya. Pattaya Beach."

"Ayutthaya?"

"The ancient Thai capital. You should go."

"You and Tanaka?" Luke asked.

"Yeah. Most times. I've gone to Bangkok a couple of times with Kingsley, from the Fifty-fourth."

"I don't know him."

Saint laughed. "He's a crazy man. I love going around with him. One trip to Bangkok we met a couple of American women, God, one of them, Julia her name was. From Nebraska. What a body. I wanted her and Kingsley wanted her and he wound up with her. Bastard. But he didn't get anything. It turned out she was living with a Thai. Do you believe it? And she had Thai breath, all garlicky."

"What was she doing in Thailand?"

Saint shook his head. "I don't know. I think maybe she was here with her family. Her father worked for the UN, I think. Agriculture maybe." He paused. "So, Lieutenant. Got any with you?"

Luke looked at him, confused.

"*Guncha*," Saint said with a laugh.

Luke was startled, then he remembered what he had said just a few moments before. "Shit!" he said.

"O come on, Lieutenant," Saint said. "Don't worry. I was just wondering. I was thinking it would be great to be stoned right now. Maybe some of these Thai have some. I hear this Thai shit is great. I hear you don't even get the munchies."

Luke shook his head. "'Fraid not," he said. "I haven't smoked anything over here."

"When did you? College?"

"Not really. It wasn't there that much when I was there, and that was just a couple of years ago. Last year I went back for homecoming and it was everywhere. That was my first time."

The train reached the top of the incline and started down, returning to speed. They entered a cut, the face of the embankment so close it felt like they could reach out and touch it. The light from their window danced over rocks and boulders like fairy sprites. As abruptly the embankment fell away again and they were on a bridge crossing a deep gorge. They couldn't see the bottom. The air became almost cold. Luke shivered. "Can you believe it?" he said. 'Makes me wish I'd brought a jacket." He paused.

"My hootch girl asked me about snow once," he said.

"She can't imagine it. She knows about it, but she doesn't understand where it comes from. How it happens. Except I think they get snow sometimes up in Chiang Mai. She knows that. She's seen it in pictures. She's funny like that. She even asked me once when we were gonna to the Thai moon. She was looking at a picture of an Apollo launch in *Stars and Stripes* and she said, 'number one gee eye,' and pointed at the picture of the launch. 'Number one,' she said. Big smile. She knew we were going to the moon, she knew that. And then she said, 'when you go Thai moon?' 'Thai moon?' I said, and she nodded and said *'Chai ka,'* all serious. I tried to explain that there is only one moon. 'No no no, rootent,' she said. 'Thai moon, when you go Thai moon?' So I drew a picture of the earth and the moon and explained about the earth turning, trying to show that the moon over the U.S. was the same moon she saw over Thailand, and she just wasn't buying it. When I was all done and I thought I'd nailed it, she said *'khap khoon ka,'* thank you, and then she said, 'But when you go Thai moon?'"

Saint laughed. "You know what, Lieutenant?" he said, "I almost don't want to say it, but the truth is that I don't give a shit about going to the moon. I don't care. It's nowhere on my radar. Nowhere. I know I'm supposed to care, and feel proud and excited and all that, and back home everyone is paying attention, but I'm not. I don't give a shit about it. This whole moon and space travel thing is about as far away from me as anything can be. I don't even know what comes next, 'cause what comes next for me is getting my young ass home in one piece. They've orbited the moon and come back, right? And next time they're going to go all the way, right? I don't know."

"I don't' know what comes next, either, 'cause I don't care

either. I don't give a shit about it. And I don't know anyone over here who does."

"The other night I was in the Sawadee Club playing cards and Armed Forces Television was on and they were showing a splashdown in the Pacific and I barely looked up. I'm not sure anyone did."

Luke nodded.

THEY PAUSED, comfortable in their silence. Then Saint said, "So it's the middle of the day and I'm sleeping, I got into the rack maybe five in the morning, and Mah-li, my hootch girl —I say my hootch girl, but she's not just mine, she takes care of our whole bay—she's banging around the bay, tearing sheets off other bunks, throwing boots down, slamming drawers shut, putting clothes away, and I know her, she wants me to get my ass out of the rack, the sun's been up for hours and she figures it's time for me to get up. So I pull my pillow over my head and she comes over and pulls the pillow off my face and starts screaming, 'God damn you, Awrence, you number ten gee eye, you number ten, you get up, I make bed!' And I said 'No. No God damn you. Buddha damn. Buddha damn you. And she goes nuts. She starts saying 'no Buddha damn, no Buddha damn, God damn, God damn,' and I started laughing, so then she really goes ballistic and storms out of the bay and a moment later she comes back hollering 'God damn! God damn! God damn!' and I say, 'Buddha damn! Buddha damn! Buddha damn!' and she goes stamping down the aisle saying 'Awrence damn, Awrence damn, Awrence damn!'"

.   .   .

LUKE RECALLED the chill of the moment before. "Do you ski?" he asked.

"Oh yeah," Saint said. "All the time. At home, when I was in high school, I went nearly every night. There was a slope just outside of town and it was lit at night. It was just a little slope, with a rope tow, but it was so easy, I'd put my skis on my shoulder and walk down the street and I'd be there. Then on weekends, once I got my license I drove farther west, far enough to get away from all the Boston assholes, and the Portland crowd that doesn't really know how to ski...the ones that ski all over your skis in the lift lines."

"I didn't start 'til college," Luke said, "when I went with some guys. I loved it. I even got to ski powder once. Just once. You know how it is in the East."

"So, maybe, Lieutenant, maybe when we get back we can go skiing," Saint said. "I want to go to Colorado. I want to ski powder." He fell silent. "In high school, I'd go with my girl-friend, and on the way back we'd stop at this bar where'd they serve you as soon as you could put a dime on top of the bar, and we'd sit by the fire and drink Tom and Jerrys. Then we'd go out to the car and fuck our brains out."

"In high school?" Luke was incredulous and more than a little jealous.

"Yeah," Saint said.

"You know that's not normal, don't you? Fucking your brains out in high school." His loins stirring, a vicarious thrill from Saint's story. He remembered Sandy, his high school girl friend, and a magical moment in autumn, sun-dappled maple leaves falling quietly in the red-leafed forest, crunch of dry leaves underfoot. Coming to the Gunn's sap house where they jimmied a door to break inside. After-noon sun streaming through chinks and cracks, lighting the dust motes floating in the air. They sat on a bench next to the evaporator and made out, passions rising. "Are you feathered up?" she asked. "God, yes," he said, and slid his hand to her crotch. She caught his arm. "No." Always no.

"Yeah, my friends hated me because I was getting laid and they weren't. Charlene Kemp," he said wistfully. "She loved to fuck. We'd even go over to her house at lunch sometimes."

"Jesus! Where is she now?"

Saint paused. "We broke up when I went to college. Not right away. I came home weekends that first semester to be with her, and she came over to the college a couple of times. She said she was waiting for me but I found out she was fucking one of my buddies back home. She said she was in love with me and couldn't wait, she wanted to get married, and it turned out she was pregnant and it wasn't me, it was my buddy."

"So, where?..."

"Pittsburgh, I think."

"Did she marry the guy?"

"Yeah. It didn't last. She came back home, and when I was home on leave, she called. She wanted to see me."

"Did you?"

"Yeah. We fucked and it was as great as ever. She was always so damn horny. She said she was safe and I didn't need a condom but I didn't take a chance. She loved being on top. She would close her eyes and just ride my cock forever."

"And no one since, since you joined the Air Force?"

"O yeah. A girl I met on the beach in Falmouth. She wrote for the first few months after we left."

"I met a girl in Falmouth," Luke said. "At a piano bar. I picked her up, which is pretty amazing right there, 'cause I'm terrible at picking up girls. She was nice. I really liked her. I started driving up to Boston to see her, weekends and even some weeknights. I thought it might go somewhere. I liked her a lot. And she came down to the Cape once. I was living in a cottage off base, near Pocasset. It was a two-bedroom and I had a roommate, Reynolds. From the Fifty-fourth..."

"Yeah, I know him."

"He was from the city and he went home every weekend and I had the cottage to myself. I brought her there and I thought we'd sleep together but she insisted I get a room for her at a nearby motel. I was happy to do that, it didn't matter to me where we did it, but that's not what she had in mind. Truth is, she didn't have anything on her mind. No passion, no passion at all. She never warmed up past kissy face and huggy bear. It was like I was back in high school. Here I was in the Air Force and flying and in a couple of months I'm leaving for Vietnam and she's still back in high school saving herself for the guy she's going to marry..." Luke paused. "I dunno," he said, thinking warmly of her. "She was always happy to see me. She lived in an apartment on the top floor of a building on Beacon Hill, and after she buzzed me into the foyer she'd come out to her landing and lean over the railing and call down to me and it always made me feel welcome and home. Maybe I should have given it more of a chance. She never gave me a ration of shit about going to Vietnam. She said she told her little brother about me and what we're flying and he wanted to meet me, he knew the names of all the fighter planes." He remembered, too, the tuft of an ever-present Kleenex poking out from under the wrist bands of her sweaters and blouses, like a kindergarten teacher ready to dab a leaky nose. He smiled.

"That happened to you? Someone gave you shit about going?"

Luke nodded, grimaced. "Yeah. More than one. I stopped in Boston on my way to the Cape to see an old girl friend from college and she laid into me. She just started about how could I go, didn't I care about anything, didn't I believe in anything, and then she started about how I was just a fraternity fuck and all I wanted to do was get laid. And then she finished it off by saying I was the kind of guy who only went to art museums to look at the titties on the nudes."

"Fuck her," Saint said.

Luke laughed. "Yeah. But I think maybe she was right about the nudes. I had to remind myself that I didn't like her all that much anyway. I think maybe the only reason I stayed with her in college was the sex, such as it was." He paused. "Thing is," he said, "I'm not sure she was wrong. Sometimes, late at night, I don't care very much for myself and what I'm doing. I'm not sure I even want to be with a girl who doesn't have issue with me and this war."

"Jesus, Lieutenant. Lighten up! Give yourself a break."

"It's not that easy, is it."

"What was she like?" Saint asked. "In bed, I mean."

"Ahhh," Luke said, just as happy to think of something else. "She was good. The first time we fucked was in the party room at my fraternity, down in the basement while everyone else was upstairs. On a Sunday morning. She was a virgin. Shit, what a mess. But she was pleased as shit. I'd been trying to get in her pants forever, and she says, 'why didn't you tell me it was so good?" He paused. "She had long brown hair, and when she was on top it would fall around my face and it was like we were in this little room all our own. She loved it. Maybe not like your skiing girl, but she loved it. Once, she was lying in bed and I had just taken my pants off and I was walking across the floor to the bed and I had a real high hard one and she looked at it and she says, 'O boy.' She didn't even look at me, she was just looking at my dick."

Saint laughed. "She said that? And she lives in Boston? We have got to look her up when we get back. Maybe she'd be up for a two on one."

Luke laughed. "Now? She probably wouldn't even open the door." He wanted to say more. Talking about her made her feel real, and almost managed to chase away the loneliness that had become a constant thread of his life in Thailand.

"Lieutenant, you know what? We have got to get laid this trip. I need to get laid. You need to get laid."

"Yeah," Luke said. "But I'll tell you, funny thing is, I don't feel anything for these Thai hookers. You know what I mean?"

"No, I don't know," Saint said.

THE TRAIN ROLLED out onto the plains. A small village sat on the near horizon, perhaps a half-mile away, buildings dark against a lightening sky. A single light shone in what looked like a central market. They could see movement, perhaps people setting up tables for the day to come.

DAWN. The sky clear, pure. Luke remembered sunrises in college, when all-nighters were his habitual way of studying, the only way out of the jam he got himself into all the time, wasting time when he should have been studying, leaving everything until the last minute. The dawns almost made it worthwhile. Seated at his desk. looking out the window, listening to the dawn chorus. His mind wandered to thoughts of his roommate, Em, still up as well, studying with him. They did everything together, classes, road trips. All-nighters. Luke had thought of them as David and Jonathan, though he never said it that way—biblical references were lost on most of his classmates, as were metaphors of the land and farming—it was all simply beyond their ken. Em, the only person besides the Boston girl who rejected him because of Vietnam. Almost a year ago, and it still hurt. He pushed it out of his mind; enough time had passed that he could at least do that.

THE WIND through the open window now carried smells of urban Thailand, of cooking and sewage-filled ditches, the bitter smells of mold and mildew. Wood shacks and houses appeared among palm trees and scrub. Beyond the trees people were walking along the roads, riding in the occasional *tuk-tuk*, the motorized samlahr.

"Yep, I need to get laid this trip," Saint said.

"I DO, I REALLY DO."

"YOU KNOW MOST of all I just loved those trips up and back to Boston. I'd drive back late at night and sometimes the fog would close in and it made my car feel cozy and separate, the instruments glowing, almost alive, and I'd zip through those rotaries and I was the only car on the world."

Saint nodded. "Did we ever fly together back at the Cape?" he asked. "I can't remember. I don't think so."

"I don't think so, either. I flew some with Molino, and with Tolliver and McAuley. But not you."

"I don't think so, either. I flew with Lieutenant Fachevsky a lot."

"I remember the first time I saw you. You and Tanaka were coming out of the BX. You had on a madras shirt and white jeans and black Converse tennies and I was thinking the black tennies were so cool. No one was wore black tennies then; everyone was still wearing white."

"That's what the California guys were wearing."

THE THAI in the galley began waking, moving around, banging metal against metal. One came into the dining car and roused the men on the tables. They dropped the chairs to the floor, nodding sleepily at Luke and Saint. The train began stopping at outlying stations and young men boarded, clerks wearing dress pants and short-sleeved white shirts. As the train started out of each station, hitch-hikers jumped onto the platforms between the cars, gripping the railings tight. Luke stuck his head out the window to see what was happening; the hitchhikers were hanging on to the handrails on the ends of the cars, behind him, like firemen hanging onto their trucks, or like Keystone cops. He marveled at their number, and that no one fell off.

At the last station before Bangkok a young girl crowded their open window with a tray of pineapple pieces on tooth-picks. They bought a few and ate them at their table, loving the freshness, the sweetness and succulence. The train rolled into Hua Lamphong station and they went back to second class to retrieve their bags. The bunks had been broken down and Tanaka and Gropper and Bronfmann were sitting together, staring sleepily in front of them. Tanaka looked lost and out of place.

They walked down the platform together, Gropper and Bronfmann followed by Luke, Saint and Tanaka.

"So where are we going?" Luke asked.

"He walks, he talks," Bronfmann said. "All that Mekong. I'm surprised."

"The Chao Phya," Gropper said.

"Really?" Luke said. "Their air conditioning smells like mildew."

"Like half the hotels in Bangkok," Bronfmann said. "What do you want?"

"I can tell you what I don't want. Where are you guys going?" he asked Saint and Tanaka.

"The Prince, probably."

"On New Petchaburi? I don't think so," Bronfmann said. "Not with the enlisted."

"Enlisted scum, you mean," Tanaka muttered.

"I didn't say that," Bronfmann said.

"We can't go to the Chao Phya," Saint said to Luke. "That's officer country."

"Why don't we stick together?" Luke asked.

"Listen," Tanaka said. "How about we forget Bangkok and take a limo to Pattaya Beach? You have to get down there and pick up your stuff, anyway, right?" he said to Saint.

"What stuff it is that?" Luke asked.

"A water ski," Saint said. "A slalom. I'm having a guy make one for me. I'm not sure it's going to be ready."

"How about you guys?" Luke said to Gropper and Bronfmann.

"Nunh-unh," Gropper replied. "I've got stuff I've got to do here in Bangkok. I want to go to the Thai Celadon factory and pick up a set of dishes. You should come, too, Luke. They're gorgeous. The glaze on the green ones will blow you away. Cheap, too. Set you up for when you get back."

"Lieutenant," Saint said, "We go to Pattaya, to the Army rec camp, there's officers' hootches and decent barracks for the enlisted. And a snack bar on the beach that makes great pizza. We can water ski and there's a couple of hotels with good restaurants. It will cost sixty, maybe seventy bucks for a limo. We can be there by noon."

The idea felt good, refreshing. Open to possibilities. He nodded.

5

Bangkok gave way to tall trees and dense vegetation, endless Gauguin green crowding the road. They lowered their windows and let the heat and humidity overwhelm them. Soon sweat was trickling down Luke's back and into his undershorts and he was sticking to the burnished leather of the Mercedes' back seat. He asked Saint and Hugo if they wanted the windows rolled up and they said no. "It's Thailand," Hugo said. "I want to get into the spirit of things." He nodded at their driver. "Like him." Which was only sort of true, because the air-conditioning was on and their driver hadn't lowered his window.

Massive cumulonimbus dominated the sky, rising like ancient cottony pillars into the upper atmosphere as high as they could see, holding up the heavens. They drove past paddies where men and women were hard at work, knee deep in the water, hems of their sarongs pulled up and tucked into their waist bands, wearing the flat-top Thai straw hats. Nearly naked children played beside them. Farther on a pool with an older boy washing down a water buffalo and two children splashing in and out of the canoe-shaped styrofoam packing of a fighter plane tip tank. Then a *klong* where fishermen stood in the shallows casting circular nets with sweeping artistry.

"Whattaya think they're fishing for?" Saint asked.

"Question is, would you eat it?" Hugo said.

"WHEN I WAS A KID," Saint said, "in the summer my Dad and I went fishing every Saturday. He'd get me up before dawn and make us breakfast, bacon and eggs and hash browns and toast, and we'd be on the water by sunrise."

"What'd you catch?"

"Perch. Some walleye and some sunnies, but mainly perch."

THE OCCASIONAL DOPPLER *VRUMMM* ANNOUNCED cars speeding by in the opposite direction. Toyotas and Datsuns, a few Mercedes, black like their own. Slab-sided trucks hauling huge burlap bags stuffed like pillows with unknown cargo, their open-sided floral-painted cabs crowded with a driver and hangers-on, the driver often sitting at an angle half out the open doorway to make room for the others.

"THE THAI HAD A REGIMENT IN VIETNAM," Hugo said, "the Queen's Cobras. I heard that when they flew home and realized they were back over Thailand they went ape-shit, jumping up and down in the aisles and over the seats and laughing and hugging."

"There's Aussies, too," Saint said.

"And Kiwis."

"And South Koreans," Hugo added. "Mean-ass motherfuckers. They had to send some of them home. They were fucking-a crazy. Still, it's like world war three. Got some Filipinos, got some of them. No Canucks. Or Brits."

"One of my instructors in the mountains in survival school was a Brit," Luke said. "From Kenya," he said, adding in a put-on accent, "Keenya."

"A British soldier?"

"No. A Brit, grew up in Kenya, joined the Air Force."

"Ours?"

"Yeah."

"Doesn't count," Hugo said.

"There's some Brit advisers in Saigon at Mac-vee," Luke said. "Imparting their learning from the Maylay war."

"Bully," Hugo said.

They laughed. "Bully. Wooly Bully!" They slipped into spontaneous song.

"Sam the Sham and the Pharaohs," Hugo said. "Bully. Wooly Bully. Wooly Bully."

"Watch me now!" Saint said, wiggling his butt on the seat in half a dance step.

"A one, two, three, four, boom, boom, boom, boom," Hugo added.

They passed an aging, beat-up Land Rover, double-skin top, aluminum body, straight out of an African safari. UNESCO and a palm tree stenciled on the driver's door, Thai driver and a bearded, safari-shirted *farung* in the passenger seat wearing a weather-beaten bush hat, ready for deep jungle. He saw them in their Mercedes and it startled him. He looked surprised, maybe disappointed—no longer was he the only round-eye out in the bush, his life-dream penetrated by three Gee Eyes in button-down.

"Bwana," Hugo said, laughing and waving.

It's the twilight zone, Luke decided, parallel worlds of

Connies and the war of Vietnam juxtaposed with a UN missionary. In a year this guy is going to be gone, and anything he might have accomplished will be gone with him.

THROUGH A LEAFY and cool-shadowed market town of two-story whitewashed and verandahed buildings straight out of the ante-bellum South, or maybe a rubber plantation in Vietnam. A great banyan tree, vendors' tables and blankets spread beneath the limbs, presided over the four-cornered heart of the town. Piles of chilis and dried fish, naked chickens hanging from lines strung branch to branch. Old women dressed in black squatted next to the piles, waiting, not a customer in sight.

A small Buddhist temple sat at the edge of town, where a dozen or so young bonzes busied themselves building a low concrete wall.

"Looks like they've got every young man in the village," Saint said.

"Classes in how to torch yourself," Hugo said."

"That's the guys in Vietnam," Luke said. "These guys are Theravada. They don't get involved in politics. They don't go torching themselves."

"How the fuck do *you* know?"

"I read a book about it."

"Oooh. Look at the Lieutenant," Hugo said. "See what you learn when you're an officer."

Luke shrugged. Remembered being in the back seat of the Clyde's '56 Chevy, riding home after church in Mount Brookville. Passing the parish priest walking up the dirt path to Ethel York's. The widow York, who daily walked the short distance from her bungalow to Ransom's for her groceries, except that she hadn't been seen for weeks. The Clydes lived across the Nine-mile swamp in Tucker Hollow, and didn't know her, nor that the Mount Brookville kids mowed her lawn whenever she asked, for free, and that she always gave them popcorn balls on Halloween that she never had ready when they arrived and that they helped her make. Nor did they know that Ethel was Roman Catholic. The priest's black cassock swayed back and forth in rhythm to his steps. And Joe Clyde, with whom he played baseball at church picnics, called out the window, "Hey, mister, you left your dress on!" At which point old man Clyde laughed uproariously and pounded his steering wheel in delight. Luke was flabbergasted and embarrassed. This was Ethel York's priest they were making fun of. Ethel's! And by Brother Clyde, the founder and sole inhabitant of the Amen corner in the Mount Brookville Baptist Church, the self-appointed judge of Reverend Goodfellow's sermons, the only one to whom everyone was 'brother' and 'sister.' The moment marking the beginning of Luke's slide from his religion. He tried to hold the saffron-robed *bonzes* in the same thought as Brother Clyde. The inconsonance was painful. *Bonzes* walking the roadsides of Khorat, beggar's bowls in hand; Brother Clyde beating on his car steering wheel in laughter.

A few months previously he and Gropper had decided to tour the Bangkok temples—*Wat Pho* and *Wat Arun* and the temple of the emerald Buddha. The temple of the golden Buddha closed for repairs, encased in serious scaffolding. The temples all squeaky clean and newly painted and tiled and gilded, reflecting an economy floating in American dollars. In the visitors' center at *Wat Pho* he bought a pamphlet explaining Theravada Buddhism. Stapled pages, green poster-paper cover, the English rugged, the syntax awkward, the meanings often unclear. He resolved to stay with it. Perhaps here was the answer. He knew where it wasn't.

"So what about you guys? What are you?" Luke asked.

"Catholic," Saint said.

"Oh. Priests and convents and tunnels," Hugo said.

They laughed.

"And you, Tanaka?" Saint asked.

"Me? Nothing."

"By choice?" Luke asked.

He shrugged.

"Well, really. Did your parents practice something?"

"Yeah. Maybe. Who knows. Maybe it was animism. I never did."

THEY CRESTED a rise and suddenly the great scimitar swath of Pattaya opened before them, white sand beach dotted with tall palms, the sun off the water so strong it stung their eyes from even a half mile away. Fishing boats were working their way across the bay towards the shore, and the few hotels stood tall among the palms, a large hotel on the north and a second to the south, just before a jutting promontory. One or two scattered in between. They descended and drove under the palms along the beach road; the road narrowed and deteriorated, became a paved track, humping over tree roots. Midway down the beach they turned into the Army Rec camp. The camp office was a bungalow of low wooden walls topped by screening, replete with a screen door on a spring that slammed shut with a bang behind them. Gee Eyes in bright Hawaiian shirts greeted them.

"Tough duty," Hugo said to the desk clerk while he signed in. "How'd you manage this assignment?"

"Just lucky," he responded curtly to what was clearly an old and tiresome question.

A soft breeze wafted through the building, temperate and pleasant, rich with the soft swish of palm fronds rubbing against each other and the splash of wavelets touching the nearby shoreline. Time fell away, talk slowed, pauses lengthened. They finished signing in and the desk clerk nodded towards the enlisted barrack and Luke's bungalow, one of several on stilts across the road. They agreed to meet at the beach.

LUKE WAS the last to get it together. He climbed the stairs to his room, opened the shutters, and turned on the fan high in one of the corners to banish a stuffy, attic smell. Paused to take in the view of the water as he unpacked. By the time he reached the beach Tanaka was sitting comfortably at a picnic table in the shade of a palm-frond beach umbrella, back to the table, and Lawrence was water-skiing across the bay, arcing towards the shore and past a rough-hewn wood shack up from them that they learned later was the Royal Varuna Yacht Club. The boat was piloted by a young Thai, and a second sat in the stern, spotting. As they cut towards shore Lawrence angled steeply into the boat's wake. He waved at Luke and Hugo and cut back and forth across the wake, throwing up a rooster tail. The boats at the rec camp dock rocked in the wake of his passage.

"You ever water ski?" Luke asked Hugo.

"Lieutenant," Hugo replied. "I'm from Hawaii. Remember? We don't water ski. What we do is take a waterski-looking board, and we go out and we wait for a wave to come up and then we ride the wave to the shore."

"All right, smart ass. You any good?"

"I'm okay."

Luke sat down next to Hugo and leaned back into the table and relaxed, stretching out his legs, burying his feet in the sand. "This is more like it," he said. "As far away from Khorat and the recon wing as we can possibly get. This was the right idea," he added.

"Stick with me, Lieutenant," Hugo said. "I'll never steer you wrong."

The beach was nearly empty. Three Thai men in bathing suits were hosing down sunfish-like sailboats pulled high onto the sand near the rec camp dock, and the boats' red-striped sails flapped softly in the breeze. A larger sailboat with a cockpit and small foredeck sat beside the sunfishes, its saffron mainsail and jib hoisted and uncleated and swinging free; the boom slapped randomly against the stays. Fishing boats continued to putt-putt in from the gulf, small and clear-decked, bows jutting purposefully upwards. Some few had tiny cabins towards the stern. They tied up to a long, ramshackle dock that sagged out far into the water, and the dock swayed to the rhythm of their footsteps as they carried their catch ashore. Earlier arrivals, now unloaded, swung from buoys; some few closer to shore had been left high and dry by the receding tide and rested on their sides, canted this way and that like work-exhausted animals.

Up toward the Royal Yacht Club three *farung* women walked down to the beach from the Nipa Lodge, the hotel anchoring the northern end of the beach, and a covey of pale-skinned and light-haired children ran before them. The children charged down to the water, stopping abruptly in the shallows to splash and play.

"Odds look good, Lieutenant," Hugo said.

"You think? Whatta we do with the kids?"

"They can watch," Hugo said, adding, "Ain't it great? Can you believe there's a place like this anywhere in the world that isn't crowded? Bustling with people? Smelling like suntan lotion? There'll be more here on the weekend, after we leave, but not many. No one knows about this place. Come night there'll be some Gee Eyes on R&R with their Thai honeys down from Bangkok, and some of them on the beach during the day sleeping it off. But not many. This place is about as undiscovered as you can get. It's like it's been this way forever. It's like it's Bali Hai."

Saint came ashore and they walked together to the beach snack bar for a late lunch. The snack bar entrance was level with the ground, the front door opening directly onto sand. Three of the outside walls were screened, and there was a distinct feeling of being outside, like maybe they were camping out, soon to indulge a can of Chef Boyardee over a campfire. Instead they ate cheeseburgers with pickles and tomatoes and onion and drank Pabst Blue Ribbon and shared an order of fries.

After eating they walked up to the road and caught a *baht* bus—a canopied pickup truck with bench seats along the sides—down the beach to the woodworking shop that was making Saint's water ski, a barren, hole-in-the-wall shack of tools and sawdust and an island counter. Saint's ski lay atop the counter, an unvarnished duplicate of the one he had been using at the Rec Camp.

"Twenty bucks, Lieutenant," Saint said, stroking it gently. "Twenty bucks! Do you believe it?" Big grin, laughing eyes, sheer delight.

In broken English, the carpenter said that he would be starting the varnish that afternoon. Saint held the ski up for inspection. "Twenty laminations," he said. "See? The thinnest layers. He shook his head in wonderment." Chatted

in pidgin with the carpenter. "It's going to be several layers
of varnish, too," he said. "But it won't be ready before we
leave."

"Too bad," Hugo said. "We're just going to have to come
back."

They walked down the road towards the promontory. An
ancient and traffic-scarred tree grew incongruously in the
middle of the road, the lanes of the road split around it, as if
it were a median strip. They were like teenagers, which is
what they had been not so long before—relaxed, essentials
taken care of, three squares and a place to sleep every night.
Open to possibilities. They started kicking a rock back and
forth and around the tree, using the tree to block, a pushing
and shoving game of keep-away.

A row of shops faced the road and the beach, open-
fronted, meager merchandise in the interior shadows, boxed
dry goods mostly, some in familiar colors but with Thai
names—Pepsodent toothpaste, Ivory soap. Halo shampoo.
Penny candies in bowls inside dirty glass cabinets. Clerks
sat cross-legged on tables, half asleep, waiting. Bananas
hung from the rafters of a dirt-floor cafe, faded and torn
oilcloth on each table. Rusting signs for Coca-Cola and
Fanta. Two men sat on white plastic chairs lounging, their
faces expressionless. A cur wandered under their feet and
the men kicked it away. Next door a garage more an open
shack, sweet smell of hot oil, a motor scooter under repair in
front, oil-coated parts splayed across an oil-stained tarp.
Electrical and fuel connections dangled from the frame like
mechanical entrails. Mechanics nowhere in sight.

At first they were convinced they were the only ones out
and about, and wondered if maybe it was the time of the
afternoon siesta. Then abruptly, like a mosquito that had
been hanging on the underside of tree leaves waiting for

someone to come along, a decked-out hooker tottered towards them on too-high heels that she had yet to master, wearing a skirt that, depending on her movement, sometimes did and sometimes didn't manage to cover her crotch. "Hey Gee Eye," she called with no preliminaries, "you come me I show you number one good time. No vee dee, Gee Eye, no vee dee." She crowded close and draped herself onto Luke and then Saint. "Oooh, *suaj mah*, very pretty," she whispered to Saint. "Me fucky-fuck big time," she said. "I brow you, you rike me big time." She walked over to Luke, straddled his leg and ground into his thigh. "Me no butterfly, okay Gee Eye? Number one." She hardly gave Luke a chance to respond before she switched back to Saint, lightly rubbing his forearm. *"Suaj mah,"* she said again, her words sing song, emphasizing the *mah*. She reached down and rubbed his crotch. Saint jumped. "You fuck me, hansome man? You fuckee me good?" She brushed his crotch again.

Saint laughed and pulled away. The three of them continued down the road and she followed. Her broad smile and her spiel were infectious and they turned around. She caught Luke's eye and hooked onto his arm and walked with him, again moving in front of him to hump his leg, rising on tip toes to whisper in his ear, "You rike maybe brow job?"

"Hey, Lieutenant, you better watch out," Hugo said. "She's got you on her radar. Pretty soon you'll end up on the incurables ward in the Philippines."

"Me no butterfly you, Gee Eye," she whispered in Luke's ear. "Number one fucky fuck, aw day, aw night, sucky suck, how you rike dat? Pretty good, huh?"

"I don't think so," Luke said.

She looked at him in dismay. "Whassa matter you," she said. "You queer?"

"I don't think so," Luke repeated. He had to work to keep a straight face, afraid a smile would coax her on.

She went back to Saint. "*Suaj mah*," she whispered again, rubbing his crotch. "Number one."

"Jeez," Saint laughed. "Maybe later," he said, trying to disentangle her.

"Okay Gee Eye, maybe rater." She latched onto Hugo. "You fucky-fuck, Gee Eye? You Thai boy?"

Hugo laughed, throwing back his head. "No, no Thai boy. Japanese boy. No fucky-fuck. Maybe rater," he said. He added "Rittle Ruru," for the hell of it.

She scowled at him. "You Thai boy," she said. "I no rike you." She dropped his arm and finally let them walk on. "Maybe rater," she called after them.

"Yeah, maybe rater," they called back. She walked away. After a few steps, she called again, "Maybe rater," a questioning note in her voice.

"Okay," Saint called back.

"She's serious," Luke said. "Better watch out. She'll hunt you down."

They took a table at the promontory bar and ordered Singhas. Settled back in their chairs and watched the coming and goings in the bar, the boats in the gulf, the few people on the beach. They felt no compunction to talk, and conversation meandered. They talked about the hospital ward in the Philippines where it was said the guys went with hopeless strains of VD, who it was also said wouldn't be allowed back in the states until they were cured. They talked about sailing around the world after they got out, maybe going to New Zealand where they could ski in the morning and swim in the afternoon. And what kind of car they wanted to buy when they got home. Vanquished waves lapped at the foundation of the bar, and they watched the sun drop towards the horizon. The waves changed to a soft sibilance. Their world felt complete and they knew they were all sharing the same feeling and they didn't say another word until finally their stomachs growled and they decided it was time to get something to eat and they decided to go back to the snack bar again, pizza this time, even if it was frozen.

6

He walked into his room thinking he was alone. Humming absentmindedly the theme song from *The Bridge on the River Kwai*. Dah dah, dah dah dah dit dit dah. He chuckled to himself when he realized what he was singing, now, here in Thailand. He flashed back to high school, Memorial Day, marching back up main street in Sangerville. After the ceremony at the statue of the Union soldier on the village green. Something cheerful and bright after the somber ceremony. Dressed in purple with brass buttons, wearing his white bucks, cleaned for the occasion. Twirling his bass drumsticks on the offbeat. And after getting back to the school, sneaking out still in uniform, strictly verboten, hitchhiking back to Mount Brookville feeling cock of the walk, the man in uniform that every woman loves. Up Faulkner Road to Sandy's, road dust clouding his bucks. The day sunny and warm, not a given in central New York in late May. Then strolling back down the road with Sandy. Stopping at John Hawkins' abandoned farmhouse, making their way around back to the ancient apple orchard, where they lay in each other's arms in the soft orchard grass, midst a drifting cloud of falling apple blossoms. While across Mill Creek valley cows grazed in the shadows of giant sugar maples, and on the far hill a solitary tractor methodically mowed a field, first cutting, the tractor's rhythmic putt putt kissing their ears like the burble of a stream. At that moment the falling blossoms were with him still, a contented thought far removed from flying, from yesterday's mission; they fell like a soft grace note to the train ride to Bangkok, the drive to Pattaya, their time on the beach, wandering through the town. The great adventure, the grand tour. Not even aware how long it had been since the war had crossed his mind, his head filled now with the magic of Pattaya and his friends.

Suddenly he realized a man was sitting quietly on the other bed, lost in the shadows, staring into space. He jumped. "Jesus," he blurted.

The man was imposing in size, but seemed somehow less so, deflated, hardly there. At first Luke thought he was bald, perhaps older, maybe a major, or, god help him, a colonel, but no, as he took shape in the shadows, he realized he was his peer, age-wise, at least. His head shaved, a farmer's tan of white forehead and forearms. His shaved head put Luke off. Seldom did he encounter this in the Air Force, and when he did it was almost without exception men who fancied themselves gung-ho in the fashion of Marines, self-styled hard-asses who made Luke nervous. The man's barracks bag lay open and untouched on the bed next to him.

The man looked at him. "Sorry," he said. "Didn't mean to startle you." He smiled, and, almost as an afterthought, stood and reached to shake Luke's hand.

Luke's first reaction was irritation: Now he had to share the room, and account for a roommate in his plans, his hopes of maybe spending the night in the warm embrace of a woman dashed. Then he reminded himself that that was not likely to happen anyway, especially if Maybe Rater was his best chance for a roll in the hay. He relaxed.

The man was a first lieutenant from a transportation battalion in II Corps. Burrell Evans. Pine Bluff, Arkansas. Easy to talk to.

"Well," Luke said. "Pine Bluff is a first for me. Actually, so is Arkansas. You here on R&R?"

"Sorta," Evans said. He began putting his kit away, changing clothes as he talked, shedding his fatigues, pulling shorts and a Hawaiian shirt from his duffel. His dog tags swung free as he leaned over to sort through his bag. He moved slowly, deliberately, perhaps not as much preoccupied as tired; unpacking, explaining who he was, just plain talking seemed to be things he recognized he was expected to do, but didn't want to. He paused often, sitting down to collect himself.

He was in Thailand on a three-day pass. "It's a reward," he said, "not really R&R." His accent was soft and not unpleasant. "Truth is, I sort of saved my Cee-Oh's life. We were hauling ass upcountry and drove into an ambush, maybe a dozen klicks out of Kon Tum. It was after dark and we really didn't even need to be out that time of night." Time was tahm. Night was naht. "Everyone knew it. Our Cee-Oh knew it, too, but he decided we needed to red-ball through to Kon Tum and we ran right into the ambush. I don't even know what we were carrying—it could have been Rice Krispies and toothpaste. We were pinned down but we were holding our own. I saw this VC sapper crawling under the truck our Cee-Oh was in. Still in, I should say. Everyone else had bailed out and *di di mau*ed, hauled ass, for the brush. I have no idea why he was still in there, and I shouted at him to get the fuck out, but he was frozen and I knew I was gonna have to go in after the VC. So I did, and I got him. Slit his throat from ear-to-ear. God, what a feeling. First time I killed anyone. First and last time. But Jesus. Up close and personal. I could feel the life flush out of him, the blood pouring onto my hands. So the Cee-Oh gives me three days in Bangkok and here I am."

Luke hardly knew what to say. Evans' whole experience was, for him, beyond the Pale. There was nothing about the story with which he could identify. It filled the room, becoming the darkening shadows. He began to feel like a stranger, a neophyte, the odd man out.

"There's something else, too," Evans said. "It's the stuff you read about and don't think is ever gonna happen to you. Our Cee-Oh is a complete and total asshole and I shoulda just let it happen. No one woulda known. Everyone hates him, and when the men realized I saved his life they just looked at me, like what the fuck were you thinkin, boy, and now I'm just the same as he is, and I'm thinkin' when I get back I'm just gonna get my ass fragged. Maybe it'll take a couple of days, but it's gonna happen. Shit, I'd frag me myself for being so stupid!"

The odd thing is that Luke began to feel ashamed. He and Evans were both in Pattaya enjoying a break, for all intents and purposes the same, at least viewed from afar. But really, compared to Evans, Luke felt he had not right to be there. Nothing about what he had been doing, nothing about flying recon, compared to Evans' experience. He made the appropriate comments and let the conversation die. Thankfully, Evans did, too. He finished changing into his civvies and left. Luke followed shortly behind.

7

The breeze had died and the heat of day lingered still in the snack bar, smelling somehow of a remote attic in late summer. They finished eating —pizza and beer, as they had planned—and left, wandering over to the rec camp dock. Luke motioned towards the sailboats and said that he had sailed a small boat a few times on a lake more a pond back home, and they decided that maybe they'd give it a try, in the morning rent the boat with the saffron sails and a cuddy where they could stow beer. Having settled that they walked across the road to the rec camp just as people were filing into the movie theater. The poster outside the door advertised *The Sound of Music*, incongruous to everything about them, but what the hell they said, and went inside.

The small theater was nearly full and the only seats available were in the front row, too close to the screen for comfort, but with no other choice. Where did all the people come from, all round-eyes, all Americans. They slouched into their seats with their heads against the chair backs and got as comfortable as they could. Thai workers from the rec camp lined the outside of the screened walls like a circle of staring, ancient caryatids, their faces glowing in the flickering light from the screen.

They sat next to a young girl and her younger brother. The girl was cute with long blonde hair that she tended constantly, twisting it in her fingers, full breasts obvious despite the camouflage of a cotton print blouse, her tanned legs set off by white short shorts. She smiled at Saint when he sat next to her.

Julie Andrews burst onto the screen, clean and fresh and innocent and captivating, beautiful and sexless, midst mountain grandeur far removed from Southeast Asia. The simple plot of good and evil wrapped itself around Luke like a cosseting blanket. Within minutes he was consumed, the Alpine meadows painfully like the hills and meadows of Mount Brookville. He suspended judgement, sat back and indulged, as did everyone around him.

Sometime in the middle of the movie Luke noticed that Saint and the blonde were holding hands, and not long after that she was resting her hand on his thigh. Then her legs were splayed open and she was moving slowly and rhythmically back and forth, Saint's hand buried in her crotch, her eyes closed, her mouth open, breathing heavily. Her brother watched with great glee.

Luke felt like he was back in junior high on a Friday night at the movie theater in Sangerville. He poked Saint and muttered that she was a child and Saint whispered I know I know she was all over me and she is so fucking wet!

When the movie ended Saint left quickly out the side exit with the girl, trailed by her brother, and he looked back and grinned mischievously. Luke and Hugo shared a look of bemused bewilderment and it *was* funny and painful all at the same time, and the truth of the matter was that Luke was jealous and wished it were him, the finale of a day's escape into innocence. He and Hugo wandered down to the beach where they took up their daytime place at their picnic table. Wondered if they should go to the bar at the Nipa Lodge for a drink without Saint. Then he was scrunching in the sand towards them.

"Nipa?" Luke asked, waiting for him to say something. When he didn't, he said, "Well?"

"Oh, boy."

"Oh boy what?"

"Nothing."

"Nothing? That's a shitload of nothing in my book," Hugo said.

"Nothing. We made out a little, and then her brother said they had to go, their mother would wonder where they were, and they left."

"Her brother? Her brother was still with you? Where? Where were you?" Hugo asked.

"In the playground."

"There's a playground?" Luke asked.

"Yeah. Right outside the theater."

"So you're with her in the playground," Hugo said. "Where? Where in the playground?"

"On the edge of the sandbox."

"On the sandbox. You have got to be fucking kidding," Hugo said. He started laughing.

"So what'd you do?" Luke asked. "What happened?"

"What do you mean, what happened?"

"You know goddam well what he means," Hugo said. "What happened? We want details, man. What happened?"

"Nothing happened, that's what happened."

"That's it?" Hugo said. "Nothing? All that and that's it?"

"Her brother was right there."

"I got that. It didn't matter in the theater."

Luke and Hugo laughed. Saint smiled sheepishly, his eyes twinkling.

"This is all in the playground," Luke said.

"She started it. She pulled my hand to her crotch."

Hugo began laughing so hard that he slipped off the bench and onto the sand. "Lawrence," he said, "you fucking slay me, you really do."

WALKING to the Nipa Lodge they ran into Burrell Evans with Maybe Rater. Burrell greeted Luke warmly, smiling in a way that suggested he would be happy just to get laid, if he hadn't already. For Maybe Rater it was like seeing old friends. She waved at them and Burrell looked at her and smiled, getting a kick out of her. They moved on and Saint asked who Burrell was.

"My roommate," Luke explained. "Came in this afternoon." He told them the throat-slitter story. They didn't say a word and he couldn't tell if they felt as divorced from Burrell's experience as he did, nor if they shared his own sense of guilt about the unchallenged safety of their mission.

8

When does an event, a day become memorable? How does is happen? Is it singularity? Or multiple singularities—some accumulation of circumstances that cuts through the mundane and stands out? Or, funny thing, *when* do you realize that you're experiencing something special, and you realize you've been in the muck of a dismal swamp so deep and so long that you've forgotten that you're even there, and suddenly you're in another world, a brighter, fresher world? After endless, fruitless, *useless* days flying mind-numbing recon, Luke bobbed to the surface into crystal clear, clean air that literally sparkled in the sunshine. And then the best part...he realized he was not experiencing this moment alone, he was with friends who were also going to remember, for as long as they lived as well, however long that might be. When a time became timeless.

They signed the sailboat out at the rec camp office. Stowed their beer under the foredeck, pushed off, wading barefoot through the shallows, hopping aboard each in turn in a coordinated ballet, lastly Luke, tiller in hand, pushing against the transom. The morning breeze popped the sails full and in but a moment they were free of the shore and sailing, settling into an easy reach towards the open bay, heeling slightly. Listen to me, Luke said to himself, this is it. Just like that. Yes, just like that. They cleated the jib and agreed they should go out to the island or whatever it was on the horizon that seemed to mark Pattaya Bay from the deeper waters of the Gulf of Siam. And then maybe beyond. Saint held the main sheet while they looked for the main sheet cleat and then they realized there wasn't one. "Fuck!" they universally said, fearing they might have to quit and go in, but no, Saint said "Nevermind," and it didn't matter. Luke tried to guess the stress of the sheet on Saint's arm. "How long do you think you can do that?" he asked, and Saint answered, "*Mox nix,*" *Mox nix,* and grinned his toothy grin and wrapped the sheet around his forearm and looked and acted like he could do it forever and Luke certainly hoped so, because he hoped never to quit, and that they could sail on and on forever.

A soft chop drummed against the hull and gurgled in the centerboard housing. They cut towards the island. Before long Pattaya Beach shrank to a thin line, the beach, the line of trees, the hotels, few as they were, poking above. They didn't talk, not yet, anyway. Each was totally invested in the moment, and the moment was returning all that they could hope for. Hugo sat forward, holding his new Canon camera, scanning for the perfect photograph. He took one of Saint and Luke, Saint holding on to the main sheet, leaning back, looking at the sail, Luke smiling, looking at Saint. Another of Saint alone. Others. When they got back to the base Hugo developed the pictures. The photo of Saint looking at the sail, Luke at him, was a surprise. The look on Saint's face was pure, unencumbered joy, and on Luke's, adoration. It was all there—the boat, the gently rolling water, enough but not too much. How was it that the movement of the water could be apparent in a still photo? But it was, an arrangement of water and sky in a paradisiacal setting. A simple boat of clean lines. Sails of priests' saffron. Hugo gave them each a copy of the photo and Luke filed his in his photo album that would turn out to be his album of his Vietnam years, and every time he opened it and thumbed to that page the day enveloped him yet again in its singularity, there was never another like it, not before, not after. One day he took the picture out of the album and slipped it behind the screwdriver rack over his workbench in his basement. Next to it he placed Hugo's photo of the small, rocky island. The two photos spoke to him of what had been. They were real and true; everything that followed was hollow, and echoed with loneliness.

Once past the island the water changed from jade to blue and the sun sparkled and shimmered deep into the water, flashing like an underwater curtain blowing in a watery breeze. The wind freshened. They hauled in the main and tightened their tack, increasing their heel. They picked up speed and Saint and Hugo moved onto the gunnel for counterweight and balance. Saint began to strain under the pull of the main, holding onto the sheet with both hands, his hands and forearms beginning to turn white.

"You okay?" Luke said. "You want me to ease off?"

"You crazy?"

Hugo slid down from the gunnel and leaned toward the center of the boat to get his camera bag, momentarily upsetting their balance, and the boat abruptly heeled farther over, perhaps too far, and there was a moment of panic.

"Whoa," Luke said. Hugo scrambled back atop the gunnel and they stabilized. Luke's stomach settled down.

"You think this boat has a name?" Hugo asked.

Luke strained and looked back over the transom. "Nunh-unh," he said.

"Grins," Saint said. "Let's call it Grins."

The wind became visible on the water, pushing up small waves with horse manes, and they tightened their tack yet again. Their wake deepened and they began to take spray over the foredeck. Clouds massed on the horizon. The boat danced on the edge between wind and water, the stays sang, the bow slapped the water in a primitive drumbeat as it cut through the waves.

"Woo hoo," Hugo called. He wrapped his arm around the stay for balance to better take a photograph of the fore-deck angled steeply against the horizon. The muscles on Saint's forearms bulged with stress. He planted his feet against the centerboard housing and threw his head back in sheer joy. Hold on, Luke thought to himself, we can do this forever.

And so it seemed. The boat was sturdy and perfect for their day, though Luke wondered about the saffron sails. They hardly looked like canvas, let alone some modern synthetic. They really are bonze's cloth, he said to himself, adding, without hesitation, surely not. Truly, surely not. Can they hold? The wind filled their ears, the clouds on the far horizon drew closer, the waves grew and the air began to smell richer with the scent of the sea. The waves became gentle rollers and the boat climbed each in succession, speeding down the other side, bow burying into the next oncoming wave. Water began accumulating in the boat, sloshing back and forth. Soon there would be so much that it would become its own force, erratic and uncontrollable.

Saint and Hugo hiked out past the gunnels and over the side of the boat, Saint still holding on to the main, Hugo to the stay. Luke decided it was too much.

"Ease the main," he said to Saint, and they fell off, settling into a calm reach. "Let it out some more," he said and they took a breath. Saint relaxed and loosened his hold on the main, alternately shaking out his arms, flexing his fingers.

Hugo looked at the sky. "Think we could sail to Cambodia?" he asked. "How far do you figure, anyways? Fifty miles?"

"A hundred and fifty? I don't know," Luke said.

"Yeah, okay, so we could do it. We could. We're heading in the right direction, aren't we? Whattaya think? Pull an Orr to Cambodia?" Citing the character from *Catch-22*, that everyone was reading, the chest-pocket *New Testament* of their war.

"Yeah," Saint said.

They laughed and held the tack. The sun moved directly overhead. The clouds increased and they were thankful for the shade. Luke wondered how far they'd come, how close they were to the shipping lanes to Bangkok.

"I think, guys, we ought to work our way back," he said.

"Bunky," Saint said, "relax."

Luke hesitated. "Okay," he said, "but we're going to change course." He pushed the tiller away and the boat's stern presented to the wind. "Haul in the main," he said to Saint, "and when the wind catches it and starts to push it to the other side, don't let it go too fast, and switch over to the other side while you do it. Hugo, you switch sides when Saint does."

"Aye, aye, Lieutenant," Hugo said, briefly touching his hand to his forehead in a mocking salute.

"Fuck you," Luke said.

"Yes, sir. Fuck me, sir. Aye, aye, sir."

They jibed and Saint smiled. "I liked that," he said. "We're getting pretty damn good, aren't we?"

"We are," Luke said.

"We're fucking sailors," Hugo said.

Now they were running with the wind, heading towards Pattaya Bay. With the wind at their backs they couldn't feel how fast they were moving. They started surfing down the rollers and each time, for a moment, Luke lost steerage, and he became a little nervous. Still the feeling of the day stayed with him, and he sensed that everything was okay. After a time they could see the southern promontory of Pattaya Beach.

"We're not going in, are we?" Saint asked.

"I just want to bring us in sight of the island, that's all."

They began sailing back and forth near the island, sometimes in sight of it, sometimes not. Hugo leaned into the cuddy and brought out the beer. He held the first can and paused, looking around. "Say, ah, Lieutenant. You don't just happen to have a church key in your pocket, do you?" Continuing to look around the boat. The woodwork was smooth and clean and it was apparent that there was nothing available to open a can. "How're your teeth, Lawrence?" Hugo said. They laughed. Then Hugo reached over and without warning pulled out the nail holding the centerboard in place. Almost immediately the centerboard slid up and the boat began pitching over. Hugo and Saint scrambled to get ready to jump clear of the boat now tilting way past 45 degrees.

"Jesus!" Luke said. He pushed the tiller over to bring the boat up into the wind and at first the maneuver further tilted the boat, but it was only a moment before the boat righted itself. Through it all Hugo lost track of the center-board nail. He dropped down to his hands and knees in the bottom of the boat to find it. Finally having it in hand he said, "We still need to open that beer." He held up the nail. "What's your pleasure, Lieutenant?" Without waiting for an answer, he took off one of his loafers and began hammering a hole in the top of a can.

"Okay, loose the sheets and we'll sit here and drink," Luke said. They settled back against the gunnel, listening to the sail flapping in the breeze, the banging of the center-board, now free and floating in the housing, scraping the insides. They felt good about what they had just done, responding to the situation with what they had at hand. When they finished their first round they began sailing again, pointing high to recapture the rapturous feeling of earlier, then running before the wind, sometimes coming up into the wind and letting loose the sheets to open yet another round.

Mid-afternoon a squall began working its way across the water towards them, a low cloud darker than the surrounding sky, grey skirts dragging the horizon. They came about and headed towards Pattaya. Then the squall was upon them and the wind and rain were strong but not more than they could handle. They sailed across the last skirts of the squall on a broad reach, heeling over farther than they had all day, hiking out, and they loved how they looked from the shore and hoped there were people watching the beauty of their moment.

After the squall moved on they decided to stay in Pattaya Bay. Off in the distance three black dots appeared just above the horizon, stacked one behind the other, and they realized they were aircraft approaching U-tapao, the airbase inland beyond Pattaya. They watched in curiosity, wondering what they might be. The aircraft closed slowly, then, doppler-like, sped up as they drew nearer. Then they were there, B-52s with their enormous wingspans spreading ever wider the closer they flew. Once overhead they seemed to block the sky, fearsome beasts permitting no other thought, black metal crosses and roaring engines, landing gear doors opening—they were real and nothing else existed in their presence. Then they were gone, leaving nothing but stunned silence in their wake. The three of them looked at each other, their expressions a look of awe and disappointment that with the departing aircraft had gone the feel of their day.

THAT NIGHT they ate at the Nipa Lodge. Drank dry martinis in the teak-paneled bar, shaken not stirred they said to the Australian bartender, not knowing what the difference was except that that was what James Bond said, and ate outside in the dimly lit darkness under the arbor, and the monkeys they had heard chattering in the trees when they had walked up to the Nipa came swinging down, grabbing at their food. The waiters shooed the monkeys away and they told the waiters not to bother because they couldn't imagine anything more exotic in all the world, eating steak medium-rare in the candlelight and fending off monkeys and marveling at how quickly the waiters flipped their zippos out whenever Saint or Luke moved a cigarette from pack to lips. They drank McWilliams Claret Bin 19 from Australia that the bartender had said would be perfect, and it was, and they had no idea that it would be because it was the first real wine any of them had ever drunk, something other than

Ripple or Mateus Rosé in a ceramic bottle. They were all smiles and knew as the day was ending that there had not been a moment in it that they would change, except for the B-52s, the recollection of which, of how they took over the sky and drove out all rational thought, never went away.

9

The crew bus pulled up to the enlisted barracks, last stop before Squadron and Wing and pre-brief. Late morning of a day already oppressively hot and humid. They were all full of life as they boarded, revived by the five-day break just past. Saint bumped his head on the stanchion at the top of the stairs, knocking his barracks cap askew and onto his forehead. He splayed out his arms, tossed his head back to hold his cap in place, took a Maurice Chevalier dance step, and sang, "Sank heaven, for leetle girls."

"No bragging, Lawrence," Tanaka said, coming up the stairs right behind him.

Luke laughed quietly.

The bus turned onto the street leading to Wing and the two squadrons. The day was hot, the close horizon shrouded in haze, the sky flaccid and ancient, tinged with a sickly yellow. They rode with the windows closed, air conditioning blasting. Thai groundskeepers worked along the side of the road, moving slowly, pruning bushes, mowing, moving almost imperceptibly, as if they were at the bottom of some great tepid pool. Not for them the false bravado of useless speed in this tropic heat. Mad dogs and Englishmen went out in the noonday sun, as the saying went.

The air conditioning at Wing was cranked high and the crew put on their flight jackets as soon as they entered. Colder yet in the windowless briefing room; John Constance made a show of blowing towards the ceiling, as if to see his breath. All save Woody sat in folding metal chairs, Woody sat in the aircraft commander's throne in the front row, a jester's reward of sagging cushions, torn fabric and leaking stuffing that looked like it had been retrieved from a third world dump, and that would surely one day pop a spring into some a/c's ass. The floor lamp next to his chair leaned precipitously towards him like a tree about to fall, casting a cone of warm yellow, bathing Woody and Gropper and the navigators.

Colonel Reilly waited for them on the podium, smiling as they walked in, practically rubbing his hands together in glee. Very unlike him. He unveiled the mission map. Southern South Vietnam, III and IV Corps spread out before them, centered on Saigon. The men leaned forward. Southern South Vietnam was something they had never seen before, and it begged attention. Reilly passed a rolled-up map to Luke and took his collapsible pointer out of his pants pocket, dramatically pulled it to its full length, and began waving it at the Delta.

"Tonight," he said, "you're going to the Parrot's Beak." He paused and looked around, visibly excited to be the bearer of such news. Something not only different, but maybe with the potential to break their shared boredom. "You'll be flying south to the Gulf of Siam, southeast along the coast of Cambodia and then northeast across the Delta to the Parrot's Beak." He traced the route with his pointer. "Four hours out, four hours back, eight hours on. You'll get there not long after dark." His sentences were short and simple and straightforward, perhaps purposely chosen to convey immediacy. There was no judgement, no agenda other than to communicate. "This mission you're going to report directly to Army artillery." He paused, again swept his gaze across the assembled crew, making sure that they were grasping what he was saying, meaning, among other things, not TFA. Not NKP. "You're going to be covering the area where the North Vietnamese are moving supplies into Saigon. The Army has cleared the area, and by the time you get there all the peasants will be in their fortified hamlets. Anyone moving outside after that is a bad guy. Sensors have been placed at every strategic point, along major roads and trails, at crossroads and fords over streams, and an artillery piece is zeroed in on each one of them. Tuttle, take a look at your map: you'll see where the sensors are set up. Everything's covered, and it's simple."

He paused while Luke unrolled his map. "When a sensor activates, all you have to do is call in the location and the Army'll pull the lanyard and ordnance will be on its way." He scanned the crew again. "Questions?"

Luke waited for more, but there was nothing. He spread the map out on his lap. Sensed eyes on him. Exciting, yes, if only to break the monotony, but already he had doubts, as the reality of the mission dawned on him. So simple a monkey could do it. He suspected his men were beginning to feel the same. For a brief moment he had warmed to the idea that they would not only be out of TFA's grasp, they'd be contributing useful intelligence. Now he understood that this was just another job for automatons, a game of *Whack-a Mole*. Worse, they would have no idea what they were hitting, a tactic based wholly on the Army's ludicrous

Hamlet program. He looked at Colonel Reilly, trying to cover his skepticism, wondering how he could be so enthusiastic.

For whatever reason, an incident from college, with his roommate Em, came to mind, the last time he saw him, just before he deployed. Em, short for Emerson. Sitting across from him in the living room of the house he shared with four other med students. DC, early on a Friday evening, autumn dusk falling early. The room graduate student sparse—a couch, two stuffed chairs. Faded wallpaper. Cold and dank to the point where it felt uninhabited. The light from a single lamp on a side table barely held off the darkness. Awkward silence save for the soft strains of Simon and Garfunkel 's *Sounds of Silence* drifting from some or other room. Em's, most likely; *Sounds of Silence* was their favorite album senior year, and they had played it constantly, that and Nina Simone at Carnegie Hall.

Luke had flown in on the Eastern Airlines Shuttle for a quick visit, a chance to say good-by. After desultory and perfunctory conversation about where their mutual friends of Colgate were now, Em worked the subject around to something clearly on his mind, and got quickly to his point. "I've thought about you in this war. I don't know where you've been, except on the Cape, and I don't know what you've been doing, and frankly, I don't want to know. I don't want to hear about it, whatever it is. I know what it's for. At Colgate, when you dressed up to play soldier, I didn't give it a second thought. I mean, Colgate wasn't real, life there wasn't real. Stuck in the boonies of central New York. It didn't matter. But now? This is it. This is real life. This is war. Bombing the North, napalming the villages. LBJ calling in all his chits to get other countries involved to make it look like a world war, which it isn't. Mention the word communist around here and off we go. Once again we can't see beyond the label. And the corruption. Jesus! The South Vietnamese government is about as divorced from their people as you can get. Look at the goddamn hamlet program, shoving the Vietnamese farmers into fortified enclosures every night. They hate our guts! And the worst of it, the most insane, is that we're trying to bomb North Vietnam into oblivion—how do you Air Force people say it—bomb them back into the stone age? I don't know what you're about to do, but you're in it and I don't think there's any difference between you and some officer in Hitler's Luftwaffe." He paused, took a breath in what Luke thought was probably a rehearsed speech. "I'm sorry," he added slowly, "but this is it. I don't think we have anything in common anymore."

Luke was taken aback. "Just like that," he said.

Em nodded.

Luke tried to explain himself, making it clear how increasingly distraught he was becoming. How playing soldier in ROTC had led inexorably to this, how he hadn't had a choice. "It isn't that simple, you know. I agree with everything you've said. It's a shitty situation, and somehow I've gotten myself into it, up to my ass. But comparing me to an officer in Hitler's Germany? Really?" He watched Em to see if his words were having any effect, and he could tell there was nothing he could say that would change Em's mind. But this...this was as if they had never even known each other, as if they hadn't shared years of college and everything associated with it. He had told himself that the year past and the one to come would probably be just a temporary break; he was looking forward to the day when he would come back and they could again share their lives. When there'd be time. They would do great things together again, go to football games, Colgate-Princeton, an easy drive from the City, where Em was from, or maybe vacations, the Catskills, maybe, or the Adirondacks. Just the two of them in the beginning, and then with their wives, and then their families. Maybe they would stand as each other's best man. Maybe they'd take trips to Europe, or share a beach house at the Jersey shore, or the Cape. Their years at Colgate had been road trips to Caz' and Syracuse, Skidmore and Wells. To Smith. Senior year had been cathartic afternoons driving the back roads and hills of Madison County, land that Luke knew like the back of his hand, and that Em learned to love through Luke's eyes, or so he thought. Surely all that counted for something. He paused in his thinking. He couldn't believe it was over, pulled up short. More than having gone separate ways, now there was something between them that Em clearly believed could never be breached, and Luke already missed the Em he had known, and frankly, still loved. He looked at Em, stared at him, easily done without embarrassment, because Em was looking only at the floor, as if he was alone, and Luke wasn't even in the room.

Finally Em stood, looked at Luke with resolve, and left the room. Silent. Soon Luke could hear him climbing the stairs, presumably to his room, leaving him alone. Dramatic. A door closed, the music stopped. Luke waited a moment for no other reason than emotional exhaustion, then resigned himself. He left.

And now here was Colonel Reilly laying out a mission so absurd it was laughable. Hitler's Luftwaffe? Hardly. He wanted to ask Reilly if he believed that all the Vietnamese would dutifully file into their hamlets each night like contented Eloi. But then the ultimate question: Did he really want things to be done better, putting aside the question of if, in this fucked-up war, things really *could* be done better? It was a dilemma greater than any he had ever imagined. True irony. Now, for him at least, the only reason to do things better was to save American lives. He knew he couldn't ask those kinds of questions of Reilly. He imagined the scene—everyone in the briefing room would look at him as if he had jumped his track, even if in their heart of hearts some might agree with him. What good would it do? No one would pass a message up the chain of command suggesting that they were losing the support of their men. A first lieutenant in Khorat? Really? And he knew that Reilly had no answers, even though at times his comments suggested that he harbored doubts himself. Reilly looked at him again and Luke nodded to suggest that he understood. Reilly collapsed his pointer. He gave them the code letter of the day and dismissed them.

THE BUS DROVE ONTO THE CONNIES' parking apron and down the long avenue between the aircraft. In spite of everything, Luke loved this moment, driving down the ramp, the aircraft facing each other like sphinxes guarding the entrance to the sky, their green and brown camouflage, the graceful upturn of their fuselages, the three vertical stabilizers. What genius, he thought, what an incredible confluence of materials and ideas that resulted in a plane that looked like it could fly by itself, just spring into the air and take off.

They pulled up to their assigned aircraft. The portable air conditioner was roaring, its yellow ducting snaking up the stairs and into the plane like an umbilicus, supplying relief. Most of the crew filed off; John Constance and Rolfe went with the bus to the in-flight kitchen to pick up drinks and enlisted food and then to the armorer for that crew's pistols. Luke and Gropper ducked under the plane, Luke to check that the row of stubby sensor antennas were still securely attached to the underbody, Gropper that the undercarriage and engines were in working order. Luke was finished in but a moment and boarded, happy to be out of the heat; Gropper finally boarded a half hour later, sweat dripping off his face and down his back, with great dark patches under his arms.

Next the intelligence compartment—posting the sensor numbers above the screens, preparing the logs and work schedule. Luke set the code of the day in the communications-security paddle and handed it off to the in-flight techs to plug it into the encryption box. John Constance and Rolfe returned, carrying the pistols and food and jugs of coffee and water. Packages of Kool-Aid. This mission Jolly-Olly Orange and Rootin' Tootin' Raspberry. John Constance wrote the names on masking tape on the jugs. A few minutes later Bronfmann came aft, stopped at Luke's position. "I don't like that with the jugs," he said.

"What?"

"What are you talking about, sir!" Bronfmann said.

"*Sir*. What are you talking about, *sir!*"

"The names on the jugs."

"You don't want to know what's in them?"

"Of course I do. Orange and Raspberry; that'll do."

"You don't like Jolly-Olly and Rootin' Tootin?"

"No, Lieutenant, I do not."

"Jesus, Bronfmann, give it a break!" he replied. "You came aft just to tell me that? Are you shitting me?" He wanted to add, "Get a life," but did not. Nor did he tell John Constance to change the labels. Idle minds, he thought. Or uptight ones. He shook his head as Bronfmann walked away.

They finished pre-flight long before takeoff. Most of the crew relaxed at their positions or in the passenger seats at the front of the aircraft or at the galley table, avoiding the sweltering heat. Then the smokers began an exit that the others followed. Soon they were all sitting on the edge of the apron in the shadow of the Connie's tail, feet dangling, chatting, kicking at the tall weeds beyond the concrete.

A flight of 105s rolled slowly down the taxiway in front of them to the run-up point at the end of the runway, two by two, canopies open like knights' visors, their camouflage markings like war paint. The aircraft halted and the pilots lowered the canopies. The planes sat quietly for a moment, as if they were about to gather their courage to enter the lists, then their afterburners burst into flame and boomed and they began accelerating down the runway, quickly picking up speed. The roar was overwhelming, filling the flight line like the B-52s in the sky over Pattaya, driving out thought of anything else. Then they were airborne, quickly becoming only brilliant lights in the far distance, heading for Laos or North Vietnam. A flight of F-4s followed, then another, an awesome display of seemingly invincible power, far removed from their own spectator seats.

The crew filed back onto their plane. Strapped in, waiting for their plane to come to life and begin their takeoff roll. Feeling the confidence of Fourth of July parades. Airborne at seventeen hundred, headed south to Bangkok.

The flight out was long and boring, the windowless and barren bulkheads of the intelligence compartment isolating Luke and his crew. As so often Luke settled back in his chair to read, this day *The Count of Monte Cristo*. He was working his way through all the old classics in the base library, all the books he felt he should have read years ago. *Dracula. The Man in the Iron Mask. Don Quixote.*

The Collected Poems of Wilfred Owen sat buried at the bottom of his flight briefcase. Rarely did he take it out, and when he did it was when he thought no one would notice, certain that those who recognized the book would think it incongruous, the moment overblown. He didn't care. He saw the similarities between then and now, the patterns fitting to a 't'. Except for the numbers, that created a dimension all their own. Always he turned to *Dulce et Decorum Est,* as a moment of private penitence. Here we are again, he said to himself. Here we are again, he said in apology. Forgive us, forgive us all. Again. Maybe not on this plane, maybe not on this mission. But down below, down in the jungles and paddies.

And this night. The mission roiled his gut like a meal gone bad. He couldn't concentrate on *The Count.* Halfway to the Parrot's Beak he gave it up and put it away. Took out Wilfred Owen, paged to *Dulce.* Read it slowly, thoughtfully. Connected the eternal questions and came up empty, but at the least, not alone.

Dulce et Decorum Est

    Bent double, like old beggars under sacks,
        Knock-kneed, coughing like hags, we cursed
        through sludge,
        Till on the haunting flares we turned our backs,
        And towards our distant rest began to trudge,
        Men marched asleep. Many had lost their boots,
        But limped on, blood-shod. All went lame; all
        blind;
        Drunk with fatigue; deaf even to the hoots
        Of gas-shells dropping softly behind.

Gas! GAS! Quick, boys!—an ecstasy of fumbling
    Fitting the clumsy helmets just in time,
    But someone still was yelling out and stumbling
    And flound'ring like a man in fire or lime.—
    Dim through the misty panes and thick green
    light,
    As under a green sea, I saw him drowning.

In all my dreams before my helpless sight,
    He plunges at me, guttering, choking, drowning.

If in some smothering dreams, you too could
    pace
    Behind the wagon that we flung him in,
    And watch the white eyes writhing in his face,
    His hanging face, like a devil's sick of sin;
    If you could hear, at every jolt, the blood
    Come gargling from the froth-corrupted lungs,
    Obscene as cancer, bitter as the cud
    Of vile, incurable sores on innocent tongues, —
    My friend, you would not tell with such high zest
    To children ardent for some desperate glory,
    The old Lie: *Dulce et Decorum est*
    Pro patria mori

10

They arrived over the Parrot's Beak at twenty-one hundred. For the first hour there was nothing, not a single activation, and Luke wondered if there was something wrong with their equipment, some kind of technical glitch, or maybe even if Woody and Gropper had their coordinates wrong, and that they were orbiting over some patch of jungle far from their target. He asked the in-flight techs to check out their equipment, and after a short time they reported back that everything was in order. Still they waited, and Luke felt like all his moralizing about the mission was laughably meaningless. He wondered if they were going to be twiddling their thumbs for the next eight hours.

Sergeant Tolliver roamed the positions, watching. Finally there was an activation at Rolfe's console. He called it in and a moment later the sensor flashed again, echoing his call, presumably from an exploding artillery shell. "Rolfe got one," Tolliver reported. It occurred to Luke then that maybe each exploding shell would wipe out their associated sensor, and by a process of elimination in a short time they would have to head back, having expended all their so-called ammunition. Ten minutes later a sensor activated on Tanaka's console, followed by the echoing explosion of a shell, then another on Rolfe's. The same sensor as previously. Then John Constance's. A certain excitement grew: Something, no matter what, was happening, if only every ten minutes or so. The pace became constant. At midnight Luke went forward to eat. When he returned, it was still busy. Molino asked if he thought it was working. Luke shrugged. "Apparently," he said. "Whether they're hitting anything...that's another matter. Who knows. Maybe we'll find out at debrief."

In the dead of night things slowed down. A few more activations after three, each followed by the flash of an artillery shell. After all that they had watched, they wished at least the feedback of the noise of a cannon being fired, the whistle of a shell through the air, the explosion of the shell hitting its target. There was none of that. They made up stories about what was happening.

"Got a water buffalo," John Constance said.

"No. That was a horny teenager off to see his honey. You know how it is. Can't keep it in his pants."

"Or VC," Rolfe said. "It could be. You have to admit it."

"You're right," John Constance said. "It could be."

Around three Gropper went to the head and stopped on his way back, pulling out Luke's jump seat. "What's happening, Lucas?" he said. "Your boys busy? Give me a tour."

Luke gave Gropper the mission map. "Go take a look," he said.

Gropper moved across the aisle to Molino's position, pulled out the jump seat, and sat down. He spread the map out and pulled the tensor lamp close, bathing the map and his and Molino's hands in light, their faces shining midst the surrounding darkness like a Caravaggio painting. As a sensor light activated, Molino pointed to its position on the map and called it in. Waited but a moment for the answering artillery explosion. But soon there weren't any activations and after a few more minutes Gropper moved to another position. Not long after he returned and handed Luke the map.

"That's it, huh?" Gropper said.

Luke shrugged.

After that McAuley took over the intelligence officer's position and Luke went aft and sat at the galley table with John Constance, Tanaka, and Rolfe. Then the engines surged and the Connie left orbit. "Well," John Constance said, "that kept the world safe for democracy." They laughed, a hollow skeptical sound.

McAuley walked up to the table. "There you are, Lieutenant," he said. "All clear. The artillery officer in charge called to thank us."

"Thanks," he said. The others burst out laughing.

"What the fuck?" McAuley said.

"It's not you," Luke said. "Don't take it personally. Did it get busy?"

"Not really," McAuley said. "What's so funny?"

Luke shook his head. "It's not worth it," he said. "It's not you," he repeated.

LIGHT GREW INSIDE THE PLANE, shadows withdrawing into the corners. Luke went forward, poured a cup of coffee and sat in the passenger seat closest to the starboard galley port-hole and watched their progress home. The coast of Cambodia took form in the dim light. The Sihanoukville peninsula. They moved slowly across the mouth of a medium-sized bay. Islands large and small bordered the coast. Inland a dark forest, tiny villages. Waves broke and swept toward the shore in biblical order. He wondered if any other American aircraft flew along the coast and if the Cambodians were watching, ready to launch a gun boat from the coast or a fighter jet from an unseen airfield.

He remembered an incident back at the Cape during the confusing days when they were getting organized. Three or four intelligence officers gathered in someone's room, the sun shining, the pleasant, salt-infused breeze wafting through the open window. Someone—who? He couldn't remember—said, "They did a risk analysis on our mission down at the Pentagon. They're saying we're going to lose one in three." He remembered the leaden silence as each of them grappled with the doom's day scenario. And now they knew it was laughably untrue. Once again the computers had screwed up, or at best, garbage in, garbage out. Earlier that year some Migs had headed their way, but in a matter of minutes three Navy fighters appeared and chased them off. Since then, nothing.

Molino and John Constance came into the galley and retrieved the brooms from behind the bulkhead and began sweeping the deck. Molino worked his way over towards Luke and nodded for Luke to raise his feet so that he could sweep under him. He grinned. "Any job worth doing is worth doing well," he said.

"Good job," Luke said.

"Other duties as assigned," Molino replied.

Luke looked out the porthole again. He decided that by now they should be off the coast of Thailand, and he looked for telltale signs. He saw a narrow strip of arable land between forested hills, then the strip began to widen. The morning sun was full up and the surf near the shore sparkled like a bright necklace. He decided it must be Thailand and that Pattaya must be nearby. The break just past came to mind: Julie Andrews singing in front of the Alps became Siam and Deborah Kerr singing to the king's children in *King and I*, Yul Brynner standing with his feet wide, arms akimbo. He laughed at his train of thought.

11

The crew bus dropped them off at their hootch, twenty-four hours since pickup. Truly fried. Luke and Gropper managed only showers before bed.

After all of that, Luke couldn't sleep. He listened to Gropper's breathing. "Tell me," he said, certain that Gropper was still awake, "what do you honestly think?"

Gropper rolled onto this back. After a minute, he said. "About last night?"

"Yeah. Flying around the Parrot's Beak."

"Who knows. Do you?"

"I just wanted to know what you thought."

"Of course not."

"So I'm not the only one."

"You must be joking," Gropper said.

The conversation lay flat for a moment. "But doesn't it bother you?"

"This is something we're going to do right now? Talk about this? Because if we are, I'm going to wake myself up. But if I don't get some sleep I'm going to be an unhappy camper in the morning, and you'll be the first to know."

"Okay, so maybe just for a minute. Humor me. I need to know if I'm a lone ranger about all this, or maybe, if I'm not, how you deal with it."

Gropper sighed deeply. "Okay. It's like, it's like...ya know...I think maybe it comes down to what you thought was going to happen. And maybe your idea of what was going to happen. We grew up on *Guadalcanal Diary,* you know? And Audie Murphy in *To Hell and Back.* All those double-you double-you two war movies. There were some that came closer to the truth, but not many. Because it was pretty clear to me from the get go that this war was pretty hopeless, from so many points of view. We've got a lot of good men, but somehow, we're lacking in the leadership thing, all the way up the line. You can see it. I don't know if it's the first time we've fought such a fucked-up war. Maybe the Mexican War. Or maybe the Spanish American War. Yeah, probably that one, too. But you know what's different, I think. All the noise from the rear echelon. Go get them commies, boys! The law of inverse proportions, ya know? The farther from the front, the louder the hounds of hell. I never thought anything good was going to happen, and I haven't been disappointed. Once again our leadership is showing themselves inadequate to the quality of our men. So what I think is...I think my advice to you is to recalibrate your expectations. Aim lower—much lower. You won't be disappointed."

Sleep beckoned. The room was comfortably cool, and the closed curtains catching the morning sun created a soft, dream-like aura. Outside, hootch girls walked up and down the sidewalk, flip flops slapping against the concrete.

"Part of my problem," Luke said, "is when we're watching the Thuds and the F-4s take off, I get excited, and I don't even think about what they mean. Going downtown, going to Haiphong and all that. It's every model airplane I ever built. You know what I mean?"

"I didn't build models. I bought old cars and fixed them up and sold them."

"You're kidding. Like what?"

"A '53 Chevy for one. And an old '38 Ford I cut up and made into a jitterbug.

Shortened the wheelbase, cut off the fenders and roof and most of the body. Drove it around the woods."

Luke felt like a child. "But it still comes down to that moment when I watch the fighter jets take off and they're flying into the real shit and then I think about what I'm doing, and I'm doing so little. Honestly, I feel a little ashamed, compared to those guys. You know what I mean? And then I feel stupid for that."

"It is exciting. And it is war, and it is dangerous. Flying those Thuds and F-4s... odds are truly against you. It's always that way in an air war. The folks in North Vietnam absolutely hate those guys. But you asked about me. So let me help you out with a funny story about heroics and changing expectations. This is how flight school works: The guys at the top of each class get first dibs for assignments, and for years the people who run the flight school have seen those guys opt for fighters. Or maybe B-52s. That's the way it always was. Fighting the Cold War. But now the guys near the top of the classes are opting for multi-engines, for C-141s and C-130s. For Connies. Multi-engines so they can fly civilian when they get out. And the people who run the flight school don't know what to do with that. All they ever wanted to do was fly fighters and drop bombs. They came up in a world that was fighting the Commies, the Ruskies and the Chicoms, and the Cold War was plain and simple and there were heroes and bad guys. They can't conceive of guys sharp enough to fly fighters who choose not to. So do I feel left out when the fighters take off? Hell, no. I worked hard not to be one of them. And I succeeded."

Luke smiled. "Connies," he said.

Gropper laughed. "Yeah. Connies. It's a safer way to get through this war. Much safer."

"But it still bothers me when I see those guys taking off and I feel so goddamn guilty."

Gropper laughed. "You gotta get over that. And now, I'm going to sleep. Got that?"

"And then I start thinking about our missions..."

"You gonna let me get to sleep?" Gropper interrupted. "'Cause it sounds like you're not listening to me."

"Yeah. Yeah, I am. It's just. We've got this huge, complicated, electronic system, the brainchild of one of McNamara's shining boys, and it's not doing anything. It's fucking useless. We're not making a bit of difference, not us and not NKP, and certainly not last night with the Army. And the Gee Eyes are getting the crap kicked out of them."

"I can make you feel worse," Gropper said. "Or maybe better. A couple nights ago I was having dinner at the club with one of my buddies from the fighter wing..."

"You've got fighter jock buddies?" Luke interrupted.

"Lots of 'em. We went to flight school together, remember? Sometimes it seems like I know half the pilots in the fighter wing. So I ran into one the other night and we were having dinner and he told me this story about his last mission, over Barrel Roll. He was going after a convoy, no doubt one that we called in..."

"You mean TFA," Luke interjected.

"Yeah, TFA. Our electronic system. Whatever. Don't interrupt. You want to hear this story?"

"Yeah, I do. Or at least I think I do. Do I?"

"Yeah, you do. So my friend, he doesn't know how it happened, but he totally missed his target. A convoy. Five trucks. I mean totally. By a wide margin!"

"Surprise, surprise," Luke said.

"Tuttle, shut up and listen, 'cause you're gonna love this. So he missed. And he watched his rocket stream off course, maybe a half mile, maybe more, maybe less, and it penetrated the jungle, and where it hit it just blew up. Multiple explosions. Huge! He had no idea what it was, maybe a transshipment point, maybe a weapons depot, whatever, but it was pretty clear to him that that was what his target should have been, but nobody knew it was there. Nobody."

"Like we're not even in the same war. Us and them."

"Yeah, something like that."

12

So many flights the same: Time slowed to funereal beats, every noise, every movement distinct—the soft swish of someone swinging his hand as he walked by Luke's position, the rhythmic hum of the engines, the creaks of the plane. The track of the sun across the bulkheads, every detail announced, every fitting, every clamp every screw every surface, the ribs in the rubber deck carpet, the on-off switch on his lamp, the chips in the paint of his console. With time to notice everything, to think about it. He watched his thoughts roll randomly through his mind, untethered. He watched his thoughts as if they were separate beings, and he thought nothing of this, he watched and didn't assess or judge or conclude. He watched his men go through their duties, and when they left orbit he still thought of nothing, his mind blank. Until finally he heard and felt the flaps deploy, the landing gear lower into place and he knew they were nearing Khorat, and soon they would touch down, most likely with a jolt, and soon they would file off the plane and step back into reality. Then they were taxiing, coming to a stop. The aft door opened and soft, humid air wafted in. He stood, gathered his briefcase, stepped onto the portable stairs, walked down to the tune of loose rattles, onto the apron. Walked away, turned, watched his men carry off their gear. Did they have everything? He sat on the crew bus. Followed everyone into Wing, dumped his flight equipment at the desk, filed into the briefing room for debrief. Listened to Woody debrief, each time the same. Were they even halfway there? Was he? Thirty missions down, how many to go? Did it matter? He watched absently as the bus drew up to its stops—post office, enlisted barracks, NCO Club, Officers' Club. Like riding the school bus home each day, Sangerville to Mount Brookville. Interminable. He followed Gropper and Bronfmann into the club for breakfast. Warmed to the banter of the Thai waiters and waitresses. Scrambled eggs. Ham. Touch of garlic. How do they do it, how did it happen, that touch of garlic in everything? Was it in the air? No coffee; time to sleep. Repeat in two days.

13

They manned positions as if they were going to be calling in targets. The same set up for each flight. Taped the consoles, inscribed sensor numbers on the tape. Posted the schedule on the Plexiglas panel next to Tolliver's position. Luke didn't know what the other intelligence officers were doing, but he thought it would be far more painful to just sit around and do nothing, wait for TFA's computers to go down. However it was happening—and he had no idea what was going on, why things had changed—TFA was not only up and running, they were staying on line, and having to jump in to cover them was becoming a thing of the past. Yes, they still tracked convoys, simple work, and they were good at it and they were ready. They paid attention, and wrote the convoys down. And to give it meaning they watched to see if the targets got hit: did TFA pick them up, call them in, and if they did, how long did it take? And then they waited to see if the trucks continued down the Trail. And too often, far too often, they did.

Green, just west of southern North Vietnam. A night

flight, moderate activity. Two positions open. Luke took them on station. After Tolliver relieved him, he stopped by Rolfe's and Molino's positions. Their logs were sparsely and randomly populated with x's, only a few resembling the diagonal pattern of time over distance that represented a convoy going down the Trail.

Luke pulled out Molino's jump seat and sat down to watch. Back on the Cape they had flown together many times, and in those days, when the wing was first organizing, they had spent many hours sitting in Connies out on the parking apron, waiting for no reason that anybody ever knew or told them about. Molino always carried a pack of cards and he and Luke and whomever else comprised the back-end crew that mission would play spades at the aft galley table. Money was never involved, though Molino complained that there should be, so Luke could help send his son of the future to college.

This day Molino marked an x diagonal to a previous activation, then a moment later another, reflecting a possible second truck following the first. He sat up, paying closer attention. The two were followed by a third, and then the first two triggered a sensor farther down the trail, in what was clearly a convoy heading south. Soon another truck followed. Then another. Little by little the convoy built. Ten. Eleven. Twelve. Luke wondered what the North Vietnamese were thinking. They hadn't seen a convoy like this since those first missions, when the NVN didn't grasp that they were being watched. For so long since it had been fives and less, rarely six or seven. But twelve? And then another. Thirteen. What was going on? Was it necessity? Was there a great need somewhere down the Trail? It made no sense.

He and Molino exchanged glances.

The first set of sensors went quiet. Minutes later the second set, ten klicks farther down the trail, began activating. One by one, soon reaching thirteen. "What the fuck?" Luke said.

Molino shrugged. A moment later he held up his hand and talked into his microphone. "Task Force Alpha's down," he said to Luke. "Maybe this is going to be it." There was a pause and then Luke listened as Molino called his convoy in to Tolliver.

Luke hurried back to his position. Stood behind Tolliver as he called Molino's thirteen-truck convoy in to Task Force Alpha. He stopped by Rolphe's position to see if he had any worthwhile targets. Nothing. He returned to Molino. The thirteen had moved beyond Molino's second string and, if they were still on the Trail, which was not a given, were working their way down towards Molino's third set of sensors, a good fifteen klicks farther on. Then Molino began marking down new activations at the first string. They couldn't believe it. Molino looked at him, mildly incredulous. The numbers grew to eight and he called them in to Tolliver. The trucks cleared the first set of sensors and shortly reached the second. Luke returned to his position to watch Tolliver.

In just a moment Tolliver held up his hand. "That's it," he said to Luke. "They're back up."

"Shit," Luke said. "Coitus interruptus," he muttered. Went back to Molino's position to see if the first convoy had showed up on his third string. After a few minutes, the first sensor in the third string activated. A moment later, the second. Then the first sensor activated again. In but a minute all thirteen trucks cleared the third string of sensors, at about the same time that the second convoy cleared the second set of sensors. Soon enough the eight-truck convoy reached the third set of sensors. Luke couldn't believe it. "Shit!" he exclaimed. "What the fuck are they doing? What the fuck is going on down there? I don't get it. I really don't. Those trucks were sitting ducks. What are they doing?"

"It's odd," Molino said. "It really is. Convoys this large." He shook his head.

Luke went to the aft door and looked out the porthole onto the Laotian jungle, black on black in the darkness. What was the point? he wondered to himself. What was the fucking point?

14

Early morning over Green. Gropper, Bronfmann. Luke standing behind Bronfmann. Listening to Armed Forces Radio, a live report from the Ambassador Hotel in Los Angeles. Bobbie Kennedy had just given his victory speech, having won the California primary. The Armed Forces Radio reporter walked with the Kennedy entourage as they exited through the kitchen of the hotel. On to Chicago. Luke smiled to himself. Looked at Gropper, who was smiling as well—at last, maybe, someone who spoke of ending the war. Bronfmann was growing increasingly uncomfortable. Rosie Greer was with them, and Rafer Johnson. Warmth flooded Luke—a respected football player, an Olympic decathlon gold medalist. Cultural heroes. The Gordian knot was being cut. Then suddenly they heard shots being fired, then the Armed Forces Radio reporter: "He's been hit, Senator Kennedy's been hit! He's got a gun, get his gun, somebody get his gun!"

"I hope they got him with a 105," Bronfmann said. An artillery shell.

Luke was dumbfounded. He couldn't believe what he'd just heard.

"Bronfmann!" Gropper exclaimed. "What is wrong with you?"

"Fuck you," Bronfmann said, and stormed out of the flight deck.

And that was it. Just like that. Luke and Gropper were struck mute.

"Where do they come from?" Luke asked. Gropper shook his head.

Anger and disgust displaced by enormous sadness. Not again. Surely not again. Only five years before Luke had been riding in the back seat of an upper classman's car, late fall, November, the trees bare save for a few recalcitrant leaves, driving down Route 20 to Skidmore for the weekend. Three of them, the driver, Luke, and a classmate of Luke's from his floor in the dorm. Listening to music on the radio. An announcer broke in to say that JFK had been shot in Dallas, in a motorcade, and they'd been shocked, all of them of the same accord, as was everyone they saw in every public place they went to after they heard the report, the gas station near Sharon Springs where they filled up, every-where at Skidmore. Everyone in a daze, dumbfounded, truly speechless, the girls at Skidmore hanging on each other's shoulders, crying.

But this one. This time he was there, in the way only radio could do it, he was as good as standing right next to the Armed Forces Radio reporter. He heard it all. One moment he was filled with shock and horror, and then, in the next, Bronfmann filled the air with hatred that dripped black and oily. He was dumbfounded. Another assassination, God help them. JFK's death had rent the fabric of his innocence. After that he'd heard that there were busi-

nessmen in Texas in gilt-lined golf carts who'd celebrated
his death, but he'd just chalked it up to Texas and their
worship of Baal. He'd lived there. He'd seen what it was like.
Then just a few months ago it had been MLK, and the
racists' spittle-dripping hatred, and all of it was beyond his
ken. But now. To be standing next to it. He *knew* this man.
They worked together. They *lived* together. He was a captain
in the Air Force. How had it happened? What the fuck was
he doing here, standing next to men like Bronfmann? And
then, as the reality of the situation became manifest,
sadness. Tears filled his eyes, though they did not flow.
Sadness tinged with despair. Bobbie Kennedy gone, MLK
gone, and there were no more champions left, no one at the
top campaigning to end the war, no one in the ranks. For the
first time in his life, he felt the eviscerating feeling of hope-
lessness.

NOT SO LONG AFTER, another incident. A small thing, but
not. Luke in the right seat, Gropper the left. Gropper and
Luke simply riding. Listening to Armed Forces Radio. Blue
skies, scattered clouds. The Rascals, *Groovin*, on a Sunday
afternoon.

Gropper changed the frequency to the airborne
command post. They listened as first one fighter called in to
pick up a target, and then, a moment later, another. Not long
after the first fighter pilot called the command post again.
"Hillsboro," he said. "I'm nearly bingo and heading home.
How'd I do?"

"Bingo?" Luke asked.

"On his dash," Gropper said. "The fuel gauge looks like a
bingo grid. When all three columns drop to nothing, he's
empty. Bingo."

"Roger," Hillsboro said. "I've got three explosions."

"Roger," the fighter replied. "Five explosions. Good working' with you."

Luke looked at Gropper.

"It happens," Gropper said. "Fuck with the numbers in the war of numbers. No one cares."

AGAIN IN THE COCKPIT, again a day flight. This one cut the last mooring. A contrail high overhead. Luke watched it form, then dissipate slowly into a long, linear cloud. "Who's that?" he asked.

Gropper leaned forward in his seat, the better to see. "Opium flight out of Laos."

Luke looked at him.

And again the Gropper shrug, punctuating his teaching of Luke the neophyte. "The opium flight. CIA. Carrying opium for the Thai generals. From the golden triangle."

"How can you tell?"

"It's a C-47. Specially conditioned. There's no missing it."

"Shit. I can't believe I'm that out of it. The golden triangle?"

"Burma, Laos, Thailand, China. They've been growing poppies up there for hundreds of years. Don't you know anything?"

"I guess not."

And after a few more moments, "Air America? Running drugs?"

"The Thai generals let us use their airbases, we fly their shit to Bangkok."

Luke sighed.

15

This night a monsoon storm on their return to Khorat. Woody in the left seat, Gropper in the right, Luke wedged behind Gropper, next to the flight engineer. The cockpit bathed in darkness except for the green glow of the lights on the instrument panels.

"Look at that," Woody said, pointing at the weather radar. Luke looked but didn't grasp what he was seeing—a green electronic blur growing slowly into a mass that spread across half the scope. He looked up. Far in the distance a corresponding wall of clouds was establishing its presence, billowing high and wide, an organic fortress that was soon going to fill the sky. Perhaps Woody and Gropper had seen weather like this before; Luke had not. He was startled at how quickly the sky changed, the enormity of what was gathering. Flashes of lightning jumped from cloud to cloud, illuminating the storm's innards and giving it insidious life, becoming a monstrous ghoulie of immense power that assumed a personality and presence all its own, like a prehistoric beast.

"Whattaya think?" Gropper said to Woody.

"There's no way around it," Woody said. "If we turn around it'll catch up with us in minutes and I don't want it running up our ass. I don't see any choice. We'll take it head on."

"Right," Gropper said.

Woody turned his comm switch to intercom. "Crew, we're heading into a front. We've only got a few minutes. Batten down everything you can lay your hands on." He turned to Luke. "Get your area ready, Tuttle," he said.

Luke's stomach churned. He didn't know what the alternatives might be, but there was no question in his mind but that this was going to be rough, certainly more turbulence than he'd ever experienced before. He went quickly aft, noting Brooks and Perez tugging on each piece of electronics, making sure they were secure in the racks.

Tolliver had inspected each of the intelligence positions and was strapping himself into his own seat, behind the Plexiglas panel across from Luke. Just after Luke strapped in the ride began to get bumpy; in but a moment the bumps became bigger and more forceful, great hiccups of uncontrolled movement, at first intermittent, then constant. The thrashing continued for a minute, then two, then three, each interminable. Continued unabated. Four, five. He tried to imagine where their plane was in relation to what he'd seen from the cockpit—how much of the storm they'd already penetrated, how much farther they to go. Six, seven. Great *thumps* of noise and thrusting metal. What was it like close in? Jerks and bounces increasing in frequency and volatility. The aircraft floor dropped suddenly, then with a jerk bounced back up. Fell again. Jerked up again, each bounce increasing in severity. Nine minutes, ten. A hellacious drop, a slapping return. He held on to his desktop to steady himself. Wondered what the stresses might be and if this Connie had ever had to stand up to such erratic and violent movement before. How much could it endure before metal started to crack? The plane was old. Was this the moment when something finally gave way? He could hear the electronic equipment straining in the racks behind him, the metal squeaking and grinding. Other noises of stress that he couldn't identify. He was petrified, couldn't stand the thought of the plane breaking up and him falling helpless from the sky. Beyond the thin sheet of fuselage churned a reality about which he knew nothing. The Connie could be corrupt to the core and he wouldn't know, like rotten wood masquerading as solid with a thick coat of shiny paint. He twisted around in his seat and looked forward and was shocked—the deck was twisting like a corkscrew, first one way and then another. He couldn't imagine what the plane looked like from the outside.

He looked across the aisle at Sergeant Tolliver and was astonished. Tolliver was sitting quietly with his eyes closed, holding his liver-spotted hands lightly one atop the other on his Ho Tai stomach. Luke wondered how he could be so calm, even with his lifetime of flying. His bald head glowed spectrally in the dim light of the intelligence compartment. Perhaps sensing Luke's attention, Tolliver opened his eyes and looked at him. Smiled his years of experience smile. Spoke into his microphone: "Lieutenant," he said. "The older the plane the better. They've got more give, and this one was flying when Hector was a pup."

"How do you know this isn't the time?"

"*Mai pen rai,* Lieutenant," he said. "*Mai pen rai.*" It doesn't matter.

The storm tossed them around like a die being shaken

in a cup. One moment Luke felt like he was floating in his chair, his stomach unsettled, the next his seat slapped him as it came back up. The engines alternately roared and growled as they worked their way through waves of heavy weather, into and out of clouds, and yes, the Connie seemed to be holding, but Luke wondered what was coming next, thinking always that this could be it, that ultimately natural forces reigned and there had to be a point beyond which the plane would not hold, there had to be stresses beyond that which it was designed for, there had to be a point at which the metal would snap, there was always a limit, there was a limit to everything, a breaking point for everything, human and material. He listened to the creak of metal, closed his eyes and gripped the armrests of his seat, steeling himself.

"Lieutenant," Tolliver said over the intercom, "did I ever tell you about when I flew up a canyon in Texas in a DC-2 during the war?"

Luke listened. He wanted to honor Tolliver, but he found it very difficult to concentrate.

"We lost an engine and lost altitude and fell into this canyon where we could barely manage eighty miles an hour and the headwinds were coming down the canyon at ninety miles an hour and we were slipping backwards. I thought it was all over. But the pilot managed to keep it under control and then when we were blown back out, we just turned and flew to the closest airfield."

Was that even possible, Luke asked himself? Aerodynamically? Backwards? He looked at Tolliver for hint as to the truth of the story. It could be true, he guessed; he certainly didn't know, yet somehow he couldn't believe it. Tolliver smiled, steady in the bucking plane, as inscrutable as ever.

Suddenly they were through and the turbulence ended

as quickly as it began; the engines dropped into a smooth cadence and they were flying level and even, everything calm and settled like the flat water beyond rock-strewn rapids. Tolliver smiled. "I'm telling you, Lieutenant," he said. "Don't you worry. You stick with me. We're going to be all right."

16

He walked down the aisle between the bunks in Saint's barracks. Midday, shutters pulled close, the air still and musty, faint smell of locker rooms and unwashed feet. The rows of bunks disappeared into the shadowed distance like stacks of inventory in a warehouse. From afar there was the sound of snoring. Otherwise all was quiet; nothing moved.

Saint was the source of the snoring, sprawled in his upper bunk asleep, legs entangled in sheets, the only man left in his bay, perhaps in the barracks. Mouth agape. A rhythmic rattling echoed from his throat unlike anything Luke had ever heard before. He wondered how it was that a human being could make such noise. He shook Saint to wake him.

Small, swishing sliding steps approached. Mah-li appeared out of the shadows like an apparition. She stopped, arms akimbo. "You get that number ten Gee Eye out of bed," she said, not quietly. Her voice was nasal and harsh and irritating. "I got work to do. You get him up."

Saint opened his eyes, croaked a few words. "This is my commanding officer," he said. "You be nice."

Mah-li was unimpressed. "What you do here with this number ten Gee Eye?" she said to Luke. "You get him up, I got work to do."

Saint pulled himself together. Sat up, feet dangling, eyes half-mast. He swung to the floor, took his towel and bath kit from his locker and went to the shower. Shortly he returned, revived and smiling. His freshness filled the bay. He dressed and they walked to the cab stand to catch a ride downtown. The day before break. Later that afternoon the crew would gather poolside for a party at the Sri Patana on Suranaree Road. Until then there were things to do.

"It's gonna rain," Luke said. "Bring your umbrella."

ANOTHER DAY of heat and heavy humidity, distant trees and buildings floating in the haze. The cab wasn't air-conditioned and their shirts were soon soaked through. It didn't matter; it was the same for everyone they saw. They passed the bus stop just off base where waiting Thai lined the road, each one squatting in the shade of a roadside guard posts, one per, a row of bookends laying claim to the meagre shadows. Broad ditches paralleled the road, the far slopes crowded by scrub brush and stunted trees and an occasional tall tree of unknown variety. Leaves drooped in the heat, coated with dust. In the distance corrugated tin roofs poked above the brush; waves of heat bounced off the tin like mirages. They passed an ancient and empty wooden-wheeled cart trundling ghost-like along the side of the road, pulled by a water buffalo. The driver's head and that of the water buffalo hung low, beaten into submission.

As they neared town the huts increased in frequency

and size and closeness to the road, and they were greeted by the familiar smells of clustered humanity—smoldering charcoal, garlic, open sewers. Mildew. Smells that Luke had recoiled from when first he had arrived in Thailand, and that since had become the smell of rich, tropic life. Huts became houses, grew to two stories, tin roofs became tile, walls concrete. Fences separated each house from the next and from the road, wattle and daub, bamboo and concrete. Spirit temples sat like elaborate bird houses atop posts in every yard, joss sticks smoldering pungently in the bird houses' miniature front yards, fending off universal evil.

They left the taxi in the market square on Chumphon Road near the statue of Mama Khorat. Lady Mo. Fighter of Lao, lifter of sieges. The square was crowded, busy with noise and people shopping. *Samlahr* ground by. Thai leis hung from the awning of a nearby market stall, their rich aroma filling the air. Luke snorted. This was the one smell he couldn't stand, finding it cloying and funereal. He steered clear. Saint walked over to the stall and buried his nose in each one.

"Can't do it," Luke said.

Saint shrugged. "Love it," he said.

They went to the Foremost dairy bar, picture windows and stainless steel, red and white formica and vinyl-covered booths. Air-conditioning. The U.S. in the nineteen-fifties. Fats Domino on the jukebox, *Walkin' to New Orleans*. They ate banana splits sitting at a table next to the front window and watched the afternoon monsoon sweep up the street like the advance guard of an invading army. Everything came to a stop. In the dairy bar those who had finished eating stood just inside the door and waited. Those outside stood patiently under the overhangs of buildings and the flaps of market stalls. A sole, shirtless boy rushed up the street holding an elephant-ear leaf over his head like an umbrella.

As Luke and Saint finished the last of their ice cream the rain moved on. They ventured out, swinging their umbrellas like walking canes, clicking the metal tips on the sidewalk, feeling British and colonial. To the Khorat Tailor, walls of bolts of English woolens and oxford-weave cotton. Thompson's Thai silk. The shop was air-conditioned, the owner Indian, tall, portly, dressed in slacks and an open-necked starched white shirt. His English accented and lilting. He nodded to Luke and Saint, greeting them both as friends, and beckoned his tailor, speaking to him in Thai. The tailor brought out a canvas safari jacket that Luke was having made and helped him slip it on.

"Whattaya think?" Luke asked Saint. "I found the canvas in another shop," he said. "It was the only duck cloth in town. I looked everywhere. It was too heavy, really, so they pulled out threads and washed it until they got it soft. I got some Thai army buttons in the local five-and-dime."

The tailor circled Luke, marking changes with pins and chalk. Luke lifted his arms and flexed. "Could you maybe vent the shoulders?" he asked. "Is it too late? Maybe use elastic so they pull back into place after you stretch? Like this" he said, hunching his shoulders forward.

The owner spoke to his tailor and when the tailor responded the owner laughed. "We can do that, yes, sir, Lieutenant Tuttle. My tailor knows exactly what you want. He says he made a jacket just like that for the Japanese colonel that ran Khorat during the war."

Luke nodded and smiled. When they left, he said, "Jesus, that feels funny, don't you think? Buying the same jacket a Japanese colonel did during World War Two. I never thought about the Japanese being here during the war, not

Khorat. I mean I know they were in Thailand, the Bridge on the River Kwai and all that. That was horrendous. Building that railroad north. But that was a totally different world, a different time, a long time ago. Only it wasn't. They were here, occupying Khorat, it's just over twenty years, that's nothing, and here I am, using the same tailor that a Japanese colonel used."

They stopped at a nearby cobbler where Saint had ordered a pair of custom-made golf shoes. The shop smelled of leather and wax, and the cobbler old and wizened, his brown skin wrinkled like the sheets of curled leather hanging on the walls. Mister Tsao. He smiled and wai-ed when they stepped inside. Pulled a package wrapped in perforated computer paper down from a shelf and set it on the counter. *Confidential* printed on the paper. Luke wondered how the paper had made it from the base to town. Mentally shrugged. Who cared. It was only confidential. Now *Secret*—that would be another matter. Mister Tsao untied the string and folded the paper back.

The shoes were dark grey. "Elephant hide," Saint said, running his fingers over the leather. "Aren't they beautiful? Naturally waterproof. Tough as nails."

Mister Tsao held the shoes up for Saint's inspection, turned them over. The soles were barren. "You rike?" he said.

"Yeah, I rike," Saint said. "You put on spikes, yes?"

The old man looked at him questioningly.

"Spikes," Saint repeated. "Spikes."

The cobbler knitted his eyebrows.

"I don't think he gets it," Luke said. "Didn't you tell him what they were for?"

"I thought I did. Spikes," he repeated. He swung a

phantom golf club, looked at his feet, turned his foot over to reveal the bottom of his sole. He looked at Mister Tsao.

The cobbler stared blankly at Saint.

Saint motioned as if to write and Mister Tsao gave him pencil and paper. More computer paper, again marked *Confidential*. Saint drew a side view of a golf shoe with spikes and showed it to Mister Tsao.

"Ah," the cobbler said. "Ah," he repeated and smiled. "Spi-kus."

Saint spread his hands apart, palms up, expectant. "You can do? Okay?"

The cobbler held the shoes up again. "You rike?"

"Yes, I rike. No have spi-kus."

"Number one, yes?"

"No number one, number ten. No have spi-kus."

Mister Tsao looked at Saint. "Number ten?"

"Yes, number ten, no have spikes. You have spikes?" He pointed to the spikes on the drawing.

"No have," Mister Tsao said. "You rike? You pay."

"No, pay. Shoes number ten. No have spikes."

"No have."

"You get?"

"No have."

"I understand no have. You get?"

"Pay now."

"No pay. Pay when you get spikes, put here." Saint tapped the sole of a shoe.

"No have."

"I know that. You get?"

"No have. You pay. Pay now."

Mister Tsao was getting uncomfortable, shifting his eyes from Saint to Luke to the street outside. The confrontation was growing. Luke wondered at what point Mister Tsao would call for help and what would happen then.

"No. No pay."

"Pay, pay now."

"Why don't you," Luke said.

"Are you crazy? Where am I going to get someone else to put on spikes? Do you know a cobbler anywhere in the states? You think it's something you can get done at a shoe repair store?"

"Pay him, leave the shoes, get some spikes and bring them back."

"Bullshit, Bunky. Where am I going to get spikes?" He paused, thinking, then gave in. "Okay," he said. He paid for the shoes. The old man wrapped them in the computer paper, tied the string and handed the parcel to Saint.

"No," Saint said. "I get spikes." He pointed to his drawing. "I bring you spikes. You fix, make number one."

"Number one," the old man said, and smiled. Luke was relieved; he wasn't so sure about Saint.

"That's a lost cause," Saint said as they left.

"What are you going to do?"

"I'll write my Mom. We'll see."

"It'll work. She can send you spikes instead of cookies.

17

The party was a celebration of sorts, a changing of the guard, good-bye to Sergeant Tolliver, heading to Biloxi, hello to Senior Master Sergeant John Rickey, formerly of SAC headquarters at Offut and the real Air Force, as he had already made abundantly clear, as if they were initials following his last name.

They were happy for Tolliver, sad for themselves. They were all fond of him, flight crew as well as back end. He had a way about him when he told the enlisted men what to do that they hardly realized they'd been given an order. Luke had talked to him about everything, even how to handle fellow officers, anxious to get an experienced and sane man's read on some he thought were undeniable idiots. There had even been a day when Tolliver told Luke that he liked the way he handled their men, treating them with respect, and looked forward to the day when that was how it would be throughout the Air Force. "This isn't the Army," he said. "We don't get the draftees." He was convinced it worked better, and that they would get the best out of the men that way. "Treat them like real people," he said. "Like they didn't check their brains at the door."

Rickey was another matter. Ripped and side-walled, taciturn, ultra-serious. A John Wayne wannabe, or so it seemed to Luke. Five-mile runs at dawn. Walked as if he were marching. SAC through and through, ready to fly through the gates of hell to get to Moscow. Sterling Hayden's General Jack D. Ripper. Tolliver warned Luke immediately. "He's going to be a new broom, Lieutenant," he said. "The NCO manual says not to and I told him so. It's on the first page. But he's going to start pushing for change as soon as I get out the door. You keep your eye on him!"

Suranaree Road was under construction, and the afternoon monsoon had left great ponds of muddy water in the ruts and low places among the hillocks of dirt and debris. Luke and Saint walked single file across planks thrown across the largest pond, while those crossing from the other side waited their turn.

Woody had reserved the pool and patio and the crew clustered at tables in a pecking order—flight officers and engineers on the patio, the back-end crew clustered at poolside. Woody was in the greatest of moods, laughing, full of life—his men, his crew. The flight engineers brought their *teelaghs*, mistresses, who sat together off by themselves. Sergeant O'Keefe's was attractive, her face pancaked with makeup, the arc of her eyebrows painted down the bridge of her nose to make it look larger, the way so many Thai women did to save the Americans the embarrassment of their European noses. Stevenson's was a Lao teenager going on thirty, straight hair and acne-scarred face, dressed Amish-plain in a dark dress. The women rarely looked at the rest of the crew, rarely at each other, and instead caged their eyes and gazed down at their feet. Woody treated everyone to hors d'oeuvres—pigs in a blanket, tuna on toast, fruit kebabs. Pineapple chunks on toothpicks. After eating the Thai *teelagh* demurely picked her teeth with a toothpick, hiding her mouth behind her hand, a lesson in refinement.

There were outliers. Frank Goodin, the radio op, moved about, sitting first with the flight engineers, who ignored him, then with the in-flight techs. Tolliver and Rickey sat at a table off to the side, their conversation deeply serious. Every now and then Rickey would look up, each time at a different enlisted man, putting a face to one of Tolliver's comments.

Conversation among the back-end crew was easy. Social gab at first, best cookout, best hot dogs, best brats. Regional comparisons of best beer, Olly versus UC versus Iron City. How many beers could be drunk at a sitting. How fast could a beer be downed. "I can do it in ten seconds," John Constance said, which Rolfe wouldn't buy. "Bullshit," he said. "Why do you say things like that?"

"Because it's true, that's why," John Constance replied.

"Prove it," Rolfe said.

"Not for nothing. Whattaya give me?"

"Five bucks," Rolfe replied.

"Five fucking bucks. Put your money where your mouth is. Twenty."

"I don't have twenty," Rolfe said.

"Okay, then," John Constance replied. "My statement stands."

"Bullshit, just bullshit!" Rolfe said. "Who's got a twenty I can borrow?"

"Don't do it," Tanaka announced. "It's money down the drain. So to speak."

"You know better?" Rolfe said.

"I do. I've seen him do it."

"You two work this scam together?"

"Suit yourself. He can do it. Fair warning."

"Who's got a twenty?" Rolfe asked.

"I'll cover you," McAuley said.

The others sat forward, started paying attention. "Airman John Constance," Woody called over from the table he and Gropper were sharing. "What's your trick? There's gotta be a trick. There's always a trick. Is this something you learned in college?"

"No, sir. Graduate school, sir," John Constance answered.

"Graduate school?" Woody said. "You went to graduate school?"

"Yes, sir, I did," John Constance answered.

"You have a p-h-d?" Woody said, drawing out the letters. "Piled higher and deeper?" he added. He laughed. Gropper and Howard, the senior navigator, rolled their eyes.

"No, sir," John Constance said. "A-b-d."

"A-b-d?" Woody asked.

"All but dissertation," Gropper said.

"How do you know that?" Woody asked.

Gropper shrugged.

"What'd you major in?" Woody asked.

"Philosophy, sir."

"Philosophy? You're kidding. You're kidding, right? A philosopher? On my crew? What kind of job can you get with that?"

"That's what my dad said," John Constance answered.

"So what are you doing here?"

"Well, sir, long story short, my Dad told me to check the want ads for philosophers. That's when I quit graduate school and went down to the recruiting office and signed up."

"Good man, Airman Constance, good man. What was your thesis going to be?"

"Merleau-Ponty," John Constance said. "And the phenomenologists."

"The what?" Woody said.

The conversation stalled, and John Constance turned his attention to Rolfe and the table. McAuley put a church key and a Hamm's in front of John Constance, took his watch off and dramatically held it up, his other hand raised in the air like starter at a foot race.

John Constance punched a large hole in the top of the can, then punched another in the bottom that he covered with his finger.

"Wait a minute!" McAuley said. "What the fuck are you doing?"

"Opening my can."

"But you can't do that."

"Do what?"

"Two holes. Top and bottom."

"We gonna do this, or aren't we? Cause I'm drinking this thing, and you're gonna pay me twenty dollars. Nobody said anything about the number of holes I was allowed." John Constance looked around. "Lieutenant?" he said.

"Seems legit to me," Luke said.

McAuley and Rolfe glared at Luke and the moment lost all joy. John Constance put the top of the can to his mouth and waited for McAuley to give the signal. When he did, John Constance took his finger off the hole on the bottom, opened his gullet, not bothering to swallow, and the beer sluiced down his throat in a long *swoosh*. In less than 10 seconds, he was done. He sat the empty can down and looked at Rolfe and McAuley. "Physics," he said. "Ain't it wonderful? Pay up!"

"Shootin' fish in a barrel," Tanaka said. All but Rolfe and McAuley laughed. Rolfe looked at McAuley, his face red with anger and embarrassment. McAuley begrudgingly handed John Constance a twenty.

"John Constance," Woody said. "How do you do that?"

"Besides the physics, sir? The trick is to not swallow. You just open your gullet and let it rip," he said. "Takes practice. That's what you do in graduate school. Practice."

THE PARTY CONTINUED with hamburgers and hot dogs and more beer. Late afternoon they went swimming—only the back-end crew, without Tolliver and Rickey, but also without Rolfe and McAuley, who continued their slow burn. First Rolfe and then McAuley began commenting about the swimmers, the gist being who was Luke's favorite. Soon the beer was talking and the comments got edgy, until John Constance said McAuley oughtn't denigrate the lieutenant, and McAuley said, "That's all right. I don't pay any attention to lieutenants, I only listen to captains and above."

The rest of the enlisted men cat-called and whistled, and a stone-faced Rickey made a comment to Tolliver that Luke caught out the corner of his eye. He could well imagine the words.

From there the party went downhill. At some point the swimmers—Luke included—decided McAuley needed to go swimming, and they threw him in, clothes and all. McAuley pushed and squirmed and they dragged him to the edge of the pool and it was all ungainly and it looked like McAuley was going to hit his head on the edge of the pool as they tossed him in. After he climbed out he sat at his table, dripping wet and glowering. It seemed perhaps that that was the end of it, that everyone had had enough, and the swimmers dried off and changed back to street clothes in the room Woody had rented. But later, when everything seemed smoothed over, as John Constance walked past McAuley carrying a tray full of cans, McAuley pushed him in. Luke saw it happen and the vicious look on McAuley's face, and decided to leave well enough alone. Enough was enough, and far too much beer had flowed to find justice.

18

To Bangkok in the morning, a big, black soft ride, driver attentive to the road and his vehicle, constantly, lovingly, wiping down the wood wheel and dash with an ancient chamois while he drove. Down the Friendship Highway, across open fields and farmland towards the range of hills and rocky outcrops marking the edge of the Plateau, then through the hills past the Thai-Danish dairy, incongruous with its black and white Holsteins grazing in the deep shadows under the trees, to Saraburi, for the left turn to Bangkok.

Just before Saraburi Luke noticed two World War Two Japanese light tanks guarding the entrance to a Thai army base, and it brought back a memory of jungle survival school in the Philippine mountains near Clark Air Force Base. Climbing a narrow path out of their encampment, through a densely vegetated ravine. Captivated by the primitive, untrammeled look of the place, so like the ravine in the woods behind home in Mount Brookville. Up and up, a step, another, and abruptly the brush fell away and he was in open space walled and roofed by green, a shadowy cathedral with a broad, empty floor dimly lit by soft, gentle shafts of sunlight flickering through the jungle ceiling. Suddenly a racket commenced—birds? Insects? He had no idea. A fast staccato, too much like singular and lonely machine gun fire. There was no other word for it. He knew it couldn't be, but it sounded like the real thing. The noise resounded for what was probably thirty seconds that seemed like minutes, then, just as inexplicably, stopped. He explored the edges of the open space, looking, trying to understand. Saw a small, rounded object, clearly manmade and not of nature, that, when he kicked, revealed itself to be the remains of a helmet. Japanese. Infantry. Then another that could have been a tanker's helmet. He remembered someone in the survival school saying that this was the route the Sixth Army took when it came back to Clark Air Base towards the end of World War Two. The relics made sense. He explored farther, and at the edge of the soft green wall of vegetation saw a hard edge. Concrete. He pulled at the greenery—vines, brush, saplings—and uncovered the firing side of a pill box, still black with carbon at the aperture all these years later. The staccato noise erupted again, continued, and he felt like an intruder, that he had stepped back in time and had come upon a sacred place, a ghostly ritual he had no business experiencing. He left quickly, retracing his steps back down the path through the ravine towards their camp.

With the memory of the Philippines came again his reaction when his tailor told him he had outfitted the Japanese commander in Khorat, and it felt like World War Two had never ended, it was here, still, in this part of the world, it was endless, evermore, if not here, then some-where, if not now, then soon.

"It's strange," he said to Saint, "how it all seems so recent," to which Saint replied, "I get that feeling when I run into the World War Two vets back home, they seem so old, but it's barely been twenty years since their war. That's nothing. We'll be there in a heartbeat."

Once in Saraburi they stopped at a Thai roadside stand at the intersection with the Bangkok highway to Bangkok, a dirt-floored cooking hut lined with charcoal braziers, little bowls of concrete wrapped by flattened beer and vegetable cans, attended by Thai women squatting on their haunches. The few rickety wooden tables and chairs were occupied, so Luke and Saint squatted on their haunches outside, in the shade of a tree, and ate their *khow pod,* fried rice, with ceramic spoons, chasing it with orange Fanta.

Saint waved his spoon at the building. "Thai Ho-Jo," he said.

Luke laughed. "Only lacks an orange roof."

"Ya know, when I first got here I couldn't have squatted like this. Whenever I tried, my ass was so big that I always fell backwards."

"How much do you figure you've lost?"

"Twenty, twenty-five pounds," Luke said. "Every couple of days I stop by the infirmary and check. High point of my day."

Saint nodded. "I love this stuff," he said, his mouth full. "I just love it."

"YA KNOW," Luke said, "I think I need to learn Thai. Something besides bar Thai. Wait and go fast and turn right and turn left. Pretty, and no have brains."

"Why?" Saint said.

"I just wanna. I wanna make this place feel more like home."

Saint raised his eyebrows.

"Well, I do. I like it here. Off base. Trips like this."

"DID you see those Japanese tanks at the entrance to the base we passed on our way in," Luke said.

"I did. But they had Thai writing on them."

"Yeah, but they're Japanese light tanks."

"How do you know?"

"I made a model of one when I was in junior high."

MEANWHILE, at the edge of the packed dirt parking area, in the shade of a small tree, their driver was wiping down their car.

"Funny," Saint said. "I don't think of the Japs in tanks."

"Yeah. I found a Japanese tanker's helmet in jungle survival school on the way over. Along with a bunch of infantry helmets. Surprised me."

"DID YOU GO? To the Philippines? To survival school?"

"No."

Luke nodded. "It was really amazing! Up in the mountains outside Clark Air Force Base, in the pass back to Clark. We rode up in trucks with canvas covering the backs, just like troops in World War Two, and when we went through this little village all the kids came running out and chased us and they were calling out "Joe, hey Joe, you got gum?" It was like straight out of a movie." He paused while he ate. "There's aborigines up there, too. Negritos. They helped us in the fight against the Japs, and when we asked them what they wanted, they said they wanted the rights to the dump at our air base."

· · ·

"THE LAST THING you do in survival school is you go out into the jungle and hide. They give you five chits, and each chit is worth a bag of rice. Then they send the Negritos after you, and if they catch you, you have to give them a chit. If you lose all five chits, you have to do the exercise in the jungle again."

"Did you?"

Luke laughed. "This old Negrito approached us. Me and a guy from the Fifty-fourth that I went to intelligence school with, and the Negrito bartered this deal with us. In pidgin English. If we'd give him four of our chits, he'd take us out into the jungle to a place where nobody would find us. I wasn't sure that's what we agreed to, so when we took off, I was a little edgy. And I mean to tell you, we went way the hell out into the jungle. I was starting to wonder. But finally we came to this open area with a little grass hut in the middle, and he motioned that we would spend the night there. And it was fine, except for the fact that we woke up in the middle of the night with rats crawling all over us, looking for food. Then in the morning, they sent helicopters out to pick everyone up, to give us practice signaling with a mirror and getting extracted from the jungle and all that. So the open space was good, because we could easily pick up the sun and flash it at the chopper. Then they came and lowered a horse collar and pulled us up. It was cool."

"Makes me wish I'd gone," Saint said.

"It was really cool. There's one thing that happened there that'll stick with me forever. That last morning, after they'd picked us up, they dropped us off in this field to wait for the trucks to take us back down to Clark, and there were all these choppers landing and taking off, bringing everyone in, and while I was waiting I happened to look around and there was this old Negrito sitting on top of a big rock, watching the whole thing. He only had a loin cloth on, and he had a feather stuck in his hair, and he had this little bow and arrow in his hand, I don't think the bow was longer than two feet, and he had his arrow notched into the bowstring and I wondered what he was going to do with it, if he was going to hunt with it or what. The contrast was stunning, this primitive culture overlooking these huge, noisy machines of war. I wish I'd taken a picture of it."

"Did you have your camera with you?"

"No. But I wished I'd had it. I'da loved to have gotten a photograph."

"And the helmet?"

Luke shrugged.

"Shoulda kept it," Saint said.

THEY FINISHED EATING and got in their car and headed south. The road from Saraburi to Bangkok was straight, first past paddies, then paddies interspersed with small factories and concrete storage areas, surrounded by wire fences and concrete posts, then just factories, most of them new.

19

T heir hotel was on a quiet *soi* off New Petchaburi, recently opened, exterior walls clean white and mildew-free, spartan against the soft green of the tree-lined street. They checked in, took their bags to their rooms, and met up in the bar.

"Look at this, Bunky," Saint said as Luke came in. He gestured at a row of portholes behind the bar that gave onto the dreamy aquamarine of a swimming pool. Shafts of sunlight flashed through the water and the pink legs of *farung* children churned at the shallow end of the pool.

"What's that?" Luke said, looking at Saint's drink as he sat down.

"Gin and tonic."

"I'll have one of those," he said to the Thai bartender.

They watched the activity in the pool, the children's kicking legs, the occasional adult's. Always female. There was a silent explosion of bubbles and color from which a vague shape emerged, a bright red bikini swimsuit and a blur of pink flesh.

"Look at that," Saint said, in hushed, reverential tones. "Boobs! Western boobs! Look at 'em!"

The woman swam by the portholes and was gone.

"Missed it," Luke said. But in a moment she was back, another explosion of bubbles and color, great mounds of flesh pushing to escape her swimsuit. She slipped by, her stomach her hips her kicking legs.

"Gawd," Saint said. "Do you believe it? I think I've died and gone to heaven. I'm already getting a hard-on."

Yet another explosion of color and bubbles. "Do you think she knows we're here?" Saint asked. And answering his own question, "She does. She's putting on a show!" He paused. "Boofers," he said finally. Exaggerated, melodramatic. "Boofers! Boobs isn't big enough!"

The woman remained in the water, hanging onto the edge of the pool in the middle distance, red bikini bottom, legs kicking lazily. Talking to whom? She slipped away from the edge, began a breast stroke towards them, her eyes open, and they were convinced she was watching them. She turned and swam away, frog kicks that momentarily accented her crotch, her full pudendum. She turned lazily around, dove down deeper and headed straight towards them again, a picture of brown hair drifting back in the current of her passage, pendulous breasts moving independently, her eyes still open.

"Boo-boffers," Saint said. "Boo-boffers."

"She saw us," Luke said.

She swam to the ladder and they watched her disappear.

"Damn," Saint said.

"I think she's a bit fat," Luke said.

"Who cares," Saint said.

A few minutes later she walked into the bar, beach robe

pulled loosely closed, cleavage exposed to view, and yes, she was overweight. And teen-aged.

"What is it with you and the young ones?" Luke said.

The girl looked briefly at them. Her glance was hard and she pointedly did not smile. Luke wondered if that was her nature, if this was how she maintained distance, or if she thought haughty arrogance was cool. She walked to the bar and ordered a coke. Still she did not look at them. Once the bartender handed her the glass she left, avoiding their gaze.

"Playing hard to get," Saint said.

"She has zits in her cleavage. And her boobs are baby fat."

Saint laughed. "Thanks, Bunky."

The girl did not return, nor did she dive again into the pool. The show was over. As a last thought Saint said, "Bombastulent. That's what they were. Bombastulent boo-boffers. Hang to her knees by the time she's twenty. She's gonna wish she hooked up with me when she could."

They went outside, walking slowly up the near empty *soi* to New Petchaburi, already wilting in Bangkok's tropic heat and humidity.

On New Petchaburi they entered the world of the tourist, a madman's pinball machine of noise and activity, some slow, some fast, all unrelated. *Tuk-tuks* darted through the traffic like fighter planes among bombers; pedestrians crowded the sidewalks—school children in uniforms of blue shorts and white shirts; Gee Eyes on R&R, their arms around their Thai hookers, hands on their asses, impatient. Street vendors everywhere, shops with tables of carved wood souvenirs, elephants rearing and fucking, the three wise monkeys, miniature temples and Buddhas of cheap jade that looked like they would crack at any minute. An exquisite brass figurine of a Thai dancer mounted on a mahogany pedestal that Luke fell in love with, wondering if it might be antique. He imagined it on the mantle at home in Mount Brookville, friends impressed by its provenance.

Food vendors everywhere. They were hungry, but didn't have a clue what was good or safe to eat. Hucksters planted themselves in front of them, holding open pamphlets that looked like small-town high school yearbooks but with columns of available women. Their earlier confidence disappeared. Now they truly didn't know. The figurines, the Chinese porcelain. The women. Should they? Would they be cheated? If they didn't, would they one day regret it?

A young Thai man darted out of the crowd and was in Luke's face before he knew what was going on. Luke was taken aback, fearful. The man looked in Luke's eyes and took his hand and put something in it. Then he was gone and Luke stared after him, wondering what had just happened. He opened his hand and held up a black bead with white spots and holes for stringing.

"What the fuck?" Saint said.

Luke shook his head. Was it safe, he wondered? Was it contaminated? Was it bad or good? What was it? Did the man hate all westerners and just put a curse on him? Was it a talisman?

"Toss it," Saint said.

At first that sounded right. But what if the bead was a gift of good will? What if it carried within it all the good feelings the man had ever managed to muster? Would it be bad *karma* to toss it? He pocketed it. He never got rid of it; it sat in a bowl atop his dresser for years, along with his other odds and ends—graciously smooth pebbles, errant screws from some or other project. Pennies. Buttons from anti-war marches, a long string of them over the years. Every few years when he came across the bead he would pick it up and put it in the palm of his hand. Remember and wonder. After all this time—was it safe? Was it malevolent? What had happened to the man who gave it to him? Was it why things hadn't gone so well for him? Should he toss it? What would befall him if he did? He had jettisoned so much of what he had brought home from Thailand. Framed temple rubbings. His flight bag mildewed beyond use. Uniforms that no longer fit. Bespoke suits and sport coats from the Khorat Tailor, even the safari jacket. He had thrown his 'Go to hell' fatigue hat into the trash even before he left for Don Mueang airport to catch his flight home. But the bead remained, and he always wondered.

Late afternoon they went to a Mexican restaurant near Sukhumvit where two Thai little people dressed in scrapes and sombreros caught their attention and convinced them to go inside. The menu said Mexican, and there were tacos and burritos and refrieds and tamales wrapped in corn husks, but everything was saturated with Thai spices, strong in garlic, the sauces so hot that even rice couldn't quell the sting. By dark they were back in their hotel at the bar drinking gin and tonics until near midnight when they finally gave up and went to their rooms.

20

They ate breakfast from room service on Luke's balcony, overlooking the trees behind the hotel. Scrambled eggs and ham, toast, fresh orange juice, pineapple slices, coffee. Wheeled in on a cart with a white linen tablecloth. A rose in a tiny vase. They acted like it was normal, though it wasn't, not for either of them. They were on top of the world, body and soul. The morning air was cool and fresh, the sun spoke of promise. A new day, full of hope. In a few days they would go back to Khorat, and while that was a study in frustration, they reminded each other that it was a shitload better than slogging through a paddy in Vietnam, as they were reminded every time they walked to New Petchaburi with the hordes of Gee Eyes on R&R. Traffic was building on the other side of the hotel and the first whiffs of diesel fumes pushed up the alleys and through the fences. "This is the way to live," Saint said, and Luke allowed as how it was true.

They decided to see the sights. First to Timland to watch the working elephants and Thai folk dancers. A cobra in a glass cage that struck hard and lightning fast when Saint tapped the glass. He jumped and the people around him jumped and they all laughed nervously, and they all knew that if they ran into a cobra in the wild they would be dead.

"So which do you think is worse?" Saint asked. "The cobra or a two-stepper with venom so strong that you're dead practically instantaneously?"

They took a boat through the floating market and stopped at a little island with a shop that sold star sapphires that at first seemed pretty and then, on second glance, a little crude, the rays of the stars crooked and bent. They wondered whether these were downscale and if they should go someplace else. Then they realized they had no one to whom they could give them anyway and they pushed on. In the afternoon, they visited some of the *wats* and in late afternoon returned to their hotel, tired and satisfied. They went again to the bar for gin and tonics because of the way they cut through the crud of Bangkok and the heat of the day.

The afternoon sun streamed through a row of windows high on the wall behind them, filling the bar with too harsh sunlight that washed the color from the bottles of liquor arrayed on the shelves on the wall of the portholes, making them look like bottles of colored water from a child's doctor's bag, and highlighting the streaks and smudges on the mirrors and walls. The pool was in shadow and the water beyond the portholes looked like used dishwater and the bar felt barren and forgotten and not a place where anyone would want to gather.

The bartender was washing and drying glasses and putting them under the counter; a waiter leaned against the wall behind him, flipping through a *Playboy* magazine. As he turned the pages he paused occasionally and spoke to the bartender and the bartender turned to look. When the waiter came to the centerfold he held the magazine in the air and let the photo unfold beneath his hand. Both men stared appreciatively. They turned the magazine so that Luke and Saint could see.

"*Suay mag*, number one," the waiter said. He smiled.

"*Suay mag*," Saint and Luke agreed.

"How much you think?" the waiter said.

"How much what?" Luke said.

"How much *baht*? How much *baht* this woman?" the waiter said.

Luke laughed. "No *baht* this woman."

The waiter laughed. "No *baht*? You make joke?" He continued to flip through the magazine and stopped again when he came to another nude spread. He held it up for Luke and Saint. "No *baht*?" he asked. He laughed and reached under the bar and pulled out a small glossy magazine like the ones Luke and Saint had seen on the street the day they arrived. He began flipping through the pages. "*Suay mag*, yes?" he said. Luke and Saint nodded.

"*Suay mag*. Number one fucky-fuck." He grinned and leered theatrically. Picked up the *Playboy* and let the centerfold drop open again. "Fucky-fuck," he said.

"No fucky-fuck," Luke said.

"No fucky-fuck? No fucky fuck? Fucky-fuck. Maybe five hundred dorrah. *Mag mag* baht. What you say?"

"I don't think so," Luke said, and shook his head.

The waiter was incredulous but did not push. His look said that he knew better and that Luke and Saint had a lot of growing up to do. He slipped the *Playboy* under the bar and went out a side door.

"Whattaya think?" Luke said. "Are we being naïve? Do you think maybe they do?"

"I don't know," Saint said. "It's possible. What do we know?"

They sipped their drinks and watched the bartender continue to wash and dry glasses.

"So," Saint said to the bartender. "Where do you meet single women in this town?"

"What you mean, sin-goh?" the bartender asked. He reached under the bar for his magazine.

"Maybe *farung*," Luke said.

"Ah," the bartender said. "Maybe Brass Foor on New Road. Many *farung*."

"Single," Saint said. "Alone?"

"Oh yes, many *farung* women."

The waiter returned and the bartender asked his opinion. The waiter nodded. "Yes," the bartender said. "Brass Foor. Many *farung*. Many *farung* radies. Big tits," he said. He winked and bounced imaginary ponderous breasts in his hands, very un-Thai, or so it seemed to Luke. "Number one Firipino band, number one. Pray Beatle. Many *farung*, many *farung* radies. Good Beatle."

THE BRASS FLOOR was as promised, *farung*, but mainly couples. The brass-plate dance floor was nearly full.

"Where do they come from?" Saint asked. Luke shrugged.

"Really," Saint said. "What are they doing in Bangkok? Embassy?"

Luke was too engaged in checking out the women to answer. There were a few Thai, prostitutes with Gee Eyes who groped more than danced. Back home their behavior would be thought lewd. Here? Well, they came from a war zone; this was a war zone, wasn't it? Home rules didn't count. Besides, who knew the local rules of propriety anyway.

A semi-circle of booths and tables on a raised floor

surrounded the dance floor, matched by a balcony over-head. Couples at every table, or so it seemed. The walls black, the lights ultraviolet. Colors glowed fluorescently. Cigarette smoke hung like early morning fog. The Filipino band was tucked against the wall just past the far end of the bar and was playing 'Yesterday'. Stairs in the corner beyond the band led up to the balcony. Thai waitresses in elegant, coarse-silk tube skirts and simple silk blouses wended their way among the tables, drink trays high.

They found two open stools at the far end of the bar and sat, backs to the band. Ordered San Miguels and began looking.

The band changed to Jaobim, a Brazilian samba that Luke had heard just before leaving the states. He liked it but didn't know how to dance to it, and feared that if someone agreed to dance, he would make a fool of himself out on the dance floor. Then the band moved to 'Light My Fire' and Luke thought, yes, I can dance to this, this I like, this will be fun. He scanned the tables more earnestly.

"Over there," he said, nodding towards a blonde *farung* at a table in the corner behind the railing.

"And she's not alone," Saint said. He picked up his beer and started towards the stairs, Luke quickly following. And yes, they were *farung*, the blonde that Luke had had his eyes on taller and heavier. As they approached the blonde smiled and her teeth glowed spectrally in the black light. She guided Saint in with her eyes, and he sat next to her, leaving Luke to her companion, a shorter, darker-complected girl with round, Celtic features, soft cheeks, full lips, dark hair long in yesterday's soft flip. Her blouse hung loose and sensuously over her breasts, and he thought maybe this would be all right, until he realized that she didn't look at him as he sat down, instead stared at the dance floor, as if he wasn't even there.

The blonde slid close to Saint in a light-hearted, flirtatious manner. "It took you long enough," she said, her words and accent communicating that she was American.

Saint laughed defensively, caught off guard by her forthright comment. He stumbled over a response.

"We've been watching you since you came in," she said. "We wondered how long it would take you to come over here."

"Well, gee," Saint said, protesting.

"No, silly, it's all right. Are you here on R&R?"

"We live here," Luke said. "Up country. In Khorat."

"The recon wing," the blonde said.

"Are you shitting me?" Saint said. "How did you know that?"

"We've met your buddies," the blonde said. She mentioned two names that Luke didn't know but Saint did. "Yup," he said. "Sixty-fourth. We're Sixty-third. What happened with them?"

The blonde laughed. "I don't kiss and tell."

"Ah, but you do dance, right?" He laughed, and she smiled and nodded. They slid out of the booth and made their way through the forest of tables to the dance floor.

"What about you?" Luke said to his Celtic girl. She half looked at him and shook her head.

Bummer, he thought. He wondered what signal he had missed or if there was something wrong. He watched Saint and the blonde dance. The band was playing *All You Need Is Love* and Saint was moving effortlessly, recalling his Maurice Chevalier act stepping onto the crew bus. The blonde smiled appreciatively. Luke wished he could dance as well. He began mimicking Saint's moves to himself, slightly, trying to make them his.

"I'm not dancing," the girl said.

"I got that," Luke said, determined not to let her coldness ruin his enjoyment of the moment. Knowing as well that because Saint and the blonde were getting on, it was going to be a long night, with him stuck with the lump beside him.

She watched Saint and the blonde and didn't say a word.

"He's good," Luke said. Still she didn't respond.

The band switched to a slow tune and Saint and the blonde moved close. She wrapped her arms around his neck and Saint put his hands on her hips. She was grinding, ever so slightly. Luke couldn't stand it. He focused again on the woman beside him, fetching for something to say that would engage her.

"How do you come to be in Bangkok?"

She looked at him but didn't answer.

"Do you like it here?"

"It's all right."

"How do you know your friend?"

"We're neighbors."

Luke waited for her to add something. She said nothing.

"What do you do here?"

"Look," she said, "I don't want to talk."

He wanted to ask her why she had bothered to come out this night, but refrained. He decided that the problem was him. He watched Saint and the blonde. "What's her name?" he said, jealous of Saint's good fortune.

"Vicki."

"And yours'?"

She stared at him, silent.

"O for Pete's sake," he said. "All I want to do is be able to carry on a conversation. Make up a name if you want. I don't care. Just make it possible for me to catch your attention. Those two look like they're in for the duration, so it might work out better if we both kinda climbed on board."

"Hope," she said finally, and Luke suppressed a snicker. He watched Saint and Vicki; Saint looked at him and grinned. He glanced at Hope as if to ask how he was doing with her and Luke shrugged. Saint whispered to Vicki and she looked at Luke. She smiled and waved. They stopped dancing and made their way back to the table.

"Let's go, Bunky," Saint said. Vicki hung on his arm. Luke slid from behind the table and Hope followed. As they walked away Hope caught up with Vicki and Saint dropped back to walk with Luke.

"What'd you say to her?" Saint asked.

"Say? Nothing. I can't get her to talk. She's the coldest fish I've ever met. What's up with her?"

"We're going for a ride. Then we're going back to Vicki's place. All right?"

Luke shrugged, agreeing to himself that he had called it right—it was going to be a long night.

VICKI'S CAR was parked just up the street from the bar, a plain grey Datsun sedan. She and Saint sat in front, Luke and Hope in back, Hope as far away from Luke as she could get, melting into the corner. Vicki pulled out with a screech. The street was narrow and tortured, a dark and jagged canyon with cars parked haphazardly on both sides like rocks jutting into a stream. Vicki slalomed between them, close but never touching. Luke was impressed. "Where are we off to?" he asked.

"Nowhere," Vicki said. She reached across and opened

the glove compartment, pulling out a white paper bag that she handed to Saint. "Here," she said, "make yourself useful. You roll. There's paper in there, too."

"I'd rather use a cigarette," Saint said. He worked the tobacco out of one of his own, opened the bag and smelled. "Ahhh," he said. "*Guncha*." He crumbled the marijuana and sucked it into his cigarette. Twisting the end, he lit up, dragged and passed the joint to Vicki. She took a drag and handed it to Hope, who dragged, coughed and sputtered, then handed it to Luke. He wondered if she had inhaled a thing.

"I really prefer menthols," Vicki said. "You smoke menthols?" she asked, looking at Luke in the rearview mirror.

"No. Sorry." And apropos of nothing, added, "The King smokes menthols. Salems. Bhumipol. Rama nine. I can't stand them."

"Do you think he smokes *guncha*?" Vicki asked.

Saint took a deeper drag and passed the joint to Vicki. Then to Hope, Luke, and around again. Saint was about to take yet another drag when Vicki said, "Be careful, cowboy. This is Thai stuff—we don't get anything like it in the states. It's better even than Hawaiian gold. You'll crash so far you won't be able to get up in the morning. And we don't want that, do we," she added, reaching over and squeezing his thigh.

They turned onto a modern boulevard of grassy medians and strips between street and sidewalk. Most unusual. Streetlights cast pools of light through which they drove in and out. Luke wondered if Vicki was driving to a plan. They stopped at a traffic light and a Thai police jeep slowed to a stop beside them, accompanied by the crackling of the police radio.

"Oh, God," Hope said. "They can smell it, I'm sure they can. What are we going to do?" She looked away from the police jeep and ducked her head, trying to hide. Surreptitiously rolled up her window.

"*Sawadee*," Saint called across to the two policemen. He nodded his head as he put the joint in the ashtray and then nonchalantly turned toward Vicki. "What are they doing?" he asked.

Vicki leaned forward to see around Saint. "They're laughing," she said.

"Laughing?"

"Yes. At us."

"They are," Luke said. "You can come up for air, now," he said to Hope. "They could care less." He watched the policemen: the passenger-side cop was smoking. He took a drag and handed his cigarette to the driver. "Shit!" Luke laughed. "They're smoking *guncha*!"

The driver looked at them and smiled. Nodded his head. "Number one, Gee Eye," he called over. "Number one Thai *guncha*." The light changed and they drove away, leaving all save Hope laughing.

"You have to admit that was funny," Luke said to her.

"Vicki, you take us home," Hope said.

"You need more *guncha*," Vicki said. Saint handed the joint back to Hope.

"I don't need it," Hope said, but she took the joint and dragged anyway. She held onto it and continued to smoke.

"Where'd you get it?" Luke asked.

"This? The drug store," Vicki answered.

"Off the shelf?"

"Not really. Behind the counter. They all sell it. So do street vendors."

"You hear that, Bunky?" Saint said.

"I do, I do," Luke said. "I think things are going to be okay now," he said, and realized as he said it that it was true, it was if he had been holding his breath for months, anticipating the worst, and now his head was slowing down and he was becoming absorbed in the moment, and all his concerns, his loneliness, his distress about their useless exercise in supposed intelligence gathering, his angst about the very idea of the Vietnam war, was slipping away, inconsequential and ephemeral. Even his apprehension about Sergeant Rickey was gone, nowhere to be found. Now is real, he said to himself. Now is beautiful and full and enough. "Fuck Sergeant Rickey," he said.

"Fuck Sergeant Rickey," Saint echoed. "Three cheers for Sergeant Tolliver," he added.

"Who's Sergeant Tolliver?" Vicki asked. "And Sergeant Rickey?"

Vicki began driving randomly, asking for decisions whenever she came to a cross street...turn here? Turn there? Right, left? Go back? They were the only car on the street, and Luke wondered how that could be in what he thought of as downtown Bangkok, or so he guessed, without another car in sight. They came to a traffic circle with a fountain in the middle. "We put soap in that last week," Vicki said. "We brought a box of laundry soap and made bubbles. Bubbles," she added. "Bub-*bles*, bub*bles*, bub*bles*. Bubbles. Don't you just love the sound of that word? It's perfect. Bubbles. Bubbles."

"Boofers," Saint said. "Bombastulent boo-boffers."

"What?" Vicki said.

"Bombastulent boo-boffers. It's a word I invented for really great tits."

"Like these?" Vicki said. She pushed her chest towards Saint. "Do these count?"

"Vicki!" Hope blurted.

Saint reached over and caressed Vicki's clothed right breast. "Yeah," he said. "Yeah," he repeated. "They count. They count big time."

Luke looked at Hope, wondering still where she was coming from, what she was even doing with Vicki, they seemed such an unmatched pair. "I don't get you," he said finally. "Honestly. You and Vicki."

She didn't bother to respond. It was like it had been at the Brass Floor, and he wondered if he had actually said anything or if he had just imagined it.

Vicki pointed to a building bathed in soft colored lights and set back from the road in a copse of palm trees. "That's the Thai generals' opium den," she said. "You want to go?"

"Really?" Luke said.

"You wanna try it?" Vicki said.

"Unh-unh." He recalled Gropper's story about the Air America plane heading to Bangkok. "Have you been there?" he asked.

"There's always a first time."

"You're sure?" Luke said.

"Everyone knows," Vicki said. "Hope, am I right?"

"The Thai generals? Yes."

"And what do they do there? Tell Luke."

"They smoke opium," Hope said, practically her first full sentence. Maybe she was getting engaged.

"Like I said," Vicki said.

Hope shrugged as if to say it was simply a known fact, and that the opium den was like a neighborhood ice cream parlor. For whatever reason, perhaps the marijuana, perhaps just the passage of time, she began at last to loosen up. She pulled away from the door, though she didn't move very far. She pointed at the opium den and the line of cars pulling up out in front. "Look," she said. "Aren't you curious?"

Luke merged into the tour of Bangkok, fixing on the existential meaning of everything he saw. "Look," he said to Hope. "Look at the way the buildings run one into the next. They're like all different but all the same. This is great," he added. "Don't you just love the way things are slowing down? It's like the mortar between our thoughts is melting and now we can see through to eternity." He basked in the feeling of the night, hot and humid and close and rich and alive and exotic, the breeze through the open windows of the car caressing his skin. He spread his arms across the back of the seat and closed his eyes. "This is nice," he said. "I could live like this."

"Do you always talk about it so much?" Hope said. There was a note of disapproval in her voice.

Luke was taken aback. He was loving the moment and his feelings, and her comment crashed through like an electric shock, disconnecting everything. He didn't even want to respond and give credence to her comment. "Is that bad?" he said. "It's how I feel. Is that bad?"

"I don't like it. It's silly. I don't like silly. Do you always get silly when you smoke?"

"I don't know," he said. "I've never thought about it." Truth being that he smoked marijuana so seldom that he didn't know what was normal for him. "I like it. I like what's happening. I like the way things are slowing down."

"See," she said.

He lifted his arms off the back of the seat. "*Mai pen rai*," he said.

"What does that mean?"

"It means nothing matters," Luke said. "It means that in

the end green slippery vines are going to grow over everything anyhow, nothing lasts, so why bother."

"I don't like that," Hope said. "I don't like that at all."

"Well, okay. It means Bangkok cops don't care if you get stoned on the city streets."

Luke indulged in everything he saw, each passing utility pole, the cones of street lights, the sidewalks, storefronts, and shadows, the darkness. Vistas between buildings opened and came alive and abruptly closed. They turned a corner and suddenly all of Bangkok, all the glitter and bright lights, seemed to open before them. A huge neon SEIKO sign atop a tall building filled his view.

"Holy shit!" Luke said. "Stop!" He got out of the car, the better to see the whole of the sign.

It was the biggest neon sign he had ever seen and it was gorgeous, the colors gleaming even in the dense humidity, becoming sounds, singing to him, green *SEIKO*, blue background, red vertical stripes. The stripes began to move and it startled him. He laughed and sat down on the curb and watched, oblivious to the others waiting in the car. O my God, he thought. O my God, and his eyes filled with joy. Better than the Fourth of July.

Vicki and Saint got out of the car, walked over and sat next to him on the curb. Hope reluctantly followed. The background began changing again, the red vertical stripes moving from left to right, then right to left. Yellow stripes joined, then green. The sign took on life. "O, man," Luke said. "O, man, O man, O man. This is so-o-o-o cool." The colors began alternating, red stripe blue stripe yellow stripe green stripe ganged together trekking across the screen, "Man," he said. "Will you look at that." The letters *SEIKO* now changing, outlines layering onto the letters, growing bigger. Taking over, a paean to capitalism expanding beyond the frame and into the darkness, flashing sequentially, as if every carnival midway of his youth had merged into one.

Hope sat next to his feet, her back against the curb.

"Look," he said, pointing. "It's gorgeous. It's beautiful."

"It is," she said. "Come down here." He slid down and sat on the road and now she was soft and open. She slid closer to him and he could feel the warmth of her thigh and he let himself love it. The stripes moved left to right and then abruptly from top to bottom with SEIKO SEIKO SEIKO flashing like a cheap no-tell motel. "This is so cool," he said. She put her hand on his thigh, though he soon realized it was just a place to rest. He decided it was okay that it was nothing more.

Saint and Vicki continued standing, heads lifted in awe. At that moment, the sign resolved into horizontal and vertical stripes and became a modern plaid. "Would you look at that," Luke said. "It's a fucking Asian tartan, do you believe it? Have you ever seen anything so cool? It's like the whole Seiko advertising department was stoned and just went nuts. Can we stay here? I want to stay here."

"I want to go home," Hope said. She put her arm through Luke's. Tugged just a little. Luke was surprised but thought, what the fuck. At last. "Okay, then," he said.

THEY TURNED onto a *soi* and then onto a bumpy dirt road that led across an open field to a multi-storied apartment building standing sentinel tall by itself, surrounded by a parking lot and a tall spear fence, balconies on every floor, windows dark, the lights of Bangkok in the distance. The ground floor was open air and lit like a Hopper painting; light fell on a bank of elevator doors and a guard asleep at a nearby bare desk, head on his arms. He woke and nodded at them as they walked to the elevator.

Vicki's apartment was spartan—two stuffed chairs, a sofa, a side table—leather, wood and chrome shining in the glow of a stereo system that sat on the floor. A scatter rug mimicking Mondrian. Vicki turned on the tape deck and led Saint to the couch. Hope and Luke lay on their backs on the Mondrian in front of the speakers. Frankie Valli singing 'Can't Take My Eyes Off of You'. Music to make out by, Luke thought. He was pleased. He closed his eyes, letting the music envelop him. Saint was lying between Vicki's legs.

After a while Luke decided that listening wasn't enough anymore. He rolled over onto his elbow and smiled at Hope. She smiled in return. "You're beautiful when you smile," he said, and dropped down beside her. She shifted closer and he put his arm around her waist. She snuggled closer. He moved his leg over hers and she jumped. "Vicki. Vicki!" she screamed, "he's trying to rape me!" She sat bolt upright. Pushed Luke off and ran out of the apartment, slamming the door behind her.

Luke looked at Vicki, astonished and shocked. He was still high but now he was confused. "Jesus Christ," he said. "I wasn't. What the fuck was that all about? I didn't do anything." And didn't add that the thought of getting inside her had certainly crossed his mind.

Vicki and Saint looked very much like they'd been interrupted. "Don't worry, Bunky," Vicki said. "I know."

"I know? Fill me in. You know?"

"She's like that, that's all there is to it. It isn't you." She smiled but clearly was more interested in getting back to Saint. She lay her head back down. Luke felt left out, and in another moment, ignored. He lay down, closed his eyes. Listened to the music. Soon he could hear Saint's and Vicki's heavy breathing and the rustling of their clothes and the movement of their bodies. He got up on all fours and crawled over to the couch and rested his chin next to Vicki's head.

"Whatcha doing?" he said, trying to be cute.

Vicki smiled and kissed his nose. Luke decided he should crawl onto the couch with them. They were his friends and loved him and maybe somehow the three of them could be together. He didn't know what that meant, but it seemed like a good idea. He kissed Vicki on the mouth, inserted his tongue, which she enthusiastically allowed.

"What the fuck are you doing?" Saint said. "No, Bunky, no," he added, laughing. Luke realized his idea wasn't going to work. He crawled back to the speakers. Looked around the room, fixing everything in his mind. The furniture that he hadn't paid any attention to before, a sliding glass door out to the balcony. The drapes were open and he tried to remember if they were when they came in. A *chinjok,* a chameleon, was resting halfway up the wall above a small lamp beside the couch. "There's a *chinjok* near that lamp," he said. "I love *chinjoks.*"

Vicki crooked her neck. "Yeah," she said. "He's been here awhile."

"Has he caught anything?"

"I don't know. I know he hasn't moved."

"I never see them catch anything," Luke said.

"Bunky," Saint said.

"I see them crawling up the walls and the columns but I never see them catch anything either," Vicki said.

Luke went over to the wall and examined the *chinjok.* It didn't move. He flicked it with his finger and it fell to the floor, a hollow husk.

Saint whispered to Vicki and the two of them went into the next room. Luke waited for a few minutes and then went to the couch. In a few minutes he was asleep. Later, when he woke, he had no idea where he was, or what time it was. Once he got his bearings he let himself out, walking to the *soi* where he caught a *tuk-tuk* back to their hotel. The streets were empty and wet and shone from the lights of Bangkok, and he felt very much alone. He didn't like it, not now, not tonight, and wished he and Saint were together.

21

Saint took Vicki's pageboy-length blonde wig from its stand on her dresser. Donned it. Struck a pose in the mirror, took a drag from his roach.

"No, wait," Vicki said. She took a necklace of rough wooden beads off her dresser and draped it around Saint's neck. Stepped back to admire her handiwork, shook her head. No; more. She rummaged in a drawer until she found a headband that she tied around his forehead. Again she stepped back. Shook her head. "Don't have it yet," she said, as much to herself as to Saint and Luke, as if she were dressing a mannequin in a store window and was responsible for the best presentation she could put together. She unbuttoned and removed Saint's shirt, slowly, cutely seductive, rubbing her hand across his bare chest. Sang a stripper's song. *"Da-dun-dun-dun, da-da-da-dun."* She dawdled. Then she pulled her dashiki over her head and slipped it over Saint. He put his roach in his mouth again and struck a pose. "Hey, man," he said in the casual sing-song of a hippie. Slouched his shoulders, relaxed his head. Extended his arm, let his wrist go limp. Toked, replenishing the heavy smell of burning *guncha* in the room. They laughed. Vicki found her camera and took a photo.

Luke couldn't take his eyes off Vicki's now near-naked breasts, covered only by her bra. Her skin was light gold, flawless, her breasts large; they jiggled as a soft grace note to her every move. He tried to be discreet, told himself that she had as much on as she would if she were at the beach. It didn't matter. His penis began to stiffen and push against his pants. This was different, this was a process, now one step from naked, which surely was coming. He wanted to pull down her bra and put his lips around her nipples. Bury his face in her cleavage. He drove himself nuts with his thoughts. Saint put his arms around her and pulled her over to her bed.

Oh, shit, Luke said to himself. Here we go again. He went back into the living room. Sat on the edge of the couch, hunched over, nourishing a bad case of blue balls. He couldn't stand it. He knew the situation wouldn't get any better, at least not for him. As if to emphasize his aloneness, he could hear the soft sounds of lovemaking, made more poignant by the singularity of thought brought on by the marijuana. He couldn't shut it off and decided once again that the only thing for him was to leave. He took the elevator down, walked out to the *soi* and caught a tuk-tuk back to their hotel.

At first he had no idea what he was going to do in the remaining two days of leave. He could go back to Khorat, then thought of Pattaya. Yes, even by himself. He imagined basking on the beach, perhaps asleep on a towel on the sand, caressing breeze coming on shore. He imagined a Thoreau-esque feel to the moment. Complete escape. Alone. Complete freedom. If he hustled, he could be there by early afternoon. He packed, slipped a note under Saint's door. Once in a limo the sights and sounds of the now familiar trip south to Pattaya felt comfortable.

PATTAYA WAS AS BEFORE, travel magazine beautiful, complete unto itself, clear blue sky, pure sand, water sparkling in counterpoint, gentle waves swelling and breaking against the verge, slipping sibilantly back into the sea. Again. And again. And again. Alive, breathing. Palm fronds dipped in the breeze. A stage perfectly set. He walked to the snack bar, sat at the counter and ordered a beer. For a moment he was alone. Then, as if on que, a group of American teenagers came crashing through the screen door, a herd of Bowery Boys and girls who seemed to materialize out of the ether. For a moment he welcomed the distraction, but they were relentlessly hectic, talking all at once, to one another and seemingly to no one, and barraged the counter waiter with their orders. When they stepped away from the counter they continued to move, talking, laughing, pacing, inevitably getting in each other's way, pushing and shoving, acting with the crazed desperation of yellow jackets sensing the coming of winter. He soon had had enough. One of the boys bumped into him without apology and he nearly spilled his beer, and it was all too much. He didn't bother to finish his drink and escaped out the door and to the beach, where at least it was calm.

He sat at the round thatched-roof picnic table where he and Tanaka had waited that first morning while Saint was waterskiing. Buried his feet in the warm sand, leaned back. The rec camp marina was empty, power boats docked, sail boats pulled onto the verge, booms swinging back and forth and creaking in the stays. Beyond, the Thai fishing boats were again anchored, the incoming tide gently rocking the anchored boats in rhythmic unison, the boats aligned and pointing out to sea.

He looked the other way, down towards the Yacht Club, and saw a young woman sitting at one of the Nipa Lodge thatched-roof picnic tables, postured as he was, back to the table, legs out-thrust, gazing out to sea. She wore a cream-colored, hooded pullover, the hood pulled up, and white shorts. He couldn't see her face until she let her head fall back to catch the sun and the hood slipped back. Her hair was dark, perhaps a deep brown, perhaps black. He couldn't tell. Rose-complected, clear skin. Largish nose and mouth. Sensuous lips. Pretty, perhaps even beautiful.

Minutes passed. He looked away if only to avoid being caught staring, and then back, before finally mustering the pluck to walk over and introduce himself. With the crunch of his feet in the sand she turned towards him. By her expression she seemed to simply accept his presence, as if they already knew each other, though her look was also one of expectancy, as if it was his turn to speak. He greeted her, and asked if he could sit down. She nodded, and brushed imaginary sand off the bench beside her. He sat down a few feet away, careful not to violate her sense of comfort.

"Down from Bangkok?" he asked.

She nodded. "What brings you here?" she asked. Her voice was soft, her diction clear. "Isn't it lovely?" she added, looking out to the water and then back at Luke.

"Vacation, I guess you could call it. I'm on break. I'm stationed up at Khorat." Luke said.

"Have you been here before?"

"Just once. A month ago. I love it here. It's such a complete getaway. It's quiet, and calm, and there's not a lot of people rushing around, just the locals and a few tourists.

It's hard to believe, really, you know. I doubt that it's changed much in the last fifty years."

She looked out to sea. "You think it will last?"

He laughed quietly. "Probably not, I guess. I haven't thought about it. But I guess when I do, it's hard to imagine that it will. Last time I was here, when I was in the bar at the Nipa Lodge..."

"That's where I'm staying," she said.

"Really... Well, when I was in the bar I heard some German women talking. And a couple of Aussies. And the bartender's an Aussie. And there's Gee Eyes here on R&R..." He trailed off. "You're probably right. We're just the beginning. But it's still nice."

"It is," she said. She paused, looking at him. "You have a nice smile," she said. "I like it. You can stay." She drew herself up. "So," she said. "Are you a Gee Eye?"

"I guess so, but I've never thought about it that way. I'm in the Air Force. I think of Gee Eyes as Army" he said.

"Where are you staying?" she asked.

"The Army rec camp. Across the road. All the boats and things," he said, gesturing at the boats rocking gently against the dock in the swell, those on the sand. "All that stuff belongs to the rec camp."

She hmmed in response.

The conversation was unhurried and comfortable; he didn't feel like he had to fill every moment. It seemed that she was comfortable chatting, at least for now, and he sensed that the moment could continue.

Her name was Lonnie. Short for Avalon. Avalon Whitcombe. Old names. Avalon after a favorite great aunt. Possibly someone even before that. He smiled.

She looked at him. "Are you mocking me?" she asked.

"No, not at all. It's like where I come from, farm country

in central New York. There're all these great names that persist. Parks. Lucian. Guys named Leslie. We've got a few in our family. My mother's middle name is Augusta, named after her grandmother. Everyone called her Gussie. My grandmother, that is. Hard to believe, a hundred years ago."

"What about you?" she said.

"Luke."

"Luke? That's it?"

He paused. "Lucas. No middle name, except my mother says there is, she just forgot to register it."

"And what was that?"

"Elmer."

She burst out laughing. "I think I'd forget about registering it, too. Where'd that come from?"

"A great grandfather."

"O the burden of family," she said, and leaned playfully against his arm. He loved it, couldn't believe his good fortune.

Her father was with AID, upcountry, working with the Lao. She hadn't wanted to come to Thailand this summer, but he had insisted. "Now," she said, looking at Luke, "I'm kinda glad I did." Again she pushed against his arm. "Now don't disappoint me. You know, I should be back in the States, working at a summer resort in Maine maybe, or maybe the Jersey Shore, earning more money for college. Slinging burgers and growing zits from all the grease. Playing huggy bear and kissy face on a dock in the evenings." She said that she was a drama major, and that what she wanted to be doing this summer was summer stock. "Maybe after I graduate," she said. "One more year, then look out Broadway, here I come!" She laughed.

"Where?" he asked.

"Smith," she said.

"Smith!" he responded. "That's great. Of all the girls'
schools I ever went to, I liked it best!"

"Really? You've been there? Why'd you like it?"

"I dunno. It's lovely, of course. I just liked the feel of the
place, like something out of a Fitzgerald short story. And I
liked the girls there, generally anyway, except that I never
had a date that repeated. I struck out more times than I care
to remember. But they were all nice."

"So where else did you go?" she said.

"Oh, you know. Sarah Lawrence. Skidmore. Syracuse.
Some others. Wells. Elmira. My mother said I should swear
off Sarah Lawrence. She said the girls there weren't for me,
and I think she was right. They just function in another
world."

"And what did she say about Smith?"

"I never told her any Smith stories. I never really had
any. The best was just incidental. I was there once in the
winter, and I stayed in this guest house with a great roaring
fire and a charcoal portrait over the mantel of the owner
back in the twenties, back before the Second World War,
and he had this pencil moustache and slicked back hair, and
I think he was wearing jodhpurs, that's where I got that F.
Scott Fitzgerald feeling. I thought I'd love to have my
portrait over my fireplace like that some day."

"That's it? That's why you liked Smith?"

"O, no," he protested. "There's more. I just had this
feeling there of refined gentleness. One spring I was there
and this girl I met took me down to the power plant at dusk
to watch the swallows circle back to the chimney. It was just
neat, everyone sitting on a bank overlooking the chimney,
just watching the birds. Students, faculty with their kids,
kids playing on the slope."

"And what happened to the girl?"

"There wasn't one. I mean there was. But. I was there with a friend from college who was dating someone from Tenney House. We went for a long weekend and his girlfriend fixed me up with a different girl every night. Thursday, Friday. Saturday this girl comes out and says "Next," and I felt like a total idiot. Turns out they were even comparing notes about me. So, nothing. Except at least she took me to watch the swallows."

She laughed. "Well, we can fix that."

He basked in her promise of a shared future. "On Sunday morning we all sat around and played Botticelli and worked the Sunday *Times* crossword."

"Did you finish?"

"I don't remember. Probably not. Whatever, it was fun."

"And the girls you had the dates with? Were they from Tenney?"

"No."

"So what did you talk about?"

"You mean at Tenney? Typical college bull sessions. They were great conversations."

"Like what?"

"I remember we had an argument...I guess it was an argument. It was about whether all great artists were brilliant. I didn't think so. Artistic geniuses, yes. But brilliant? I remember mentioning Van Gogh. And maybe Picasso. Creative geniuses, that's for sure. But plain old geniuses? Score high on the SATs? I didn't think so. I thought Picasso just had an ego that wouldn't quit, and great talent, but I wasn't sure he was all that bright."

"I love the bullshit sessions," she said. "But they're not real, you know, are they?" She kicked at the sand. Again she looked out to the water. "What else?" she said. "What else did you talk about?"

"Nothing," he says.

"No, really, I want to know. I miss it. Sitting in an apartment in Bangkok, not knowing the language, not knowing anybody."

"Okay. Only I can't remember if was at Tenney House or wherever. Maybe at the kitchen table at my fraternity."

"You haven't told me where you went to college."

"Colgate."

"Colgate. Really. I've never met anyone from Colgate. All I've ever heard was that all the guys at Colgate are jocks."

"Well, that wouldn't be me. So, we were sitting around a kitchen table, and someone asked if there's any such thing as true altruism, or isn't it all just selfishness, in the end, when you get down to it. That everything comes down to what makes you feel better."

"Out of nowhere like that?"

Luke shrugged. He realized she was staring at him, smiling.

"What?" he said.

She laughed. "Nothing. I like this. I like you. So, what should we do?"

"Like what? Whattaya mean?"

"I mean like right now. What should we do?" She stood. "How 'bout we go for a walk? Let's just go take a look at this town."

They walked towards the rec camp dock. "So," she said. "If you're in the Air Force, does that mean you can use the stuff here? Like maybe the boats?"

Luke nodded. "I've gone sailing in the larger boat."

"Really," she said. "Can we?"

"Sure. Hardly any time left today. How about tomorrow, if you're still going to be here?"

"That would be wonderful," she said, and laughed. And

then, "But what about today? What about the rest of the day? What about dinner?"

Luke couldn't believe what was happening, that she could simply want to be with him, and that he didn't have to work to hold her interest. "Where?" he said.

"The Nipa Lodge?" she said. "I want to eat outside under the arbor with the monkeys. What do you think?"

Luke laughed. "Absolutely," he said. "That would be great!" He was about to tell her how much fun it was to be with the monkeys, to impress her with his experience, but stopped himself. He told himself not to act the know-it-all. Imagined the two of them under the arbor, vines hanging low, and understood that it would be more enjoyable for Lonnie if she thought they were discovering it together. He took her hand and they walked up to the beach road and she smiled at him and her smile took over her face, and it was clear that she was happy with this moment and with him.

Once on the beach road they walked down toward the point, past the tree in the middle of the road with the scars from the passing cars.

"This is perfect," Lonnie said, "a tree in the middle of the road. It's beat up, of course, but it's still here. No one has said that if they want to be a real resort town, that it has to come out."

Of a sudden they were engulfed in the afternoon monsoon. Protected from the sky by the spreading branches of the trees overhead they hadn't even been aware of its approach, the curtain of grey advancing relentlessly across the water and the sand and then atop them. They took refuge under the canvas of the dirt-floored outdoor café that he and Saint and Hugo had noticed before. They stood among the empty oilcloth-covered tables, watching, listening to the downpour. The rain was a forced time out, past gone, future yet to come, present full of promise. The air was warm and rich with moisture and ozone, there was nothing more they could see, nothing else they could hear, and they loved the isolation. Their mental view was fore-shortened, there were only the two of them in their rain-shrouded room in all the world, and they stood for the longest time close together, not talking, Lonnie's hand in his arm. Until they realized that the rain was not going to let up. "Whattaya say?" Luke said, nodding outside. "Wanna go?"

Lonnie grabbed his hand and pulled him out into the monsoon and they ran up the road towards the promontory. In but a moment they were soaked through, hair sopping, shirt and pullover plastered against their bodies, revealing. When they reached the promontory bar they sat at a table just under the overhang, water puddling onto the stone floor around them. Ordered martinis and watched the rain until it ended.

Lonnie took his hands in hers. "You have lovely hands," she said. She touched his palms, turned his hands over and began methodically pushing back the cuticles on each finger. Luke was overwhelmed by the intimacy of the primi-tive grooming. She looked at him. "This is good," she said. She drew his hands close to her face. Stared at him as if to plumb the depths of his intent.

THAT NIGHT she wore a deep maroon Thai silk blouse unbuttoned low, the depth of the shadow between blouse and skin stirring Luke's imagination. He wore only khakis and a blue, button-down shirt and he felt inadequate to the occasion, not exotic nor loose enough by far.

The chatter of the monkeys was continuous and rich,

like crickets on a warm summer night. Their waiter started to chase them away, but they shook their heads, and the waiter left the monkeys alone and they became part of their dinner conversation. Each time the volume of the monkey's chatter increased they looked up and got ready to protect their food. They finished eating and the waiter cleared their table and they sat in silence, confirming their good fortune.

They walked down to the beach. The darkness was total. The sky was clear and endless and the milky way an ancient theater. The tide was out and they walked on firm, wet sand, close to the surf. After a few minutes Lonnie chanced to look behind them.

"Luke," she said, practically whispering. "Look at our footprints."

Their movement, the pressure of their feet on the sand, had jostled phosphorescent creatures in the sand and each step glowed in the dark. The glow lasted only a few moments, but it was a magical history of their being together, however transient, as if the world was confirming their relationship. They walked on and looked back again. And at each other. Lonnie touched his lips with her finger. "I like you," she said. And Luke realized that this was what love should feel like.

22

They launched the boat with the saffron sails. They planned to stay within the bay. The sky was clear, the breeze steady, the water inclined to gentle swells. Luke told Lonnie the names of the parts of the boat and the maneuvers. She thought his seriousness cute. He told her about the near disaster when Hugo pulled the nail out of the centerboard. "They thought I was too serious, too," he said, and Lonnie thought they were right. "So what if you'd gone over," she said. "You could have righted the boat, couldn't you? It's not that big a deal."

"Maybe," Luke said.

"I rest my case," she said.

The day warmed. She took off her hooded pullover and tied it around her shoulders. Her bathing suit was white and one-piece and set off her olive-rose complexion. She caught Luke staring and smiled seductively.

They sailed back and forth across the bay, then ventured out past the island. A cleat had been added for the main sheet and Lonnie was able to relax, lean against the gunnels and enjoy herself. "It's interesting," she said. "The difference between just sailing, letting yourself get into the moment, and having a place you have to go. It feels different. There's room to just enjoy ourselves. More casual."

"That's something I think about now and then," Luke said. "Just enjoying the moment. It's hard to do. Sailing, I think, is one of the few things that makes it possible. When you don't have a destination."

"When I can do that, when I can live more in the moment, I love it. You're right. It doesn't come easily."

Though they sailed for only a few hours, as things turned out Luke wished they'd gone in earlier than they did, because they were still out when the B-52s came back, the war making its presence known like the crash of a hammer on an anvil, black crosses creeping up quickly, suddenly engulfing the sky. He watched Lonnie, certain she was going to be upset, and she was, four black crosses swooping in, voracious, enveloping, until finally and at last they were gone. Quiet returned, but their bright, fulsome mood of just a few moments had vanished, the softness scoured clean. Everything had been going so well, and now this. Luke wished there was something he could say that would soften the harshness, but he knew there wasn't.

"Was that what I thought it was?" Lonnie asked.

Luke nodded. He should have had the good sense to leave it at that, but he didn't. "On final approach to U-Tapao," he said. "Just inland." And there it was, superfluous detail that made the B-52s more real.

"Coming from where?"

"Could be anyplace," he said.

"Vietnam?"

"Maybe."

She stared at him. "You know, don't you," she said. "You know all about it. Well, I don't want to know. I don't want to know where they're going or where they've been. I want it the way it was." She stared at the horizon. Luke waited to see if her mood would improve, and when it didn't, he changed course and headed for shore. They beached the boat, loosed the lines and furled the sails. He walked her back to the Nipa Lodge, up the drive and to the front entrance, still not a word spoken between them. Luke feared the worse. At the front door of the hotel she managed a wan smile. "Later," she said. "I'll get over it."

PERHAPS FORTUITOUSLY, the Nipa bar, with its hard and empty walls, was cold, the air conditioner turned down much too low, and they went again to the patio. A gentle evening breeze off the water bathed them in soft tropic air. They were alone save for the monkeys, it was quiet and their martinis slowed the evening to a languorous pace that begged indulgence.

"I think you need to know something about me," Lonnie said after a while. She looked at him poignantly. Luke wondered what was coming, couldn't imagine anything so bad it would adversely affect what was happening. "This spring, back home at Smith, I got really involved in Bobby Kennedy's campaign. I was only a volunteer, but come summer I was going to go wherever I had to to help. Once he came out against the war, that was all that mattered to me. A bunch of us even drove down to DC to go door-to-door for him." He thought he saw tears welling in her eyes, catching the flickering light of the table candle. He reached across the table to hold her hand, and was relieved that she did not pull away.

She paused, gauging Luke's reaction. "I'd do it again," she said, to make sure he understood what working for

Kennedy had meant to her, and what she supposed were the implications of that for their relationship.

"I'm not sure what you expect me to say," Luke said.

Lonnie looked at him. "I don't expect you to say anything," she said. "I'm just letting you know how I feel, where I stand. So you can decide if you want to see me again."

"Listen," he said. "I'm glad you did it. I wish it had worked. There's nothing I want more than an end to this war."

Lonnie looked relieved. Their legs touched under the table and a spark jumped between them. It was a pleasant surprise. They looked at each other, knowing what it meant. Luke paid the bill and they went to her room. Lonnie held the door for him, led the way to the bed, sat. She patted the bed next to her and he sat down. They embraced and fell back on the bed, but nothing more.

"We'll see each other again, won't we?" she said. "In Bangkok?"

"I'm here until January. It would be great if you were here, too."

THEY SHARED a limo back to Bangkok, thigh to thigh in the back seat, oblivious to the driver and the tropical kaleidoscope flashing past. She rested her head against his chest in a gesture of platonic trust that consumed him. He closed his eyes and indulged the moment and the feeling of wholeness that he couldn't remember when last he had had, knowing he didn't need to worry about his next move or what he had to do to win her over. As they reached the outskirts of Bangkok, like airplane passengers about to touch down, they began to think about the practicalities of what came next. "I'll tell you what," Lonnie said as they joined the melee of the traffic, "at least I know what I'm not going to do. I'm sure as hell not going back to school, at least not this fall."

They said their good byes on the street in front of her apartment compound, on a *soi* off Sukhumvit. Held each other close. Lonnie listened to the beat of his heart; Luke buried his face in her hair. He explained that he thought he could get back in a couple weeks, if only for a few days. He started to explain about how his flight schedule worked, but she didn't want the details, only that he could. Then he reluctantly got back into their limo and continued to Khorat.

23

Being on position for hours without anything happening, without anything to do, became the devil's playground, and Luke's mind wandered inevitably to thought of Lonnie. Were she back in the states, he would have had to deal with the frustration of not seeing her for months, most likely a year, but it would have been a frustration that would have dwindled to only an occasional pulse. And if that had been the case, he thought he just might have been able to push her out of his mind completely, except for the occasional letter, and making plans to meet in someplace like Hawaii or maybe Hong Kong, on R&R. Instead she was only a few hundred klicks away, a long hitch-hike in college, now just a morning's limo ride, and he was haunted by her, not by images, not by scenes from their short time in Pattaya, but by possibilities, and he couldn't shut them off, except for brief moments— pre-flight inspection, coordinating changeover on station, questions or comments from whomever was on position— before he slipped back into his reverie of what the future might bring, and it was torture. He couldn't believe his good fortune. He, who could never pick up a woman of any consequence. They were such a fantastic match, in temperament, in sensitivities, and really, basically, in their view of the world. And the physical attraction—they'd only had a moment alone the evening before they returned to Bangkok, and of course on the ride back, but the sparks, truly, literally, had flown, and his desire was becoming impossible to tamp down.

McAuley took over for him a few hours after coming on station, and finally the immediacy of the real world engaged him. He tailed John Constance and Tanaka and Lawrence into the galley, where they sat down to eat. Box lunches, Luke's plain Jane from the officer's club—sandwiches, an apple, a cookie; the enlisted pretty much the same except for the addition of a hard-boiled egg and extra bread. White, of course. Luke eyed John Constance's egg and salivated over the idea of an egg salad sandwich. He couldn't remember when last he had eaten one. "What'll you take for it?" he asked.

"Whattaya got?" John said. "Better said, whattaya got that I might want?" He slid Luke's box lunch close, peered inside. "Not lookin' so great in here, Lieutenant," he said.

Luke rummaged. "I've got baloney," he said, holding up one of his sandwiches. "When's the last time you had baloney?"

"That's the best you can offer? Are you kidding?"

"I've got an apple."

"Lieutenant, we've all got apples."

Luke was facing aft, and at that moment looked up and saw Sergeant Rickey leaning against the counter, watching, his face expressionless. It seemed to Luke that he had appeared quite suddenly, almost like an apparition, making no entrance, just being there. A moment before he hadn't been there, and now here he was, in all his stern-faced glory. Luke couldn't recall seeing him since takeoff, when he had sat across from him in the Assistant's seat. Tolliver's seat. Where he went after that was anyone's guess, and as ridiculous as was the thought, Luke had the feeling that he had gone into some room off the aisle down to the intelligence compartment, to the right...or left. It didn't matter which, it was just a feeling. And now he was here, thin-faced, staring, looking for all the world like a bird of prey come to perch, waiting for the juicy leftovers.

Tanaka brought him back. "Why such a hankering for a hard-boiled egg, Lieutenant?" he said.

"A want to make an egg sandwich," Luke answered. "I haven't had an egg sandwich since we got here."

"You got mayo?" Tanaka asked. He held up a small sealed packet. "You got some of this? You got plain bread?"

"No, nothing."

Tanaka shook his head. "Sad," he said.

"How about favors?" Luke said. "I can bestow mucho favors. Scheduling. Maybe no more trips to the in-flight kitchen?"

"Lieutenant, Sergeant Rickey here hands out those duties," Saint said.

"I have influence," Luke said. Sergeant Rickey allowed himself a quiet laugh.

"You've got me thinking," John Constance said. "I'm starting to like the idea of an egg salad sandwich myself."

"Come on. You guys?" Luke asked Tanaka and Lawrence.

"On white bread? That sounds good. I'm thinking John Constance has the right idea," Saint said, cracking and peeling his egg. Thoughtfully, carefully. He opened his plastic utensil bag and took out his knife with a flourish, slicing his egg into a paper cup. He opened his mayonnaise packet and squeezed it artfully overall. "Looks good, Lieutenant, don'cha think? Great idea. Salt? Pepper?"

"Fuck you," Luke said. He was enjoying the little melodrama unfolding at the table, the play of humor, and felt good about their ease with each other. He glanced at Sergeant Rickey, wondered his reaction. He tried John Constance again. "Well?"

Saint stirred his mayo and eggs, added salt and held up his pepper packet. "How much do ya think?" he asked.

"A soupçon," John Constance said. He looked at Luke. "Bet you didn't know that was in the enlisted vocabulary."

"I don't think it's in most officers' vocabulary."

Saint carefully put his sandwich together and took a bite. "Taste?" he said to Luke.

"Maybe rater," Luke said.

Saint and Tanaka laughed. Saint closed his eyes and dramatically chewed. "You're right, Lieutenant, it's been a long time." He wiped a fleck of egg off his lower lip with his finger, looked at it, and licked it. "Good," he said, drawing out the drama. He looked at Luke. "And good for you."

"Don't you officers get roast beef," John Constance said. "Au jus? Maybe a dram of port? Your baloney's just an appetizer, right?"

"Right."

"I'll tell you what, Lieutenant," John Constance said, getting into things. "You get milk, too, don't you? We don't get milk, not real milk. Just that reconstituted stuff; you can taste the powder. Don't you get real milk? I heard you do."

"This is something in the enlisted grapevine?"

"Oh, yes. You'd be surprised what's in the enlisted grapevine. I'd love a glass of real milk," John Constance said. "Where's yours come from?"

"Cows," Luke said.

"Oh, thanks. Never knew that."

"The Thai-Danish dairy," Luke said. "It comes in a plastic bag, looks like a little pillow. It's the cutest thing you've ever seen. I've never seen milk in a plastic bag before. Have you?"

"It's not reconstituted, right?"

"Nah. That reconstituted stuff is just for enlisted."

"Scum. You forgot to add 'scum'," John Constance said. "Come to the mess hall, I'll show you reconstituted. Tastes like chalk. You get me a glass of real milk, I'll give you my egg."

"Now you're talking," Luke said.

"When?" John Constance said.

"You get off the bus with me, we'll go to the club and I'll buy you a glass of milk."

"They won't let me in," John Constance said. "I'm unter-mensch, remember?"

"I'll get you your milk."

John Constance handed Luke his egg.

"What about mayo?" Saint said. "It's no good without mayo, Lieutenant."

"What do you want?" Luke said. "I'm fresh out of bargaining chips," he said to John Constance.

"Well," John Constance said. "Here ya go, on the house. And bread. Consider that you owe me a favor."

Luke took the packet and bread.

"So, Lieutenant," Saint said. "How was Pattaya?"

Mouth full, Luke nodded and made a grunting noise of approval.

"Really?" Saint answered. "That good?"

Luke swallowed. "I met someone," he said.

"And?" Saint said.

"And it was a girl."

"Really. Well?"

Luke smiled. "She was...is...really nice. I like her. We ate at the Nipa Lodge. We rode back together. We even went sailing, on the boat with the saffron sails. We're going to see each other again."

"Finally," Saint said. "It's about time. She going to be around a while? When you gonna see her?"

"Next break, maybe, at least. Sooner if I can."

"She a round-eye?"

Luke nodded.

"American?"

"Yeah."

"You're not very forthcoming," John said. "Is she ugly or something?"

Luke laughed. "No. She's really very nice. She's pretty. Her father is working with the Laotian police up in Vientiane. I don't have a clue what he's doing. And she's here for the summer. Maybe longer. Depends."

"Sounds promising," Tanaka said. "Cha' get anything?"

"Jesus, Hugo," Saint said. "Really?"

"You're no one to talk," Tanaka answered.

LATER, after Luke was back on position, Sergeant Rickey joined him, pulling the jump seat down, sitting. Luke twisted his earphones askew so that he could hear both his radio and Sergeant Rickey. Last hour of the mission, screens blank, as they had been all night, zilch going on, as if they weren't over Laos at all and were instead sitting on the ground in Khorat. Luke couldn't recall any night as quiet as this, and said so. Rickey ignored the comment and went directly to his own agenda.

"It's been my experience, Lieutenant, that it's never a good idea to get too close to the enlisted; they'll take advantage of you."

"You're referring to, what? Our gathering in the galley?"

Rickey nodded. "Among others."

Luke had been expecting this conversation since Tolliver had given him the heads up about Rickey. He thought for a moment about Rickey's statement, and realized immediately the difference between him and Tolliver. He figured that Rickey had probably never flown with such an extraordinary group of men before. He thought about how fond he was of each of them, how each stood out, each for their own reasons, every one of them, even McAuley and Rolfe and Brooks. He tried to imagine a situation where his faith in them would boomerang and he would regret how close they had become, and couldn't. "No," he drawled slowly, pensively. "I don't think so, Sergeant. I really don't." He watched Rickey chew over what he had said, and waited for a response.

Rickey pursed his lips. Luke imagined he was rifling through his memory, reliving his experiences, gathering an answer. "Let me give you an example of what I mean," Rickey finally said. "This mission tonight, plus the one's since I arrived. This is how you do it? This is how you and Sergeant Tolliver did it?"

Luke nodded.

"I draw up the schedule and post it and we trust that the men will check it out and take their seats when they're supposed to?"

Again Luke nodded.

"And if they don't, what do you do?"

"It's never happened. It never will."

"See, that's my point, Lieutenant. That's not how it should work. We should do our own pre-brief before every flight where we go over everything and everybody knows exactly what they're supposed to do and there's a common understanding and you can be certain that everyone is going to do his duty." Rickey paused, looked at Luke. "It's called order. It's called discipline. If nothing else, it reminds them who's in charge."

"Sergeant..." Luke said.

"I'm sorry, I didn't mean for it to come out that way. I'm not a smart ass. It's just what we need to do if we're going to build a cohesive unit that we can depend on."

"And what makes you think we don't have one now? Maybe, if we had a bunch of new guys, what you're suggesting would make sense. And maybe, if the new guys weren't too sharp, it would make even more sense. But these guys are sharp, every one of them. And we've been together for months. In the beginning, way back, we worked through all the steps. And now they know to check the schedule. They know their jobs and they just do them. See, here's the thing that I keep in the back of my mind. I'm not sure how to say this, 'cause I haven't had to verbalize it before. We're in intelligence, even though we haven't seen hardly anything since Khe Sanh, and we basically haven't been on our own since the computers came on line at the command center. But I still believe the mission could come where something happens that doesn't make any sense, and I want these guys to feel free to venture any idea they can think of. That's what's important. Ya know what I mean?" He watched Rickey to see if any light was coming on, and decided there wasn't. "Look," he said, "I don't know what you were expecting to run into over here, but let me tell you, this is a fucked-up mess of a war, and every one of these men knows it. Nothing makes any sense. We've got officers who came to Southeast Asia just to get their tickets punched, and that don't care if what they're doing makes any sense at all. And us, we're all just sitting back up to a computer at Nakhon Phanom, at Task Force Alpha. To go through some kind of inspection just to make sure everyone's got the order of command is just bullshit, and they'll know it. The way I see it, our main job is to protect these guys from the bullshit, so they can do the real work, and if we manage to do that, we'll have accomplished what we need to. And we'll be able to send them home with some semblance of sanity. So, bottom line, I think you need to back off." While he was speaking, it occurred to Luke that maybe Sergeant Rickey was one of those careerists he was describing and that he was here just to get his ticket punched. He had no idea what Rickey had done in SAC, but given the legacy of the cigar-chomping Curtis Lemay, who had nearly brought the nation to war with the Soviet Union, sending bombers in all on his own, and that Rickey had earned his stripes in that kind of charge-the-cannons environment, it seemed possible his worst enemy was sitting right next to him. Certainly the lack of recognition in Rickey's eyes hinted that it might be so. He waited to see how he would respond.

Rickey stared at the blank screens in front of him, then, for a moment, at Luke. "You know, Lieutenant, I've been down to Training and looked at these guys records, and it's not a pretty picture."

Luke was taken aback, thrown off his pace, if only just a little. In truth, he didn't even know there was a training office, and had never thought to check on his men's records. He waited for Rickey to continue.

"Since these men left radio operators school, they have

not moved one inch towards their next level of certification. Not an inch."

"All of them?"

"No. Just your boys. Constance, Tanaka, Rolfe. Lawrence. The others have all already achieved it."

"And you think they care?"

"It doesn't matter what I think. They need to stay proficient. If they have any hope in the world of putting on another stripe, they need to get with the program. They need to be reminded that they belong to a system, and that there's certain things the system expects them to do."

Luke closed his eyes, practically picturing the gulf between Rickey's and his point of view. He thought for a minute. "Listen, Sergeant. Here's the thing. You may have me there about watching out for all these guys. Making sure they keep up their radio op proficiency. But first off, I don't worry about the careerists. They're all good, and you and I will write them good performance reports, and they'll get their next stripes, every one of them. Molino, McAuley, Brooks. As for Constance and Tanaka and Rolfe and the rest...this is their last assignment. They're gonna go home and they're gonna get out, and they have no interest in earning another stripe, and that's that. And in the meantime, we'll be ready, and we'll step in when we have to, and I know we'll do a damn good job...at intelligence. And I'm not going to bug them about training, and neither are you. Do you understand?"

Rickey didn't respond. He sat quietly for a few moments, then stood, put the jump seat away and went forward. Luke wondered if that was going to be the end of it. He tried to get his mind off Rickey, wondering what might come next, but couldn't. Even thought of Lonnie didn't work, leaving him to ruminate about whether he was doing the right thing, or if Rickey was going to come back and bite him in the ass.

TWO DAYS later they flew Blue, over one of the main infiltration routes off the trail into northern South Vietnam. Throughout the time before takeoff Rickey kept to himself, on the crew bus to wing, filing in to the pre-flight briefing, collecting their parachute harnesses, the bus to the plane. Luke wondered what he was thinking, if maybe he was going to explode in resentment or maybe just take his grievance to Woody. And truth was, Luke wasn't sure what Woody would say. The way he approached his crew was his own, and it seemed to be working. He'd never discussed it with Woody.

Once at the aircraft, he and Rickey drafted and posted the schedule. The enlisted men stopped by to look. Luke watched Rickey to gauge if he was taking in what was happening. The enlisted men chatted among themselves as they taped and marked their screens; when they were done, they told Rickey they were ready. Rickey nodded. His expression seemed neutral, but it also seemed possible that he was softening as he realized that things were as Luke had said, that the crew's casual demeanor was but a veneer over a self-discipline that got things done.

Not much happened that night. In the wee hours they tracked numerous trucks, none in convoys above five. Most were attacked, a few were hit. Towards the end of the flight, on the way back to Khorat, Rickey stopped by Luke's position, pulled out the jump seat as before, and sat down. He went straight to their previous conversation.

"Lieutenant," he said, "I'll give it to you. It's clear what you say is true. These guys know what they're doing. It was tough listening to you last flight. I've never had an officer talk to me like that. Pull me back. Never in my whole career. I've never had anyone pull me back from what I thought were my duties."

Luke avoided rejoining the old argument. "I suspect you've never been in a situation like this before, Sergeant Rickey. Gung ho just won't wash here."

Rickey nodded. "I have an idea, Lieutenant," he said. "Here's what I'd like to do: I need something, something useful that helps occupy my time. Here's the thing. I'm a good cook, so I was thinking why don't I just cook meals for the crew on each flight. I'll collect the money and get things together. Maybe some of the men can help me with that. I'll tell you beforehand what I want to make and you run it by Woody. I'm not sure my wife would admit it, but I'm the chef in our house. I love it. I don't think you'll regret this."

Luke was surprised, near flabbergasted. It all seemed too good to be true. He wondered how the man could do such a complete one-eighty. "You sure, Sergeant? I like the idea, and I suspect everyone else will, too. I just want to make sure you're convinced you really want to do this."

"Yes, sir, I am. At home my holiday meals are legend, and when we were on standby in SAC, I often cooked for the crew. I enjoy it. So, yes, I think it will work."

"All right. I'll run it by Woody, but I know he won't care. He'll be tickled pink. But let's not look for menu approval. You know what that's like; we'll never get agreement on anything. You decide what you want to make and let us know.

RICKEY STARTED SIMPLE AND EASY, spaghetti Bolognese, sauce from scratch, his own special recipe. A real supermarket had opened in Khorat, plate glass windows, air-conditioning, fluorescent lights; vegetables in trays, aisles of canned goods. Fresh tomatoes, pasta. Recognizable spices. Rickey sent John Constance and Rolfe for his ingredients; they brought everything aboard in the ubiquitous woven-plastic Thai shopping bags, a strange sight boarding a camouflaged aircraft. Next the crew bus would have a rack for chickens and pigs in wooden cages.

Rickey started cooking not long after they went on station. In a moment he came back to Luke at his position. "Take a look at this, Lieutenant," he said. He was holding a garland of garlic, a couple dozen bulbs or more tied together. "I told John Constance I needed some garlic and he brought me this." He draped the garland around his neck. John Constance was on position one and Rickey waved at him. "What do you figure, John Constance, a life-time supply?" He laughed. "Dracula will never come near me!"

John Constance shrugged. "What do I know from garlic," he said.

It all seemed to work, though Luke remained trepidatious. He was amazed the change had come so quickly and easily and hoped it was for real. It was tough for any professional to admit that what they were doing added little or no value to the war, not directly at least. Tougher still to come to grips with the fact that the war was a senseless loss of lives, men dying for no good reason, snafu from start to finish, situation normal, all fucked up. And that the stench of it was a yellow bile that would never go away. Still, it seemed to be working out, and Luke was grateful.

· · ·

THE NEXT MISSION was beef stroganoff, now with linen on the table and metal eating utensils. At the end of the mission, Rickey received an ovation on the crew bus as he boarded. "Good work, Sergeant," Woody said. "What's next?"

"Don't know yet, sir," Rickey responded

"A hymn for Sergeant Rickey," Major Howard said.

To which they all responded, singing their Gregorian chant-like response: "Him, him, fuck him!"

Rickey smiled.

24

Luke woke in early evening. Gropper was already up and out, presumably gone to the club for dinner. He didn't feel much like moving. He got up and sat in his desk chair, waking. There was a loud knock at the door, too loud and insistent for the occasion, as if some unknown authority wanted entry. A pause, then the knocking began again, but now more intermittently, as if the person knocking wasn't so sure after all. He opened the door to Saint, who was holding himself up by the door jamb. For a moment Luke wondered if he was injured, then noticed that his eyes were bloodshot, his look unfocused. He stumbled in and fell onto Luke's bed, banging his head against the headboard. He moaned. Closed his eyes. Luke wondered if he was out cold. The tart smell of beer wafted his way

"I'm wasted," he said.

"Really. I couldn't tell. Whatcha been doing? As if I had to ask."

"Drinking."

"How much?"

"Dunno."

"Whattaya mean, you don't know? Where've ya been?"

"Sawadee Club. I went over after breakfast."

"So you were there all day? And then you came here?"

Saint nodded, groaned.

"Any lunch? Any dinner?"

Silence. Then, "I don't remember."

"No, really. Have you had anything to eat?"

"I don't remember."

"Dunno?"

"Dunno."

"Who was with you?"

"McAuley. Tanaka. Rickey."

"Rickey? You're shitting me. Are you all wasted?"

"Dunno."

"That's it? Dunno? Rickey went drinking with you and that's it?"

Saint swung his legs to the floor, sitting up. "I wanna go downtown."

"In your condition?"

"I wanna get laid."

"Tonight?"

"I wanna get laid right now." Saint looked Luke in the eye, squinting conspiratorially. "I wanna to get some girl to do some really weird shit. I wanna do some really weird shit."

"And Vicki? Where does she fit in this?"

"Really weird," he said, ignoring the question about Vicki. "I wanna find a whore and do some really weird shit. Maybe we do some two on one. Whattaya think?"

"Not me. But don't let that stop you. You should get showered. Clean up. Brush your teeth. Your breath smells like the whole Russian army marched through your mouth. I'll come with you, but that's it."

"But it would be good. I'm sure we can find someone."

"I just don't feel like it."

Saint pulled himself together enough to think about what Luke was saying. "Is this 'cause of what's her name?"

"Lonnie? Maybe."

"D'you fuck her?"

"No."

"And you don't want to get laid tonight."

"I'm not feeling it."

"Hmmph," Saint said. "Hmmph," he repeated. "That's it then, for us guys?

"No, it's not it for us guys. I'm gonna go with you tonight, I just don't have any desire to get laid. Besides, you certainly went off with Vicki. And here we still are."

"Vicki doesn't count."

A LONG HOT shower and a shave later they made their way into town, to a bar that had to be the largest in Khorat, at least as far as Luke knew, a cavernous, high-ceilinged barn with a bar at each end, a band in the middle, full of Americans, some at every table, most sitting with Thai women. More Thai women stood against the walls, mainly in small groups. Luke had never been to the bar before, in fact didn't even know where he was, a *soi* off a larger road that he also didn't know. The noise was deafening. He recognized no one; Saint seemed to know them all.

They found an empty table. Luke noticed a young Thai woman standing alone against the wall across from them, barely noticeable in the shadows. Her eyes were roundish, nearly *farung*, her hair short in a page boy. Incongruously, she was wearing a double-breasted grey pinstriped suit, but without a blouse. She was reserved and standoffish, as if she had never been there before, and was there for some reason other than picking up a trick. She seemed to be avoiding eye contact with anyone.

"You see her?" Luke asked.

Saint nodded. He pushed his chair back and was gone, making a beeline for the woman in the shadows. He talked to her briefly and then brought her out to the dance floor. Luke settled back to enjoy the show. The band was playing the chorus of "Hey, Jude", and it seemed like every man in the place was singing along, on the dance floor and at the tables. *Take a sad song, and make it better.* Ringing out *Na, na, na, na-na-na-nah, na-na-na-nah, He-ey Jude, Ju Ju de Ju-de Ju-de Ju-de Ju-de.* Saint was dancing more than singing, his eyes closed, his body rhythmically fluid, head moving slightly back and forth in time to the music. The woman smiled, enjoying him. Luke recognized the moment, the same as when Saint first met Vicki. He knew that from here on he would be the odd man out, that for him the night was over.

He stayed for the rest of *Jude,* joining in, singing along with all the other men. The band continued long past the typical ending, playing endless codas in time with the men. They sang as if mesmerized, whooping and stamping until finally, one by one, they quit, and after a time, the band quit, too. Luke left, walked to the taxi stand in the central square, still singing *Jude* in his mind, knowing that in the morning Saint would regale him with everything that had happened with the girl in the pinstriped suit and he wouldn't be gloating or bragging and Luke would feel like he had been there, and he would laugh and once again get a vicarious thrill. Things could be worse.

25

They lost hydraulics a third of the way to orbit, most likely from a leak somewhere in the system. Woody sent Gropper searching for spare cans of hydraulic fluid to replenish the reservoir. He looked in every nook and cranny on the plane—the cans had to be there, were *supposed* to be there, somewhere, for just such an eventuality. In the head, maybe, or maybe in the storage space next to the head, or stuffed in the curved space between the galley and the inner wall of the fuselage, in with all the odds and ends. The cabinets near the aft bunks. Nothing. It seemed impossible. This was important stuff, but no, they couldn't find any, and Woody swore there'd be hell to pay.

They turned around and headed back to Khorat. Not long before descent the crew began manually lowering the wing flaps, using a long crank reminiscent of the engine crank for an ancient car. Everyone pitched in, one at a time, officer and enlisted, huffing and wheezing and spelling each other as they fought to bring the flaps down. Truthfully it was a lark, something very different, something besides riding back and forth to station and flying around in circles.

After landing Woody worked the brakes as they rolled down nearly the entire length of the runway. Finally he was able to bring the plane to a stop.

A firetruck met them, ready to smother the brakes should they burst into flames. Colonel Crawford and Colonel Milque, chief of maintenance, drove up in Crawford's jeep and stood by a distance from the aircraft.

Woody gave the order to evacuate. Sergeant Rickey popped the aft hatch and was loosing the evac rope from its case when Woody called Luke forward. "We're having trouble hooking up the tow tractor," he said. "Move your men as far aft as they can so we can take pressure off the nose wheel."

Luke hurried aft and gave the order.

"Are you serious?" Tanaka said, incredulous.

"Just do it!" Luke said, raising his voice.

"Aye, aye, sir," Tanaka said, still giving Luke the eye.

Woody came back on the intercom. "Got it!" he said. "Now evacuate!"

One by one the crew slid down the rope to the ground and moved a safe distance from the plane. Like a captain prepared to go down with his ship, Woody was last. As soon as everyone was clear, the tractor driver began rocking the plane, shifting forward and reverse, pulling and pushing the Connie. Woody was apoplectic. "What the hell is going on?" he said, and started towards the tractor. Then he stopped, turned. "Tuttle," he said. "you come with me."

Luke couldn't imagine why, but dutifully caught up and followed Woody to the tractor.

"What do you think you're doing?" Woody shouted to the ground crewman as they walked up.

The ground crewman was clearly intimidated and

squeaked out a response. "Sir, the manual for the Connie says to rock the plane back and forth to cool the brakes."

"Bullshit!" Woody said. "Not my plane," The ground crewman was convinced he knew what he was doing, and protested, citing the manual again.

"I don't care what you think it says," Woody said. With Crawford and Milque looking on from afar, he reached in to the tractor's dash and turned off the engine. The ground crewman burst into tears, which was far beyond anything Woody had expected. Exasperated, he walked off to the waiting crew bus. Luke followed, still wondering why Woody had insisted he join him.

LATER, in their room, Luke asked Gropper what he thought it was all about, why Woody had insisted that he go with him to talk to the tractor driver.

"I dunno," Gropper said, "but maybe...I think maybe Woody thinks you're too palsy with your men. I think he thinks it's one thing to be friendly, you know, we're on these long flights together and it's probably inevitable, but once... when we're off duty I think he thinks that we need to maintain our distance. I think maybe he wanted to show you how to handle enlisted men."

"Really?" Luke felt a twinge in his gut. "Why? Just because I don't bust their balls every now and then? I don't think that's the way you build a team. All he managed to do was intimidate the tractor driver to the point of tears."

"He cried?" Gropper said.

Luke nodded. "Yeah, he did. If that was supposed to teach me something, it sure as hell failed." He paused. "What do you think?"

"About fraternizing?"

"Yeah."

"I dunno. I've gotten to know your guys and they're good men. They're bright. And you're with them for hours at a time. I guess you've got to answer the question yourself. What do you think? Are you too close to them? Will they lose their respect for you? I mean like the roughhousing at the pool party. And going off to Pattaya with Lawrence and Tanaka."

"Are you serious?"

"Cool down! I think it's something you should think about, that's all. I don't know. I mean I do. I can't imagine a situation where it would be an issue on the plane, not with our crew, anyways. Maybe, if some other men come in, it won't be the same. But now? I'm just not sure."

Luke recalled his brief interchange with Tanaka on the plane when he was marshaling all his men to the rear, and he wondered if the situation wasn't just what Gropper was talking about. Then he reminded himself that Tanaka had done what he told him to, and to expect him to smile and salute brightly was over the top. Then he wondered, maybe, if Rickey had gotten to Woody, but the more he thought about it, the more he doubted it: Rickey seemed to have settled into the way things were. Still, he harbored a vague feeling of apprehension, wondering if maybe he didn't need to comport himself differently. It pissed him off, and he resolved that he wouldn't back off, devil take the hindmost. And now more than ever he knew that the military wasn't the place for him.

26

H e bounded up the stairs to the covered veranda that ran the length of Lonnie's apartment building. It faced a courtyard surrounding a garden abundant with green trees and bushes and a wandering path spotted with benches. Early on a Friday evening, due back in Khorat Sunday night. He knocked at Lonnie's door, nervous with excitement, and was taken aback when an older, grey-haired man greeted him.

He checked the number on the door, compared it to his hastily written note of a few weeks before.

"And you are?" the man said, holding the door carefully, purposefully blocking Luke's entrance.

"Luke Tuttle."

Immediately he heard Lonnie, a little squeal followed by running feet and there she was, pushing through. "This is Luke, Daddy, this is the guy I told you about."

Lonnie's father opened the door slowly, giving Luke just enough room to slip inside. He continued to hold the door while he looked Luke over, making his wariness palpable.

He was of Luke's father and mother's generation. Luke's

height, heavier set. Full-faced, with Lonnie's strong nose, steady gaze, commanding look.

Lonnie stood on her toes and kissed Luke lightly on the cheek. Wearing a lime green muumuu decorated with Christmas red orchids, colors that enriched her light olive complexion. She looked comfortable and relaxed, and it infected Luke. He needed it; her father had put him off, and he was feeling more than a little unsure of himself.

"You made it," she said. "For how long?"

"Just a few days," Luke said.

"Oh, I'm so happy." She took Luke's hand and led him into their apartment. Her father followed.

The apartment was eerily like Vicki's, yet another American temporarily in Southeast Asia, spartan white walls, rented Danish modern furniture, teak and mahogany, dining table and chairs, coffee table. He wondered where the furniture came from, if all Americans shopped at the same store, or maybe if the State Department had a warehouse full stuff for American citizens working for the US Government in Thailand. Or Laos, as the case might be. He'd seen it all at Vicki's, save for a small antique statue of the monkey god, Hanuman, legs spread wide, defiant, mounted on a teak pedestal and holding pride of place in the center of the coffee table. And one picture on the wall, a large framed photograph of a World War Two Hellcat F6F fighter plane flying high above an immense body of water, canopy open, pilot visible, looking towards the photographer. He looked at the photo, then at Lonnie's father.

"Yeah," Lonnie's father said, "that's me. Coming back to my carrier. During the Marianas Turkey Shoot."

Luke raised his eyebrows. "The Battle of the Philippine Sea."

Her father nodded and looked at the photograph. "Yeah.

That's me," he repeated, with wistful pride. "You know your history," he added.

"Some," Luke said. "And now?" he asked, already knowing where Lonnie's father worked, but wanting to keep the conversation going.

"I'm in Vientiane training the local police to defend themselves against the Pathet Lao. And you?" he added.

"Flying recon over Laos," Luke said. "Laos and South Viet Nam. Over the Ho Chi Minh Trail. In Connies."

Again Lonnie's father nodded. "Igloo White," he said, using the code name for Luke's program, taking Luke aback. He obviously knew what was going on, and Luke realized he would need to watch what he said.

Meanwhile Lonnie disappeared, reappearing a short moment later having changed into white Capri pants and an emerald green, scoop-necked and patterned peasant blouse. That's her color, Luke said to himself. She certainly knows —she looked strikingly beautiful, healthy and vibrant.

"We're going to buy dinner," she said. Her father reminded her where the shop was located. "Daddy," she said, her tone of voice challenging his need to say the obvious. "Chicken," she said to Luke as they went out the door. "We'll be right back," she announced.

"Well," she said, as they walked through the courtyard garden and a back alley leading to the main thoroughfare. "What do you think?"

"Your father? He's certainly imposing. And maybe protective. We only had a moment. He was nice enough. And he sure is proud of his time in the Navy. And he sure blocked that doorway."

"That's about right," Lonnie said, laughing. "All of it. Officious, not too friendly, at least not at first."

"And your mother? Do you keep her in a closet?"

"There's just Daddy and me."

"Really?" He was surprised such a vital fact had not come to light before.

"She died years ago. I barely remember her."

"Is it hard? No brothers or sisters, just the two of you."

Lonnie nodded. "Sometimes."

"And he leaves you alone for days, maybe weeks at a time?"

"It's not much different than college, is it? I'm careful. It was difficult in the beginning, freshman year, but we got past it. Smith isn't that far from Providence, and he came up a lot on weekends. But he's okay with it now."

"Providence. You never mentioned that before. Your dad worked there? What'd he do?"

"He was the police chief. Not so long ago."

After a moment of silence, Luke asked, "How far're we going?"

"Down a few blocks. I've worn a groove in the sidewalk. We get our dinner at this place almost every night. They know us now. Chicken curry, red curry chicken, basil chicken, chicken soup, lemongrass chicken, garlic chicken. Buck, buck," she added, imitating the sound of a chicken. "Those are the names I remember."

"And today?"

"Whatever's the chicken of the day."

They walked slowly, casually, window shopping as they went. Lonnie took Luke's arm. He looked down at her. With the movement of her breasts he realized she was braless. He felt a surge in his groin. Lonnie watched his eyes, his expression as he tuned in to her breasts, and smiled.

"When do you have to go back?"

"Sunday afternoon."

"Doesn't give us much time."

"No, not really. I wish it were more, but it's something, right?"

"Right."

"And will your father be here the whole time?"

"Yup. He doesn't go back for a week." After a few minutes, she said, "So we really only have tomorrow and Sunday morning. What do you want to do?"

"Wander Bangkok?"

"That would be fun. Do you know your way around?"

He shrugged. "A little. I've gone to some of the obvious tourist destinations. Timland. The floating market. I know how to flag a taxi. How 'bout the movies?" he added. "Coming into town I noticed *Romeo and Juliet* at a theatre. Presumably in English, or maybe dubbed in Thai with English subtitles. I didn't recognize any of the names, except Michael York."

"Do you really want to go?" Lonnie asked.

Luke hesitated. "No, not really."

"You've got a room, don't you?" She hitched her gait to look up at him. "You checked in at a hotel?"

Luke nodded.

"Okay, then," Lonnie said. "*Romeo and Juliet* it is."

"And your father?"

"We'll tell him it was a good movie. But tedious."

"That'll be enough?"

"Trust me," Lonnie said.

IN THE BEGINNING, conversation at dinner was casual. Lonnie's father asked Luke about himself and Luke was happy to oblige. Lonnie was content to listen—so much of what he had to say was news to her as well. He recounted growing up in Mount Brookville, the two-room school, playing in the woods, how much he loved it, how special it was to him—the hills, a place where everybody knew each other and yes, knew each other's business, but also where people helped each other out when there was trouble—getting hay in before a rain, or collecting a herd of heifers that had escaped through a broken fence into the forest. And the beauty, the green summers, the maples in the fall. He watched to see if Lonnie's father was evidencing any interest, and, realizing that he wasn't, decided he needed to cut it short. He knew the look. People who grew up in cities and suburbs hadn't a clue about rural ethos, about rural life, not really. Hell, many of his neighbors didn't. And to explain took too long.

"So your dad's a farmer," Lonnie's father said, moving the subject on.

"Was. We didn't make it. We weren't big enough, really. Once upon a time, maybe. Ours was a prosperous hop farm, but those days are long gone. And now, the price of milk keeps dropping. More and more middlemen. We still have the house and the barns, but not much else."

"So what does your father do?"

"He works in a factory in Syracuse," Luke said.

"So not a farmer."

Luke shook his head. "We've got a garden. Plus chickens. We kept one last cow for awhile, until I left for college. Dad tries to get a deer every season, sometimes in the off season."

"And he works in a factory."

"Yessir."

"How's he doing?"

"Not well," Luke said.

Lonnie's father eyed him, seemingly calculating every question. "Will you go back?" he asked.

"I don't know. I don't think so. There's not a lot of work in central New York. Most of the small factories are gone, the textile mills. Moved south for non-union labor."

"And you think that's bad?"

Luke recognized the pregnant question, the entre to capitalism and profits, the debilitating unions. "The farms are dying, and the factory jobs are disappearing. There's no work. That just about says it all."

"And your parents managed Colgate."

"Scholarships," Luke answered.

"And now you're in the Air Force. Have you thought about making it a career?"

Luke nodded his head but slightly, in sympathy to his lack of enthusiasm about the idea. "I thought about it for a while. Not anymore. I don't think it's for me." Which was code for not in a million years. He wasn't going to go into the why of it; there was no question in his mind that Lonnie's father would cotton to none of it.

They finished eating and Lonnie began clearing the table, wordlessly carrying dishes out to the kitchen. He heard water running, dishes clattering in a sink. He made as if to get up and help. "No, wait a minute," her father said. "I don't often have a chance for male company at the dinner table. I want to hear more. I want to hear about your mission. What you do. Is it dangerous?"

"I don't think so," Luke said, skating the surface. "Not anymore, anyway. The North Vietnamese nosed around our planes some in the beginning, but now we own the skies, at least over Laos and South Vietnam, and they leave us alone. Maybe they've figured out what we do, and don't see any reason to bother. We're not stopping anything from going into South Vietnam."

"Really? You've decided."

"Sir?"

"It doesn't work. McNamara's electronic wall."

"No, sir. It's like nobody's standing back and looking. Tet. Hue. The Battle for Saigon. The VC were everywhere, and they were well armed. And the North Vietnamese. They all were. We're not stopping anything."

Lonnie's father stared at him. Cold, piercing, eyes, putting Luke off. He could feel the tension rising in his stomach, the feeling of fight or flight that paralyzed him whenever his father was about to lay into him. Wondering what was coming next.

"I'll tell you what I think," he said. "I think your problem is that you guys, all you guys over here, are losing your war."

Luke was taken aback. It was such a blatant hit, a calculous Lonnie's father must have been turning over in his mind for quite some time. He didn't know how to respond. The implication was clear: The men who had flown Hellcats in the Battle of the Philippine Sea had had what it took, and Luke's generation didn't. There was nothing he could say that would budge his opinion. He waited a few moments for Lonnie's father to say more, but he didn't. He looked at Luke. Piercingly. If ever there was a proper use of that word, this was it. Then he balled up his napkin and melodramatically dropped it next to his plate. Stood, and left. He had spoken.

Luke joined Lonnie in the kitchen, where she was washing dishes. Luke picked up the drying towel and began to help.

"Did you catch that?" he said.

"Some of it. Not all. What'd he say?"

Luke sighed. "Basically, he said my generation, guys like me, are losers. We're all losers."

Lonnie set the dish she was washing back into the sink.

She wiped off her hands and hugged Luke. "I'm sorry. I hoped this wouldn't happen."

"It's not just that he said it, and that it's offensive. It's that he doesn't have a clue, you know what I mean? How do you stand it?"

"We have a gentlemen's agreement, sort of. We don't talk about this stuff. We don't talk about Vietnam. We don't talk civil rights. We don't talk about anything of consequence. He's in total control of his world and used to people agreeing with him and saluting and doing what he says."

Luke shook his head. "It's so damn disappointing. Another guy at the top. We're fucked."

"Us?"

"All of us."

"It sounds like you need a drink. How about a martini?"

Luke laughed. "Are you a martini drinker? Aren't whisky sours and screwdrivers the drinks of choice for college? They were for me." He paused. "Can you make it a double?"

They went back into the living room. Lonnie slid open the glass door to their liquor cabinet and took out a bottle of gin. "Vermouth's in the refrigerator," she said, heading back into the kitchen. "Olives?" she asked. Luke nodded.

She returned with his drink.

"So tell me," Luke said, "how does someone like your father wind up with such a gorgeous, thoughtful, compassionate daughter?"

She laughed. "He can be such a horse's patoot. But I have to say," she added, and paused. "I'm confused. When we talked in Pattaya, you led me to believe you opposed this war. And now here you are upset because my father said you're losing. Where are you?"

"I know, I know." Luke said. "I can't reconcile it. There's no sensible reason in the world for us to be in Southeast

Asia, but here we are. There's this mindless fear of communism. It buffaloes us. When that word gets tossed in, we don't think straight. It just kind of crept up on us, didn't it. I hate it, that no one stops to think. That no one seems to care. It's men's lives, for no good reason, and I hate what it's doing to us. I want it to end, but I'm not a loser. None of us are. We're stuck."

He downed his martini and asked Lonnie to make another that he downed equally quickly. He didn't feel them until after he left, and back at his hotel he crashed.

27

Lonnie wore a long, casual gingham sundress that brushed the floor when she walked, the skirt striped, the chocolate brown bodice held up by straps tied behind her neck. Stylish hippie. Not something often seen on the streets of Bangkok. As they walked across the lobby of Luke's hotel to the elevators, the Thai concierge stared at her. It made Luke uncomfortable. He didn't want the man thinking ill of Lonnie, as if she were some kind of street hooker, and he swung behind her to block the concierge's view.

In the room she went first to the window to look out, then turned towards him. She reached up and untied the straps of her sundress and let the bodice fall away. She watched Luke's reaction and smiled at his appreciation. All without saying a word. She pushed him back on the bed and unbuckled his belt, releasing him. Looked at him for a moment before straddling him, then unbuttoned his shirt. She dropped onto him and he tried to control himself, to last forever, but he couldn't. She smothered his face with kisses, moved rhythmically atop him, caressed him with her breasts. She nuzzled his ear. "O Luke," she said. "Luke," she repeated, and he thought she sounded both happy and sad.

THE ROOM WAS COLD, and they pulled the sheet and blanket up to their chins and snuggled close.

"I want to see Mount Brookville," she said. "Will I like it? Will I love it the way you do?"

"I hope so. But it's not all peaches and roses. There's some real poverty."

"So you said. What could be so bad?"

"Well, it's not just that some of the houses are collapsing, it's that so many of the people aren't even trying anymore. A piece of wood, a hammer, some nails. They could make it better. At least put some cardboard in the broken windows. And the abandoned barns. They were magnificent, huge maple beams, pegged joints. But the roofs are leaking and the beams are rotting. It's just sad. A way of life is ebbing away."

THEY MADE LOVE AGAIN, slower, longer. Afterwards, Lonnie went into the bathroom, closing the door behind her. When she came out she was still nude, and in no hurry to cover up. She walked towards the window and looked out. Explored the desk, flipped through the travel magazines, unhurried, unencumbered by any expectation, from Luke, or anyone else. Complete. Luke had never known a moment like this. Yes, he said to himself. Like enjoying the nudes in a museum, the smooth marble, the turn of the brush. Only this nude looked at him, smiled, and returned to the bed.

28

Night over Laos, targets frequent. Strong winds of irregular rhythm buffeted the plane. Luke, Saint and Rolfe took them on station. When they first sat down, in the beginning, they kept to themselves, hunkered down. When they did talk another violent jerk of the plane would catch their attention and stop them mid-sentence, and they'd pause and wait for calm.

Two hours in they were relieved by McAuley, Molino, and John Constance. "Soup's on," McAuley announced when he took over from Luke. "Goulash. Personally I'd rather just steak and potatoes."

The air was still rough and when Luke stood he had to hold onto his console to catch his balance. Moving forward he grabbed onto whatever was quickly at hand, feeling like a pinball being whacked by flippers. Rickey greeted him with a linen napkin over his forearm, smiled, and pointed to the table. "Seat?" he asked.

"How'd you manage in this weather?" Luke said.

"It's easy when you know what you're doing," Rickey

said. "I've made this recipe a dozen times." He started the water to finish boiling the noodles. "This is an experiment," he said. "For all that they have at the new supermarket, they don't have Hungarian paprika. I shouldn't be surprised. Maybe everyone around here just uses fresh chilis, but these Thai things are just so hot. Who knows. But I figured I could make do. It's good, but then I'm from Texas, and you can't make anything too hot for me. Everyone seems to like it so far. Let me know what you think."

He drained the noodles and spooned them into bowls, followed by the goulash over all. "Dig in," he said as he served up bowls to the three of them.

The goulash <u>was</u> spicier than Luke would have liked, but he was able to handle it. He broke out in a sweat and dabbed the top of his head with his napkin.

"Too hot, Lieutenant?" Rickey asked.

"Close," Luke said, "but I like it. How can I complain with food like this?"

Rolfe cleared the table and began washing the dishes. Luke and Saint went to the aft bunks. Luke crawled into one of the top bunks and fell asleep almost immediately, his dreams rich and vivid. It was cold in the Connie and the cold entered his dreams. Walking down the driveway to the barn, the night air freezing and stinging his lungs. The sky black and seemingly endless, full of stars, humbling. His milk pail creaked with each step, his nostrils prickled. The snow crunched under his feet, sending shivers up his body like chalk on a blackboard. The wind was constant, flinging snow across the fields, over the drifts and into his face, piling ever higher in the driveway and on the highway. The scene shifted: Lying face down on his sled, speeding down an ice-embalmed road, the ice not four inches from his nose. The snow towered beside him like canyon walls, blocking his view. He couldn't see where he was; he knew where he was—Clark Road, he could sense it. The dirt of car traffic filled the crevices in the snow beneath him. Alone, no one sliding with him, the nearby houses empty, alone in all the world, and fearful. He rounded the curve just before Ransom's general store, dragging his left foot to hold his course. He headed straight for the bridge and he knew he wouldn't make it, he was going too fast. He dragged both feet. It wasn't enough—he was airborne, flying over the snow bank, and he couldn't stop and now he was on ice, spinning uncontrollably down Mill Creek, the ice cracking, about to give way, then it did and he was in icy cold water and he was afraid he was going to slip under the ice and be trapped and freeze to death and die. Then he was under, and soft, sibilant freezing water flowed all around him, he was under the ice and he looked up and there was nothing but more ice, solid ice, without a hole through to air or an air pocket to breathe. There was no way out. He was trapped and he was going to die.

He woke. Air *sissed* past the fuselage. Almost immediately it dawned on him that it was a sound he'd never heard before, not in a Connie; always there was the rumble of engines, always, the pulse of existence, like breathing out and breathing in. And now it wasn't there. Where're the engines? he asked himself. What's happened to the engines? He felt light in the bunk, as if he would soon levitate. He realized with a start that the Connie was falling, and just like that, everything changed. He wondered how long it had been going on, how far had they fallen. How close were they to the ground? Were they about to crash? Was this it? Just like that? Was it over? Was he about to die? How long did he have?

No, he said to himself. No. This can't be how it ends,

helpless in a bed. He jumped out of the bunk and landed lightly on his feet as the floor fell away from him. Just as he landed Saint jumped out of the bunk next to his. They looked at each other and saw through to each other's fear and confusion. The Connie continued to fall, but somehow, the floor was level. The overhead lightbulb cast ghostly, other-worldly shadows, lighting the eerie capsule in which they were trapped. It was happening, this was how it was going to end, the plane falling and he and Saint and the crew unable to move or do anything to stop it!

The Connie jerked hard left, throwing him against the bulkhead, Saint against the aft table. What happened? The abrupt movement flushed the last vestige of conscious thought from his mind. He was terrified, and he could see that Saint was, too. Then an engine caught and roared, then another. Then two more. The Connie stopped falling, began climbing, climbing, *climbing*, for god's sake, O my god, he thought, Yes. We're climbing. Is it over? What was it?

The intercom crackled. "Crew, this is the flight deck." Woody. "We had a little problem with ice back there and the intakes froze up. We dropped down to warmer air and now everything's clear. We're going to fly at this altitude from here on out."

Luke could hardly grasp the thought. It was over, that was all that mattered. Everything was okay. He was okay. He sat down at the table, Saint across from him. The shock remained. They both still had fear in their eyes. They breathed deeply, sat speechless, waiting for the shock to wear off. Long moments, looking at each other. Then they stood, walked forward. Luke checked the men at their positions, Molino and John Constance, McAuley. They were all white as ghosts, and equally stunned.

"That was wild, Lieutenant," McAuley said quietly. He paused to regain his composure. "Major Woodrum called, asked me to call TFA and tell them that we're going to be flying a little lower the rest of the mission. I've taken care of that."

29

Enter Major Morgan, subbing for Woody, who had gone back to the states for a funeral. Morgan a fucking new guy, an FNG, recently transferred from the Pentagon, where he'd flown a desk for most of his career. Tall, spindly, weak-looking. Oily skin. Jughead ears. Possessor of a ridiculous Svengali mustache waxed so heavily it shone like plastic, a look so absurd that Luke was ashamed for all the wearers of mustaches, himself included. He vowed to shave his off as soon as they landed. Here was a man difficult to take seriously, with a whiff of incompetence about him that put everyone on their guard.

At pre-brief Morgan told Gropper to call the crew to attention. Gropper hesitated, wondering if he should try to explain that that wasn't what they did, that no one did it. Once at attention, Morgan scanned the crew before proudly assuming the AC's chair. Gropper said "seats," and everyone sat down. Colonel Reilly stood by, waiting for the theater to be over, a look of barely suppressed incredulity, and perhaps mirth, on his face. Then he began running through the essentials of the upcoming mission, reporting that the orbit area had been moderately active throughout the night. Morgan listened attentively, taking notes in a small book that he kept in the thigh pocket of his flight suit. After the brief was over Reilly gave them the code letter of the day. F. Morgan stood, faced the crew, and repeated the letter. "F," he said. "Dih-dih-dah-dit." He looked at the crew again, and settled his gaze on Luke, glowering at him. "F," he repeated. "Dih-dih-dah-dit. Get-a-hair-cut!"

Luke was surprised and didn't know what to make of it. He had been called out on the length of his hair so many times in his short Air Force career that it almost seemed normal. Of course it was him, it was always him. But not today. Today he was regulation and he knew it, having been to the officer's club barber just the day before. He looked around and immediately his stomach sank. John Constance was sitting in the row behind him and until this moment he hadn't really paid any attention to him. He cringed when he looked. John's hat sat on top of his head like a tarp atop a Monet hay stack. Shit, he said to himself. When did that happen? How long had John Constance's hair been that shaggy? He felt exposed and vulnerable.

Morgan led the way to the bus, strong stride, head erect, marching, in a way. The crew watched in amazement and followed at their own pace. The day was young, still waking at the horizon, and the air was cool and pleasant. At their Connie they fell into their regular tasks. Rickey worked out the manning, the enlisted men stowed the meals and the drinks, handed out the pistols, readied their screens. In a very few minutes all was ready. Most wandered outside to wait for takeoff.

Luke stayed aboard, sitting at his position reading the

Pacific edition of *Time* magazine. Onion skin paper. Rickey dozed lightly in the assistant intelligence officer's position across from him, behind the Plexiglas map screen. John Constance was catty-corner to Luke, next to Rickey, his chair tilted back, his leg resting casually on his desk, foot sticking into the aisle, reading *Stars and Stripes.*

Morgan walked up the aisle. When he got to John Constance, without breaking stride he kicked his foot, hard. "Get a haircut," he said, harshly. He glowered again at Luke as he walked by.

Luke was nonplussed. He stood, looking after Morgan as he continued up to the flight deck, unsure of what to do, how to react. He knew only that what he had just seen was wrong, and that it called for him to do something.

Rickey came around the Plexiglas panel. "There's nothing you can do that won't get your ass in a jam, Lieutenant." he said. "What he did wasn't as bad as Patton slapping a guy in a medical tent. Let it go. Anyway, It's my fault. I know better. That's the one thing I should be doing. Like you said, look out for our men. Let it go."

Luke nodded.

They didn't see Morgan again before takeoff. Luke took them on station, and Rickey replaced him. Rickey had two bags of groceries ready to cook and thought better of it. He didn't know what Morgan would say, but he was convinced he wouldn't approve. The men understood, and ate their in-flight box lunches.

Mid-flight Luke and Rickey chatted at position, Rickey in the chair, clicking through the screens, Luke riding side saddle on the jump seat. The screens were all blank. "We're going to see more like him," Rickey said to Luke. "FNGs that need to get their tickets punched if they're going to have any hope of continuing their careers. This late in the game, a lot of them are gonna be like Morgan. They'll never get promoted, and they'll never understand why."

Over the course of the flight Gropper learned more about Morgan that he later shared with Luke when they got back to their hootch. Married, seven children that Morgan took on vacation every summer in their RV, usually near some military installation so they could use the facilities—the BX, the theater, sometimes the officer's club pool. Just before he had deployed to Khorat he'd taken a last quick trip, down to Eglin where he parked at the officer's club annex next to Fort Walton Beach, and every morning his kids scrambled out of the RV and into the water. Wasn't that heaven? Once a month he went out to Andrews and cranked up a Cessna-T-41 to get his flight hours. He thought the T-41 was a sweet aircraft, and hoped the Air Force would follow the Army's lead and go to the 210-horsepower model. "A regular Chatty Cathy," Gropper said. "I mean, really, he's bragging on a Cessna?"

Luke told him about the John Constance incident. Gropper shook his head. "How do they...where do they find them? You know, you can't make stuff like this up. People like that, give them an opening, they'll drive a truck the wrong way up a one-way street." He paused. "But I've got a great story to tell you," he added, shaking his head, smiling. "Coming home, I was flying left seat. We were on final approach, practically at the runway, and there were some fighters at the end of the runway ready to take off, and the enlisted troop in the tower decided fighters taking off took precedence over a Connie on final approach, and he cleared the 105s for takeoff and told us to go around, that we were cleared for a closed pattern. A closed pattern! Which means, by the way, a bunch of tight turns. As if we were a fighter plane. Gee, thanks! At first I thought, shit, we can't do that, we're gonna have to go all the way around. But then I thought, wait, we can do this, Woody would. It's just an airplane, right? There weren't any more fighters moving up for takeoff, and nothing was coming in behind me. So I shifted the plane over a couple hundred yards so I could keep my eye on the 105s as they took off, and I told Stevenson to give me max power. Then I told Morgan to pull the landing gear and flaps up, and he gave me this look, because he didn't have a clue what I was doing, he saw these fighters rolling down the runway and his eyes were open wide and he's got this deer-in-headlights look, and I didn't have time to explain my maneuver. But he did it, he pulled the flaps and landing gear up. So then I did an Immelmann, you know, where you quickly turn around, and he's holding on to his ass and his eyes are getting wider and wider. We leveled off at 1500 feet, and the flight engineer gave me the throttles. We're just over the end of the runway and I told him to drop the landing gear. So then we were high and tight to the runway and I told him to give me full flaps, and I closed the throttles and I'm waiting for the asshole to drop the flaps and he's fucking frozen, he isn't moving or saying a thing and we're flying down the runway, we're running out of room and I waited another moment and he still hadn't dropped the flaps so finally I said, are you going to put those flaps down or do I have to do it myself? So finally he did it, just in time. So now I'm not touching the throttles at all and we greased it in and it was beautiful, we just glided in. And I looked at Morgan and I could tell now that he was just pissed, I had called him out on something and I was going to hear about it. But who gives a shit. It was a beautiful thing to see. Just like a glider. Do you have any idea what that means?" He smiled and rubbed his hands together. "Some days I just love the Air Force," he said. He paused, savoring the thought, then added: "I'll tell you what, though. Watching him. The man doesn't even know how to fly an airplane."

30

L uke was awakened by raucous laughter and the high-pitched whine of a food blender. He opened his door to clear skies, cool air and Gropper standing at a table under the portico, manning a blender full of bright green liquid and surrounded by a dozen or so men from the two facing hootches. "Bunky," Gropper said when he saw Luke. "Look what my Mom sent!" He held up a shoebox split at the seams, out of which were falling shiny green plastic envelopes. "Daiquiri mix," he said enthusiastically, grabbing to catch them. "A year's supply, she said. Little does she know."

Most of the men were sitting at the round coffee table under the portico, while a few stood at the bar or were leaning against the portico pillars. "Tuttle," Fachevsky, one of the other intelligence officers in the hootch area, said, toasting Luke's arrival. A tall, well-built man with a low Neanderthal hairline. Penn State, he was always quick to tell you, everybody's friend. He held up his glass and nodded towards Luke, but seemed to be struggling to remain standing, as if the air was lubricated and he wasn't in charge of his muscles and soon he was going to slide into a heap like the wicked witch of the west. Luke wondered how long they'd been at it, more, how he'd managed to sleep through the racket. "It's not even noon," he said to Gropper. His robe was tied loosely around his waist and he held his toilet kit. "I'm not even dressed."

"*Mai pen rai, khrup,*" Gropper said. He filled the blender with ice and poured in rum from a half-gallon jug. The jug was nearly empty; another sat next to it midst a dusting of spilled green powder. He put the lid on the blender, held it in place and turned it on. The high-pitched whine over-whelmed the air. "The gods are with us!" he said. "We have a marvelous confluence of karma!" All very un-Gropper. He lifted the carafe high and waved it back and forth. "God be with us," he said, as if blessing his congregants, "and with our men and horses."

"Connies," someone shouted.

"Our men and Connies," he said.

He filled a cup and handed it to Luke. "Breakfast, my son," he said. "In the name of Gropper and his mother." Those with empty cups held them out and he refilled them like a priest at communion, saying "Bless you, my son," as he filled each one.

"Drink up," Fachevsky said. He downed his cup. "A Gregorian hymn for Gropper!" he shouted, and they all sang the fuck him song.

"Amen," Gropper said. He offered to fill Luke up again. "You have some catchin' up to do, Lucas." He brushed away a phalanx of pissants that were making their way to the spilled daiquiri powder.

"You got a problem," Luke observed. "The ants have arrived."

"Nah," Gropper answered. "Fachevsky," he called. "Front and center. Load and lock."

"Aye, aye, sir," Fachevsky said as he approached with a can of bug spray. He sprayed the concrete floor and the legs of the table and the pissants' entry trail.

"Bunky," Gropper said, "get some dishes from the hootch girls and let's take care of this altar for real, do it the Thai way!"

Luke went out to the hootch girls' screened-in hut, and amid much tittering and discreet pointing at his robe, which by now had fallen open, made himself understood enough to get four small rice bowls. He brought them back to the table, put one under each leg, and filled them with water. "There," Gropper said. "That'll stop the little bastards!"

Only it didn't. Shortly the pissants discovered the electric wire leading up to the blender, and soon the wire was a highway covered by a steady stream of ants heading to the tabletop. "Shit," Gropper said. "Spray the wire," he said to Fachevsky, which finally isolated the tabletop and stopped the ants.

Fachevsky stared at the mass of dead ants surrounding the table. "I wanna see something," he said, slowly, thoughtfully. He went into this room and returned with a string. Tied one end to an open, full daiquiri envelope, the other to the middle of the clothes line that stretched between the porticos of the facing hootches, suspending the envelope from the line. "There," he said. "Let's see how long it takes."

Within minutes a single ant made its way up the near portico post and across the line to the packet, almost as if the location of the bag had been announced and the ant had been given directions. Fachevsky cheered its progress. The ant was soon joined by others, and in a few minutes a steady stream of ants was making their way up the portico pillar, across the clothesline to the package and back. "Do you believe it?" Fachevsky said. "They're un-fucking believable." He sprayed the ants on the clothesline. "Okay, guys," he said. "How long? Bets?"

Now most of the men watched, fascinated, as the ants found their way across the open space between the hootches and up the pillar of the portico across the way. Soon the ants were making their way to the packet from the opposite direction. The few became a stream. "Do you fuckin'-a believe it?" Fachevsky said. "You know what's gonna happen. Those fucking ants are gonna hide in the wheel wells of our aircraft when we go home, and then our year is up and we're safely back in the states, we're gonna have fucking Southeast Asian fucking ants all over the states looking for us and they're gonna take over!"

They all laughed, and then continued to watch the ants moving along the rope.

"So, okay," Gropper said, snapping them all out of their thinking. "I've got another batch here. Drink up, for tomorrow we die. Or something like that. Drown. Get eaten alive."

31

Cold air whooshed from the open vent. Luke twisted it closed and tucked his flight jacket under his chin. Settled in his chair, scanned his panel. Nothing. Niente. Diddely-squat. The Connie droned on, the flight smooth, the intelligence compartment dim, his mind wandering, randomly touching moments. Cold again, winter. Snow began accumulating in the silent corners of his mind.

He was at his uncle's farm in the Adirondacks, an old log cabin deep in the mountains, built not long after the Revolutionary War. Snow was blowing in great drifts, building slowly over the fields and road and the gravestones in the tiny cemetery at the foot of the slope leading to the cabin. Seven gravestones—his uncle's, oldest of his mother's siblings; his grandfather's, who died in the single bed tucked under the sloped-ceiling loft. And five children who died within two weeks of each other in the early eighteen-hundreds. Goodspeed, all of them. Soon the snow would bury everything, lost from until spring.

He was alone, gone to the farm in a melodramatic

gesture to sort through his life. Winter break, sophomore year. Soon he would have to decide whether to commit to ROTC. So here he was on the Adel Brook, away from everything, every distraction. Alone in the deep snow and freezing cold. So far, however, it seemed that the only thing he'd learned was something he'd never expected—he didn't do well by himself, and was floundering in loneliness. He yearned for another voice, and wandered the house aimlessly, looking for something, anything, to occupy his mind.

In the old desk in the great room he found the only prize —a recipe for making opium, together with a poem memorializing all the presidents through Arthur. The opium recipe had a few stains on it, presumably ingredients spilled in the making. *Chuckle chuckle.* Something to help them through the long winter nights, keep them from stringing themselves up on a cross beam in the woodshed. Where were the ingredients now, when he needed them? And in the dirt-floored cellar an ancient pump organ with worn leather bellows from which he managed only a haunting moan. He'd been to the farm dozens of times in his life, but never by himself, and never free to wander at his leisure, stick his nose into every nook and cranny. And even in this small house—three bedrooms and a great room—there were plenty. He had no idea how the organ got there, or even if his uncle knew how to play it. Let alone what purpose it might serve. Mid-week Prayer and Praise for whatever folks lived in Eden Brook hollow? Or even if his uncle had brought it. To an ancient farmhouse deep in the Adirondacks. Still, it held his interest, at least for a moment. There was nothing else. Nothing. Nothing else to read, nothing to do.

The emptiness became intolerable. He sat in his uncle's

favorite chair, a great overstuffed beast by the front door. Indian door, double thick and cut in the middle so you could open only the upper half if you needed to keep strong wood between you and a visitor. Fireplace flames flickered on the varnished log walls like lost souls. He wondered how the ancients tolerated it, back, way back, when the cabin was first built. And after the children died? He went to the window. It had stopped snowing, and loose snow was blowing like white dust across the drifts. He looked at the thermometer on the outside sill, visible in the light from the room. Twenty below. For sure it would drop another ten, perhaps twenty, by morning. He'd known such cold in Mount Brookville, but rarely. Besides, in Mount Brookville there were people, none more than a half mile away, serving always as a safety valve, a pressure relief in case things just got too bad.

He went out the front door without coat, hat, gloves, or boots, moving slowly through deep snow to the plowed road. Stuffed his bare hands into his pockets, hunched his shoulders against the freezing cold.

The night was pitch black, made more so for lack of a single manmade light anywhere, not from the house, not from the woods, not across the open fields, clear to the horizon. The snow was building; new shapes were growing that told nothing about what was buried beneath, and his imagination began to take flight. Creatures? Bodies? Boulders? The edges of the road had disappeared. He wondered if he'd be snowed in, or if the plow would return again before morning. Perhaps not. It didn't seem to make sense to keep the road open just for him. Maybe in a few days, as a matter of routine. He hoped.

The sky was deep and endless, at first suffocating in how small and alone it made him feel, him midst the eternal nighttime sky. He stared for long minutes, scanning the sky, and managed at last to clear his head of fear, and then of everything. He had known such a moment only once before, in Mount Brookville, on a Boy Scout camping trip deep into the frozen Nine-mile swamp. Troop 12. There were only a few of them, ten or so, all the boys of Mount Brookville. A bedraggled bunch, none with uniforms. Wearing green tartan neckerchiefs of the clan Gunn. None with a merit badge, only a few first class. Their Wednesday evening meetings were mostly horsing around under the watchful but disinterested eye of Walt Gunn, who managed to organize only one activity each year, the winter hike, an overnight into the depths of the now frozen swamp, always camping in the middle of the same circle of cedars. Potatoes and biscuits wrapped in aluminum foil cooked in the camp-fire, hot dogs on sticks. Cans of Chef Boyardee. Luke shared a tent with Fergie, and late the second night he had gotten up to take a leak when he had experienced a moment of total nothingness such as he had just felt here on Eden Brook. At Colgate he'd read Wallace Stevens' The Snow Man, amazed that someone had been there before him and put a name on it:

ONE MUST HAVE a mind of winter
   To regard the frost and the boughs
   Of the pine-trees crusted with snow;

AND HAVE BEEN cold a long time
   To behold the junipers shagged with ice,
   The spruces rough in the distant glitter

· · ·

OF THE JANUARY SUN; and not to think
  Of any misery in the sound of the wind,
  In the sound of a few leaves,

WHICH IS the sound of the land
  Full of the same wind
  That is blowing in the same bare place

FOR THE LISTENER, who listens in the snow
  And, nothing himself, beholds
  Nothing that is not there, and nothing that is.

THIS NIGHT he watched his thoughts move as solitary ships though his mind—four-masters, rigged ships, perhaps a carrack, like the Tudor Rose. Watched but didn't engage. Then they were gone, and he simply stood in the falling snow. Cold but not cold. Nothing distracted, and for a brief time he was the essence ɪof his consciousness. Five minutes, ten minutes. Twenty. He walked down the road. Nothing busied his mind. He slowly floated upwards, time-less, unfettered, free. When finally he had a thought, it was that he was, and would be, regardless of his career deci-sion. The Air Force. Alright. Alright, he said to himself. Alright.

He woke to the cold penetrating through to his bones. Shivered. Wouldn't it be funny, he thought, if he froze to death on the open road, to be found in the morning by people wondering what it was that had brought him out in the middle of the night dressed only in house clothes. Musta been a city boy, to not know better. He hurried back inside, rolled out his sleeping bag in front of the fire, curled up, and fell asleep watching the shrinking flames.

At first light he went snowshoeing, taking his uncle's snowshoes down from a hook in the garage. Rawhide and wood, still strong. He climbed atop the drift outside the garage door and headed for the pine forest. Sank down in the snow too deeply to move quickly. Came to the long depression of Adel Brook and trekked along the bank until he came to a place where the snow had blown clear, revealing ice over the bubbling stream like a window into tireless nature. Stems of brown grass waved within the current, here and there protruding through the ice and dipping in the light breeze. He crossed and began working his way uphill. Brittle cold, the snow going on forever, blanketing the world, disappearing in the deepest woods. Singular leaves skittered across the snow, collided against tree trunks. Twisted free and tumbled away.

He made his way towards a wall of pines cloaked in snow. Slipped through, careful not to bump the branches and bring an avalanche of snow down the back of his neck. Once through it was calm and close and the wind sighed through the branches. Snow cupped shallow near the trunks, encompassing a deer bed. He wanted to share his discovery. He wanted to share everything he saw with someone, anyone who would appreciate it. He ran through names, images in his head. Came to Sandy, with the forever eyes. And recalled yet again their walks on Faulkner Road and through the fields and forests of Mount Brookville. The way things caught her fancy—unusual plants, rocks. A largish piece of petrified wood, fibers frozen in time, that she lugged home and displayed on a shelf in their living

room, next to the oil-fired stove. He remembered her
kneeling in a patch of clover, methodically combing
through and finding a four-leaf clover that she brushed
against his lips and carried with her as they continued walking, absent mindedly brushing it against her nose. The next
day she gave it to him taped to a tab of paper on which she
had written, "Love always," that he had with him still. He
drew his wallet from his flight suit pocket. Not much there
besides his Geneva Conventions card. And the time-
bending folded paper with Sandy's four-leaf clover, a warp
to deep past, present and future.

32

A nd then the chill of the Rockies, the last evening of survival school, their closing dinner—a feast of steak, potatoes, and beer, reward for their days trudging through the mountains and the POW camp. The mess hall more a barn, with enormous walls that swung-away to the night, like a church-camp tabernacle, roof trusses and beams lost in shadow. Row upon row of tables noisy with men eating and drinking, and in front, a small stage, payment to be extracted for their food.

A captain strode to the stage. Blond hair cut high and tight, chiseled body emphasized by tailored fatigues. He nodded at an unseen companion and the lights dimmed. A projector hidden in the rafters flashed on, washing the captain in light.

Click: A photo appeared on the wall behind the captain, glowing in the dark: A nighttime view of a guard tower surrounded by fencing that spanned the width of the photo. A thin blanket of snow covered the ground, weeds and rocks poking through. A rabbit's eye view, the tower distorted and imposing.

"This," the captain said, "for too many people, is the face of the world. They have no freedom; they cannot leave whenever they choose. They live in countries where they want out and can't get out. They cannot say out loud what they want to say; they cannot think what they want to think. They live in fear. Some put themselves at risk to get out. Men, women. Children. Y'all remember that. Y'all remember that when the going gets tough. And it could. In six months one in ten of you will be shot down, and if you don't practice what we've taught you here in survival school, the one in ten of you who gets shot down will wind up a POW."

Click: The iconic photograph of an East German border guard leaping the barbed wire between East and West Berlin, one arm stretched wide against his rifle sling, holding it taut as he hurdles into West Berlin.

Click: Pyongyang. Stark concrete buildings, flat rectangular shapes against a barren landscape. Devoid of life, devoid of hope. A North Korean guard looks straight at the camera, transfixed in his stone-faced gaze.

"There are places in this world where there is no hope, where the communist boot grinds people's dreams into dirt."

Click: The Hungarian Revolt of '56: Soviet flags burning, the toppled statue of Stalin. Rocks and bricks litter the ground.

Click: Soviet tanks; bodies in the streets.

A film clip: Khrushchev speaking, with subtitles: "We will support wars of national liberation, especially insurgencies against imperialists."

"This war in Vietnam," the captain said, "plain and simple, is a war of communist aggression. There's very little about which we can be certain in this world, but there is one thing—the communists must be stopped."

Click: French troops march through colonial Hanoi. "Our allies, the French, tried and failed, and we are here to take up the cause."

An animated film clip: Vivid red flows like blood from China across the border into North Vietnam, down to the demilitarized zone, consuming everything in its path. The red tide overcomes South Vietnam, creeps into Cambodia and Laos, pushes into Thailand. Only Malaya to the south remains clear.

"Look at Malaya here. The Brits stopped them, and we've learned from them." The red pushed into Burma, pushed through East Pakistan into India. Voiceover, LBJ: "We must faht or lose the Pacific to communism and prepare to defend our own shores."

"Listen to me, genelmen," the captain said. "Our freedom does not come cheap. Men died for it. They died for us to be able to sit here and enjoy our steak and beer. But we must remember, we <u>have</u> to remember...there are communist heathens out there who would take away all that we have, who would enslave us just as they are enslaving their own people."

Luke recognized the captain's tone, his cadences, his certitude. He was back in Mount Brookville, in his tiny Baptist church. Billy Graham and Oral Roberts. Brother Clyde. He was leery and suspicious and resolved not to be led around by his nose yet again. He remembered his mother dragging him out of church one Sunday, insulted by Reverend Goodfellow's reference to Catholics as heathens and idol worshipers.

"This is our crusade!" the captain said. "There can be no question! If we do not stop them here, we'll be fighting them in Australia and New Zealand. Mark my words. I guarantee it! If we do not stop them here, we will be fighting in the streets of Rangoon! If we do not stop them here, we will be fighting in the streets of Honolulu. We'll be fighting in Los Angeles and San Diego and San Francisco."

Luke's stomach turned. This was Brother Clyde incarnate, self-righteous, ignorant; and his father, after a late night at the gin mill in Mount Brookville. "They've got you thinking there's one behind every tree," Luke said. To which his father replied, "I think that's the right way to look at it".

"The communists," the captain said, "are taking over the world; we've got to stop them! Look at what they're doing in South Vietnam, beheading village elders that stand in their way. We must stand behind the South Vietnamese in their fight for democracy and freedom."

Luke looked around to see how others were reacting to the captain and realized that few were even paying attention. Instead they were chatting among themselves, laughing at private jokes. They'd finished their training, they'd trekked through the mountains, they'd endured the POW camp and they didn't give a rat's ass about what this tailored-shirt captain, another Marine wanna be, was saying. Still, Luke couldn't leave it alone, and when the captain finished and the lights came back up and the bible-camp tabernacle once again became a military mess, he made his way upstream through the departing crowd to the podium. The captain was tidying up his notes and slipping them into a folder. He looked at Luke. "Lieutenant?" he said.

"So, Captain," Luke said. "I'm wondering if you're really doing these guys here a favor."

"How's that, Lieutenant?" he said. He put down his folder down, eyeing Luke skeptically.

"About your talk. I'm not so sure things are as simple as

you paint them. You're serving up some mighty thin gruel here."

"Interesting. Tell me more."

"Look, the communist stuff, the domino theory across the Pacific. Really? This is just another civil war and we've stepped into the middle of it. And monolithic communism. You do know the Soviets and the Chicoms are facing off across the Amur River, don't you? Right now? As we speak?"

"Lieutenant," the captain said. "All that shit, that'll just confuse these men. When you're being interrogated, you have to have a rock to stand on. There's no room for saying, 'on the other hand.' You start questioning, you're doomed."

"But you're confusing Asia with Europe, Ho Chi Minh with Brezhnev and Khrushchev, a civil war with the threat of communism in Europe..." He paused, looked at the captain and realized that everything he was saying was meaningless to the man, truly water off a duck's back. The captain waited him out and as soon as Luke stopped talking he finished putting away his notes. "Let's just leave it that we agree to disagree, Lieutenant," he said. He paused, looked long at Luke, as if he was filing away his countenance for future reference, and walked away.

GROPPER WALKED BY, heading aft. He banged on Luke's position, startling him, bringing him back to the moment. "Where are you, Lucas?"

Luke nodded. "Far away, that's for sure."

"Well, come on back. We're out of here pretty soon."

33

The crew bus bounced down the flight apron. Early dawn, first light breaking over the Plateau. Last flight before break. Before Bangkok and Lonnie. In the distance the headlights of the flatbed trucks carrying Thai workers to the base. The bus pulled up to their aircraft. Tail number Niner-niner. At first no one noticed. Woody and Gropper knew, of course, the tail number was on the manifest, but they hadn't said a word, as if it didn't matter. Then one by one the rest of the crew realized which aircraft they were parked in front of and a certain tension began to rise, soon becoming near tangible. Maybe they all noticed at the same time. They began to talk among themselves, laughing nervously. A comment that their time had finally come: Niner-niner, the plane with a two-volume maintenance log, necessary to accommodate the history of everything that had gone wrong. Niner-niner that had had to leave orbit early nearly a dozen times—auto-pilot dead; instruments gone haywire; sensor radios that wouldn't work, whole racks of them. Niner-niner, the aircraft where a wrench had been left behind in a nosecone and had burst out during flight, centrifugal force driving it through the fuselage like flak, breaking through the metal skin right behind the radio operator. Human error, yes. Sometimes. But more. The plane with props that wouldn't feather. The plane that lost two engines at once, both on the same wing, requiring heroic efforts by the aircraft commander to bring it back to Khorat. Niner-niner, the lemon of the wing. For sure this would be the flight where it broke down completely, for sure, and probably even over Laos, over the jungle. For sure.

The bus came to a stop and Woody stood at the front, blocking the exit. "It's an airplane," he said in a slow, impatient steam. "Just an airplane. And we'll do our pre-flights, and if something comes up we'll get it tended to, and we'll do it without any fuss. If it can't be tended to that will be it, and we'll find another airplane." He looked around, looked at each of them, driving his point home. "It's just an airplane," he repeated.

Once aboard, Woody sat at the forward galley with the crew chief and went over the most recent items in the maintenance log. As to be expected. But it took so long that it became center stage, and the crew began watching, finding one reason or another to go to the galley to watch the show. Pleased at Woody's attention to detail that was driving the maintenance crew chief to distraction. Meanwhile, Gropper was going through his pre-flight with a fine-tooth comb, peering into the wheel wells, checking the inboard engines, climbing a step ladder to peer under the cowling of the outboard engines. As always. Luke was sitting at his position when Gropper boarded and headed forward. "Well?" he said.

Gropper shrugged and popped the floor hatch in the middle of the aisle next to Luke and dropped down to the

Connie's belly. In a few minutes, he was back. "Mouse shit," he said when he emerged. He went forward to deliver the news.

The word circulated and the crew stopped what they were doing and again cocked their attention to Gropper and Woody and the maintenance crew chief. Everyone knew the drill—rodents chewed on every and anything, and all the wiring and hydraulic lines in the aircraft would have to be inspected before Niner-niner could be flown again. It was as simple as that.

A few minutes later, Colonel Milque came aboard. He smiled routinely at the crew as he walked by, lips tight, making the crew more nervous, wondering his agenda. He gave them all a thumbs up, which caused a chuckle. Once upon a time, thumbs up meant 'ready to go.' No longer. This was a new generation, and a thumb up meant 'rotate,' as in, 'shove this up your ass and take a spin.' This man was out of it. This man was in charge of maintenance. This man held their destiny in his hands. Now the volume of the conversation in the galley elevated, and what should have been a quick conversation wasn't. Colonel Crawford arrived, grim-faced and intent. The volume of conversation in the galley increased yet again, rising to the level of Crawford's occasional shouts, but only for a few minutes before Crawford stormed out, steaming.

Gropper came down the aisle to alert Luke. "Pack it up," he said, "we're going to a new aircraft. No need to hurry. The plane we're going to isn't ready, either, and it's going to be awhile before takeoff."

"So what happened?" Luke asked.

"Nothing," Gropper said. "Crawford wanted a quick look-see below deck and then for us to go ahead with this plane. Woody isn't having it."

"And?"

"And there goes Crawford's on-time takeoff schedule."

ON STATION LUKE opened two positions: TFA was up the entirety. The Connie's engines rumbled hypnotically, sunlight swept across the bulkheads with clocklike regularity, and cold air whooshed from the vents. Luke returned to Adel Brook.

He recalled sitting in the great room on the third day of his trip, looking around, imagining how he might do things differently—replacing the wood-burning kitchen stove with electric, though that would do nothing to heat the room. A furnace in the cellar. Oil-burning. Maybe a bigger window in the great room facing the white pine forest. Not a Fifties picture-window, but an expanse with mullions to bring dimension. He wanted to be able to sit in front of the fire and turn his head and look into the woods. A window so big that it would bring in the outside. He imagined snow-shoeing back to the farmhouse on a winter's evening, the drifts deep, the window aglow and beckoning, promising warmth and comfort. Something wide and tall and of course triple-paned. He knew he could find just such a window, if not in Saranac, then for sure in Montreal, which wasn't so very far away. He imagined bookcases either side of the window, with books he could easily pull down and flip through and lose himself in—art books, travel books, pictorial histories. Never again would he fetch for something to read.

He remembered snowshoeing that day. Early afternoon. Scattered clouds scudding across the sky. Still well below zero, the air sharp, the wind erasing the edges of the drifts.

Coming again to the clearing in the pines where the silence was total.

Out the corner of his eye he saw movement, at first indistinct, just something that didn't fit. Abruptly a snowmobile broke through the trees and into view, throttle down, driven by a man perhaps ten years Luke's senior, dressed not in the ubiquitous quilted down of snowmobilers, but instead in hunting clothes, red and black checked wool jacket frayed at the elbows and cuffs, faded and patched dungarees. The snowmobile worn and dented, and customized with a large, vertical muffler that dampened the engine to a whisper. The driver wore an aviator-style hat, ear flaps turned up, and was scruffy and unshaven—all in all a rough-looking character that, given a choice, Luke would never engage. Luke's father would have called him a ridge runner, or his other favorite, mountain Jaboni, without the brains to come in from the cold, or at least keep his ears covered. A rifle balanced across his lap.

Luke realized that the man was jacking deer, hunting out of season, and on Tuttle land. The man noticed Luke, of that Luke was sure; strangely, he didn't acknowledge Luke's presence, not a nod of the head, not even a flick of the eye, as if to say that all the legalities of ownership and trespassing didn't matter, this was his forest, and he sure didn't need to pay Luke any mind. In this sparsely populated rural land people greeted each other wherever and whenever they could. Not today, not this man, not this moment, trespasser or not. Luke was troubled, and considered calling the man out, reminding him that he was trespassing. Then he thought better of it: this was the deep woods, an area seldom visited by anyone. The man looked primitive, and was most likely hunting for his livelihood, and maybe that of his family. Luke was convinced that he would not take kindly to someone calling him out, especially with rules that he probably believed had nothing to do with him. He could drop Luke in his tracks with one shot, and leave his body in the snow to freeze stiff, not to be found until spring thaw, if ever. Of a sudden Luke felt vulnerable, helpless, and crestfallen that the ridge runner could so destroy his equilibrium. He abruptly turned and snowshoed back to the farmhouse.

With darkness, the wind rose, becoming a breathing baritone that sighed through the trees, seeming almost to speak, then growing stronger, buffeting the house, banging the windows in their frames. Luke feared another storm, and with plans to leave in the morning, he again worried the details of being snowbound. Little by little the volume of the wind increased, soon to the point where he began to hear banshees gathering, at first faintly and occasionally in the distance, then closer and more distinct. He imagined the moment in the cabin a hundred and fifty years ago when the Goodspeed children were dying, the banshees howling and screaming to get in, candles flickering, mother and father huddled near the children in their beds, helpless as the children succumbed, one by one, while still the banshees screamed, day after day, night after night, a fourth child succumbing to fever, then a fifth, the last date on the childhood gravestones in the nearby cemetery, leaving only the mother and father and a life hardly worth living. And now the banshees were blowing through his air vents and he couldn't quiet his mind and when he did his thoughts were haunted by a feeling of being trapped, of flying inside an airplane, not his Connie but military nonetheless, grey plastic bulkheads, going where he didn't want to go, surrounded by men as numbed as he, commanded by forces unseen and beyond all redress.

He snapped out of his daydream, but the feeling of helplessness remained, and now there was another feeling, of guilt, of having done something unseemly that he couldn't remember having done, that there was a body buried out there somewhere, in the dirt maybe, maybe under the porch of his home in Mount Brookville, maybe in the snow, he didn't know who or how it had happened, but he had done it, he had killed someone, somewhere, and they were going to find the body and it would all be over, life as he knew it, they would find him and he would be locked away forever and there was nothing he could do about it.

He sent word to Rickey that he needed to take a break. Once away from his position he paced the airplane, and try as he might he couldn't shake the feeling of being trapped; Even after landing it would not go away.

34

Early afternoon in Bangkok. Saint got out of their hired car at their favorite hotel off New Petchaburi, and Luke went on to Lonnie's, unsure yet where he would spend the night. Lonnie greeted him at the door with a hug, took his bag and instead of leading him inside, led him down to her father's car, putting his bag in the trunk. She drove through bustling commercial districts to an older section of town, non-descript back streets and two- and three-story aged concrete buildings with open air shops on the street floors and pedestrians bustling every which way on neighborhood errands. She turned onto a street more an alley that became a rutted dirt track leading to a line of trees and underbrush, and parked next to a small bungalow on stilts, one of several in a row sequestered in the tree line. "Follow me," she said. "I'd tell you to close your eyes and lead you but I'm afraid you'd trip and fall. Watch out for tree roots. Get your bag," she added when she opened the trunk to get her own.

She led them up an outside stairway and onto a balcony

that led into a room that was the whole of the second floor. The room was shadowed, the only light coming from the door and a window that opened onto the balcony, and a small window over a simple sink in back. The teak walls barren save for exposed studs. A small, unfinished table reminiscent of Shaker design, with a hot plate atop, sat in the back corner, next to the sink. A mattress lay close to the door to the balcony, made up with sheets that echoed the clean folds and lines of the newly purchased. Mosquito netting hung from a ring suspended from the ceiling and was pulled back to the head of the mattress like a bed curtain. Once they had looked around the inside, she led him back out onto the balcony and the view of the *klong* lapping quietly beneath them in the shade.

"This," she said, "is ours." She stood on her tiptoes and kissed him and smiled. "Like it?"

Luke grinned.

The *klong* was dark and shone like a mirror. Bushes over-hung the banks across the way and it was impossible to tell where the *klong* ended and land began; what lay beyond the brush in every direction was unknown: Open land, streets, another *klong*? Anything was possible; nothing could be seen. The sounds of everyday life reached them from nearby, adults and young children talking, metal-ware clat-tering, doors squeaking, a solitary splash from the *klong,* but they saw nothing. They were in their own private world, and it promoted a feeling that they were free to do whatever they wanted. There was something about the moment, too, that made it sensuous. The heat, the heavy, rich humidity, the dense smell of vegetation and teak, the dank smell of the *klong,* and from the nearby homes the smells of garlic and chili. They went back inside and sat on the mattress, the only place there was to sit. Lonnie dropped the mosquito net around them and they were in their own intimate, gauzy chamber. They disrobed thoughtfully, and held each other close, damp skin to damp skin, soft, pliant. They caressed and indulged their closeness. He was in her and their circle was complete. Then, in the humid tropic heat, they slept.

Late afternoon; the world asserted itself. Waking to the soft liquid voices of their neighbors, children yet again calling to each other in play, birds whose songs and names they did not know. The heat receded, the day drew down. Amorphous shadows moved across the walls.

Luke lay on his side, looking at Lonnie laying on her back. He ran his finger along the silhouette of her nose. "I love you," he said. He had been afraid to say it for fear Lonnie would not return his confession in kind. She closed her eyes, breathed deeply. "I know," she said. There was a long pause. Despite the deep bonding of the afternoon, Luke began to fear he had gone too far. But on the brink of the quiet becoming troubling, Lonnie said, "I love you, too. I loved you the moment I met you. I love everything about you."

Her words swept him away, his doubts, his unanswered questions. He felt safe and validated. There could be nothing more. They were the definition of happiness, and had no thought other than loving and being loved and loving the moment in which they found themselves. They made love yet again.

They woke in darkness. It was hard to believe they had filled the afternoon and early evening in such warm pleasure. Step by step, phrase by phrase, they began to tie the moment, this place, to the world of the practical.

"How'd you find it?" Luke asked.

"Do you like it?"

Luke smiled.

She poked him. "I can't take any credit," she said, "other than finding an English-speaking realtor. She took me right here. It's cheap. I can pay the rent and my father will never know."

"I'll help."

"You don't need to. It hardly matters."

They dressed, went out on the balcony. Leaned on the railing. Marveled at how different this primitive, tropic world was from what they knew.

"I almost want to dive in," Lonnie said. "I feel like I could go forever."

"Down?" Luke asked. He shuddered.

She laughed. "Not really," she said.

"I just couldn't do it. Not in my wildest dreams," he said. He told her about survival school and the simulated prisoner of war camp and being shoved into a five by five by five box and then one hardly bigger than an orange crate. "They wanted to show us we could be broken and they proved their point with me. I got my neck twisted around in the little box and passed out. They pulled me out and revived me and then stuck me back in and I just suffocated. I was sure I was gonna die. And now...now it's like a latent virus and it takes nothing to bring it back, the whole closed in feeling, the claustrophobia, everything. Just looking at that *klong* and imagining going deep into that darkness. I can't do it."

"They did that to you?" She stiffened.

"It happened," he said, trying to put the thought behind them. "I'm sorry I brought it up."

"It's just that I don't like the idea of someone hurting

you," she said. She leaned over the railing, looking down. "They did it to all of you?"

Luke nodded. "Some guys it just didn't bother. When they were first shoving me in I could hear this guy next to me, he must have been short and small, he was practically bouncing up and down in the crate," he said.

Lonnie touched his arm. "Please, no more," she said. Then, to change the subject, she asked, "How long do we have?"

"Five days," he answered. Her face was outlined in the evening light. Soft, mysterious. Life itself. He fell in love with her again. "Don't move," he said. "I brought my camera. I want to capture you and this moment." He went back inside, rummaged through his bag, and returned with his camera. Rested it on the railing and looked through the viewfinder. "There's not a lot of light," he said. "But if you hold still and I hold the camera perfectly still, widen the aperture and slow it down, I think I can get it." The railing was awkward and he moved to the side of the bungalow, securing the camera against the wall, and looked again. Then he tried the end of the balcony.

"Make up your mind," she said. "The mosquitoes have." She slapped at her arm.

"Okay," he said, snapping the photo. He led her back inside, to the mattress. He raised the netting for her and crawled in after.

"Is this the only place where we're going to be safe from the mosquitoes?" he asked.

"Doesn't sound like a bad idea to me."

They lay next to each other. "Where'd you get the mattress?" he asked.

"Furniture store. And the sheets at a neighborhood, general store, I guess you'd call it. Stuff piled high on the counters. I don't think they'd ever had a *farung* come in before...have I got that right?...*farung?*"

"You think maybe we could use some chairs?" he asked. "Someplace to park our bodies besides the bed?"

"This hasn't been so bad, has it?" she asked.

"Maybe from the same store?"

"Probably."

"You hungry?"

She rolled onto her side and faced him. "Not really. I like it like this, just laying here, talking. I want to learn all about you. We can go out in the morning."

"And get some chairs."

"And food."

"So what do you want to know?" Luke said.

"Well, for a start, what's next?"

"Besides eating? And maybe sex?"

She poked him. "For us. We're getting in deep and I want to know if your intentions are honorable." She giggled. "But really. I want to know when you're going back to the states so I can plan accordingly. I want to know where you'll be going. I don't want to scare you off, but what about after that? Are we really in love? Are we really the match we think we are? Or are we both just horny?"

"Okay," he said, thinking about the answers. "I'll be going back early next year. I suspect I'll be going to DC, to some or other intelligence agency." He looked at her to gauge her reaction.

"And then?"

"What are you looking for?"

"I want to know when can we link up. You'll be getting out?"

"Probably."

"Probably?"

"Okay. I'll be getting out. Where will you be?"

"I still have a year to go. A year and a half, now."

"That'll work. When I get out I'll probably go back to central New York. If you're at Smith or wherever, it won't be that far. I have a car."

"Really? What kind? I want to know."

"Austin-Healey 3000. Red."

"Is that a convertible?"

"Yup. Two-seater. I love it. I love how it handles, the way it corners, and the sound of it."

"Men," she said. "And what do you think you'll do?"

"I dunno." He paused. "I have a place," he said. "It's an old farmhouse in the Adirondacks. Not too far from Lake Placid. It belonged to one of my uncles, my mother's oldest brother. It's been empty for years. The main room is the original cabin that was built right after the Revolutionary War, all hewn log walls and beams. It's so classy it's unbelievable. More rooms were added over the years—a kitchen, a big bedroom on the first floor, two bedrooms upstairs. My uncle even added a screened-in porch just before the war. And a fantastic stone fireplace."

"And you'll do what there?"

"I dunno. Maybe work for the state, for the department of conservation. There aren't a lot of jobs up in the north country, either. Maybe the Lake Placid Club. I've been day dreaming about it a lot lately."

"And what would I do?"

"I don't know. Saranac's not far. Maybe work there. There's Paul Smith's, the forestry and hotel management school."

"Is there any summer stock?"

"I don't know. Maybe."

"There's a lot you don't know, you know."

"I know we can make it work," he said, getting excited at the possibilities. "And if we come up with a better idea, then fine. I'm not wedded to the idea of the Adirondacks, although I love the idea of escaping from everything."

They fell silent, both on their backs, staring at the ceiling and the apex of the mosquito netting. "So how about this," Lonnie said. "How many bedrooms did you say there are in this place?"

"Three."

"Could we add more?"

"You planning a family?"

"Maybe. No. Well, not right away. But I've got an idea. It's ski country, right?"

"And hunting. And fishing. And canoeing."

"Tourists, right?"

"Yes."

"So we could open a tourist home. Add some rooms. Couldn't we?"

"There's room. We could." The idea began to intrigue him.

After a few minutes, Lonnie said, "We could put Louis Quatorze telephones in each of the rooms. That would be lovely. I love those."

"You're serious?"

"Yes I'm serious. I think they're cute. It would be fun."

Luke didn't respond, and Lonnie came back on him. "Is that what you are," she said, "someone who rains on other people's parades? I think they're pretty and I think they'd be neat."

"I'm sorry. I just don't think it makes any sense. It doesn't fit the idea. In the north woods. In the Adirondacks." He could sense Lonnie getting tense beside him, and realized he'd destroyed the mood. He wasn't sure how to fix it.

"Well, I like the idea. Is there going to be room for me in your plans?"

"I'm sorry," he said again. "It's just that it doesn't make any sense to me."

"I repeat," she said.

"Okay," Luke said. "I get it."

He wondered what would come next. Surely they could get past it, but he wondered how long it would take. Maybe just doing something would help, go out to the street, get something to eat.

Silence ruled. After a time Luke said, "I'm sorry, I really am. I was probably being far too serious about this."

"Do you think I wasn't?"

He laughed quietly. He'd stuck his foot in it yet again. He was going to have to start thinking before he talked.

"Don't snigger at me," she said.

"I didn't snigger."

"You did, too."

"I didn't think so. Really, if I did, I'm sorry. I think we could make it work. I think we could make sense of it."

THEY WOKE to the morning sun angling through the one small window on the east. It fell on the mosquito netting and cast soft light across their bodies.

"I love this netting," Lonnie said. "It makes me feel like a little girl again, when I made tents on the couch. Nothing could touch me there." She stretched and pulled the sheet over her. "I loved that feeling. I could play there for hours."

"And here?"

"No," she said. "We need to go into town." She pulled the netting aside, slipped into a light robe and went down the stairs to the outside shower that was tucked under the bungalow. He heard her squeal when she turned on the water. He went out to the landing dressed only in shorts. "I didn't bring a robe," he said.

"Wait a little bit, and you can use mine," she said, and laughed.

35

Luke filled the one and only pot from the tap and set it on the hot plate. The cast-iron sink was like so many in the old farmhouses of Mount Brookville that he felt the comfort of familiarity. Once the water boiled he made instant coffee and carried it back to the mattress in their only two mugs.

"Lovely," Lonnie said. She scrunched her bare shoulders. "I want it to always be like this, where we're completely natural with each other."

They decided to go exploring. Luke put on khakis and a short-sleeve shirt, Lonnie loose silk pants and a scoop-necked peasant blouse. They walked to the *soi* and flagged a *tuk-tuk* and in their awkward and broken Thai and a pantomime of eating, they managed to get to an open-air market, a park, really, abundant with piles of soft and hard goods and foodstuffs, many of which they didn't recognize, or if they did, didn't know how to cook, least of all on their single hot plate. Fruit was easy, and they indulged it. Shared a mango off by themselves, under a shade tree, sitting cross-legged on the grass. Skinned with a jack knife

Luke bought. Curried bread rolls. Orange Fanta. Then on to what they might buy to take back to their bungalow. Nix to the live poultry in bamboo cages. Querying looks to each other about the piles of peppers, fresh and dried, large and small. So many sold by elderly women dressed in black, their teeth betal-nut dark. Lonnie leaned over to inspect a pile of dried fish and the front of her blouse fell away, exposing her breasts. A young boy sat cross-legged tending the pile, with a view of everything, and his eyes opened wide, amazed and delighted at his view of Lonnie's breasts. "Googly eyes," Luke said. "You're giving him quite a show. Maybe you should hold your blouse back."

"I don't care," Lonnie said. She smiled at the boy and then moved on to a pile of garlic, loose bulbs and garlands. She picked up a garland, smelled it, put it back, looked back at the boy. He was still watching her and she winked. The boy looked away, embarrassed.

Canopied carts with prepared food hugged the curbs of the nearby street, chicken and squid hanging like pennants on a line, woks of beef and vegetables. Now they were drowning in choices. "Let's just get some more fruit," Lonnie said, and they bought another mango and cut-up pineapple and then decided to buy packets of cooked rice wrapped in banana leaves.

They noticed some stacks of small birdcages, most with birds in the cages, some empty. They watched as people bought the cages with birds in them, walked a few feet away, and then released the birds, all seemingly light-feathered song birds that flew quickly away, prizing their freedom. The purchasers then returned the now empty cages to the salesman. The purchasers smiled almost beatifically, pleased to have ended the birds' captivity.

"<u>Now</u> that's a racket," Luke said. "I wonder if the birds are trained to return."

Lonnie looked at him. "It's possible," Luke said. "You have to admit."

"Maybe. I just choose to enjoy the moment."

Luke had enough sense not to argue.

They came to a pile of transistor radios and decided they needed music. After buying one they tried to turn it on and realized it didn't have a battery, and they hunted until finally they found what they needed. At their bungalow, they tuned their radio to Thai music, and for a time were content with the exotic mood it created, the simple feeling of truly having gone native. Then they found a station with a British DJ playing jazz and big band songs from the forties. They surprised each other by singing the words together. As the music slowed, they danced. "Mood Indigo". "Red Sails in the Sunset". "Smoke Gets in Your Eyes". At first they danced simply and properly, arms up, Lonnie's right hand resting lightly on Luke's palm, left hand on his shoulder. Laughing. They danced well together and were pleased at the discovery. Then they drew into a hug. Still they danced.

THAT EVENING they joined Saint and Vicki at Nick's Hungarian Number One. Bangkok's best steak house, Gropper had said. Luke and Saint had planned dinner there on their way down, and the concierge at Saint's hotel made the reservations. Gropper said that Nick's Kobe steak was the best he had ever eaten, admitting as well that he had never eaten Kobe steak before, but that that didn't matter. He was certain.

Nick's was enchanting, a dark, wooden Victorian manse sitting alone on a slight grassy knoll in the middle of

Bangkok, at the confluence of Rama IV, Sathorn and Wire-
less, across from Lumpini Park. The house was incongruous,
straight out of a Charles Addams cartoon. The female
maître d' who greeted them and guided them to their table
was stunningly beautiful, Eurasian. "Burmese and English,"
Gropper had said. "Don't make an ass of yourself," he had
added. "She's already married." He and Saint looked at each
other in shared appreciation when they saw her. Luke could
tell the wheels were turning in Saint's mind, most likely
trying to figure out how he could meet her away from the
restaurant, never mind the married part, and Vicki.

The occasion turned out to be awkward, clouded by
something festering between Saint and Vicki. They hardly
talked and followed Luke and Lonnie's lead on everything
they ate, starting with snails and finishing with Kobe steak.
Luke had never eaten snails before and was unwilling to
admit his ignorance. "Let's," Lonnie had whispered to him.
The same with the Kobe steak that they all ordered and yes
there was that moment when they all took that first bite and
it melted in their mouths and their eyes glowed in appreciation. Luke related what Gropper had also told him, that the
cows were penned their entire lives and fed beer and sake
and massaged daily for exercise. Lonnie was mortified and
put her fork down; Saint didn't care and Vicki didn't say a
word.

"They're never let out?" Lonnie asked. She looked with
distaste at the detritus of her plate. Luke feared she was
going to up-chuck.

"Apparently," he responded, claiming no reaction.

"And you're okay with that?"

He didn't answer and Lonnie looked at Saint. "What do
you think?" she asked.

"It doesn't bother me," Saint said.

"And you?" Lonnie asked Vicki.

Vicki didn't answer. She had barely touched her food, and seemed to be fading into the woodwork. Luke wondered what it was that had so curtailed her typical ebullience.

Lonnie laid her utensils down, neatly parallel, and put her hands in her lap. Luke had not yet finished his steak, but his appetite was gone. He followed suit. At a loss for what to do next, he asked if anyone was interested in a drink. Vicki declined and Saint said he'd have a beer. Luke and Lonnie agreed on scotch. Once the table was clear and they had their drinks in hand, Lonnie opened the conversation again, playing the game of figuring out who they knew in common. "Where're you from?" she asked Vicki.

"Around," she said. "I'm an army brat."

"Really? Where've you lived? Where's home now?"

"Texas. And I've lived in Alaska. And North Carolina. And Germany."

"Ooof," Lonnie responded. "Far beyond me. I've only lived in Rhode Island. What about college? Maybe we have some connections there."

Vicki stared at Lonnie. "I doubt it."

"We could try."

"Not tonight. I'm not feeling myself. Some other time."

"Well, Saint," Lonnie said. "What about you? Where did you go to college?"

The conversation was getting stilted and Luke could tell that Saint was wary. He shrugged off Lonnie's question.

"You did go," she said. "Luke told me you were in college when you were drafted."

"When I joined up."

"What did you major in?"

"I was going to major in drama," Saint said.

"Really?" Lonnie exclaimed. "No kidding." She turned to Luke. "Why didn't you tell me?" she said.

"I didn't know."

She looked at Saint. "That's my major. What have you done?"

"You mean plays? Nothing before I quit, outside of high school."

"Nothing?"

"I quit second semester. What about you?"

"I see you as a kind of Godot character," Lonnie said. "When you go back, if you go back to drama, you've got to try that. You'd be great as Godot."

Saint smiled. "I'll keep that in mind."

Luke looked at Lonnie, wondering what she was up to, what she was trying to accomplish. She had clearly divined Saint's lack of experience, and knew he wouldn't know the play, that there was no Godot. She had deliberately tried to embarrass Saint, although, other than himself, she was likely the only one who was in on the joke. Luke didn't understand; it was a side to Lonnie that he hadn't seen before, and he didn't like it. Conversation died.

She turned to Luke. "What do you think? Is it time?"

Luke nodded, wanting to get away from the table as soon as possible. Luke and Saint confirmed they'd meet at Saint's hotel to go back to Khorat. They walked out to Rama IV and both couples caught cabs.

In the cab Luke asked Lonnie what she was up to. "You knew he didn't know what you were talking about. He doesn't know anything about avant-garde or the absurd. He doesn't know Beckett."

"I didn't know that."

"Right. So what were you doing? Baiting him? He doesn't

know there is no Godot in *Waiting for Godot*. Why would you do that?"

"I don't know. It's just this whole military thing. Army brats and everything. These people live ignorant lives."

"Wow. Where'd that come from?"

"My father. Saint. Vicki. I felt like I just had to take a whack."

"But why? It seems to me like your intention was just to hurt."

"This military thing. It's everywhere and I can't stand it."

"There *is* a war going on. And you *are* in a country practically in the war zone."

"That's what I'm talking about. What does that even mean?"

"Are you throwing me in that mix?"

"Should I?"

He saw no point in pursuing the conversation. What had happened seemed incongruous; he hoped it was, and that that was that. Now that she'd gotten it out of her system, he hoped it would never come up again.

ON THE DRIVE back to Khorat he asked Saint what had been up with Vicki at dinner.

"We broke up," he said.

"Just like that? What happened?"

"She's pregnant."

"Yours?

"She doesn't know."

"So what're you going to do? You like her, don't you? At least it seemed like you did."

"I don't know. Probably nothing."

For a time Saint sat quietly next to the door, staring out

the window. When they made the turn in Saraburi, he came alive, becoming more of his usual self, clearly having pushed Vicki out of his head. "My, God," he said, "that Kobe steak was great! I've never tasted beef that delicious before. But did Lonnie keep ragging you about it? I tell you, these Bambi people, I don't understand them. How was she?"

Luke didn't feel like looking back at that part of his time with Lonnie, and he just blew it away. "We didn't talk about it again."

"Good. She looked so hot. Whattaya think? Is there something there?"

"I sure hope so."

36

The C-130 corkscrewed down to the air base at Nakhon Phanom, brief glimpses of the Mekong glistening in the late afternoon sun and the Annamite Mountains beyond flashing by. They touched down hard and sped down the runway. Then their props roared, reversing pitch, and Luke was thrown forward, followed by a hard turn onto a taxiway, a jolt and a bounce and an abrupt stop. The crew chief waved Luke forward and opened the hatch, pointed towards the now idling props. Drew his forefinger across his throat in warning and stood aside for Luke to get out. As soon as he was clear the crew chief threw him his flight bag and closed the hatch. The C-130 immediately roared back to life, pivoted back onto the taxiway and runway, took off and was gone.

What the fuck, Luke wondered. He was at the heart of it all, NKP, the northern-most U.S. base in Thailand, Laos just across the river, and he expected unchallenged strength, not wham bang thank you ma'am on a plane beating a hasty retreat, as if they were under fire.

Then he woke to the tempo of the base—the busy flight

line, A-26 light bombers and Sandies rolling out, running up, taking off one right after another. A FAC's Cessna bounced down the runway and was quickly airborne. Nearby the rotors of a Jolly Green helicopter turned slowly while crew members ran to board. All in a hurry. A time warp, a forward base in the Pacific in the island-hopping campaign, everything pointing towards Tokyo; the Ops building that looked like it wouldn't sustain a strong wind; Swiss cheese flight aprons that had been quickly laid down; metal revetments protecting aircraft against mortar attack—all a far cry from orderly, rear-echelon, concreted Khorat. He scanned the horizon and discovered a possible reason for it all: smoke wafted into the sky over a notch in the distant mountains, and Sandies circled and dove through the smoke like a murder of crows scavenging roadkill.

An Air Force blue jeep driven by a taciturn airman picked him up for the ride to Task Force Alpha, and their pace slowed as soon as they left the flight line. NKP became but a small base anywhere, Thai, maybe Lao, civilians mowing lawns, airmen in olive drab walking the streets, talking on corners. Khaki-clad officers stepped out of a jeep and walked up the sidewalk to the officers' club. Concrete. Permanent.

As they drove the streets quickly opened, buildings replaced by open fields of mown grass. Room to grow. They came at last to what the driver said was the headquarters of Task Force Alpha, only there was no there there, just a solitary guard shack in front of a stand of trees in a vast lot protected by a barbed-wire topped cyclone fence. The guard directed Luke up a pleasantly curving road through the trees that felt like a garden path leading nowhere, but that ended finally at a ramp that descended into the earth to a pair of massive steel doors large enough to admit trucks and who knew what else, in front of which was another guard shack. There he was cleared through a small door cut into the larger steel doors, like the daily entrance to a European cathedral.

Inside Luke expected a largish room, in the middle of which would be a map table surrounded by airmen or women moving toy trucks down the Ho Chi Minh Trail with long sticks. He laughed at his naiveté—World War Two at the movies: officers hovering, talking, contemplating next moves in a terrestrial chess game, radio operators at nearby desks relaying decisions to the whomever, wooden walls, low hanging lamps bathing the map table in light. Instead, a vast, cavernous and dimly lit space-age command center, massive steel beams and black-painted concrete walls built to withstand a direct hit. Glassed-in offices and a double row of raised desks faced a huge glass situation map that filled the far wall, in front of which was a bullpen populated by a row of computer printers spewing out endless accordions of paper. A drafting table sat behind each printer, each manned by a junior officer in combat fatigues who periodically stepped over to his printer, ripped off his most recent printout, and carried it back to his drafting table for examination.

The wall map drew him in. It was all there—the golden triangle of Laos and North and South Vietnam, roads and truck parks, transfer points. Numbers denoting sensors, smeared erasures from constant updates. A column on the side listed the entirety of the Fifty-third's orbits, painted permanently in the colors of their names—red, green, yellow, blue, purple—with the call sign of the Connie currently flying each orbit crayoned in. This is it, he thought to himself, this is the heart of things, the *Sanctum Santorum.* He felt oddly like a voyeur, detached yet intimately connected. Until that moment he had thought of the Fifty-third as the center of things. Here was reality: we are a satellite, an adjunct, one of many, he said to himself. We rotate around TFA. He knew it intellectually. He had always known it. But he had always held onto a naturally narcissistic feeling otherwise. Here was truth, right or wrong. They were a sideshow. He was a sideshow. Here was the center of the world that ignored his existence.

The center was cold, verging on freezing, and smelled sterile and plastic, like the inside of an airplane, or maybe the inside of an operating piece of electronics, like a radio or a television. An enlisted man stood on a stepladder behind the map, updating the locations of sensors and the latest convoy traffic, writing backwards. The junior officers standing by their drafting tables looked like modern-day monks in a scriptorium. He recognized their work as that of his own men, their pace busier than it should have been that time of day—shadows were just starting to gather in the Laotian jungle, and there should not have been any traffic of consequence moving down the trail, not before nightfall. Periodically the junior officers carried a printout to a major at one of the surrounding desks, and the two of them put their heads together and looked over the paper. From the major the word appeared to go to the enlisted man on the stepladder, who marked the convoy's track and numbers. Another major at another desk kept track of it all and lifted a telephone to—do what? Call a radio operator? Call the airborne command post? The operation was neat and well-organized and linear and, it seemed to Luke, had more steps and was taking maybe twice as much time as it took him and his crew to do the same thing. He wasn't sure he had the steps right, but here was a possible clue to what he had long suspected—this computer-based operation, supposedly faster, was, in fact, slower, with too many people in the decision-making chain.

A tech sergeant appeared at his shoulder and asked if he was the new liaison from the Fifty-third. Luke nodded. The sergeant said he was here to show him around. He took Luke to his office, the last in the glassed-in row in the back, overlooking the center, where Luke dropped his flight bag.

They went first to the radio room adjacent to the command center—five men at tables in front of radios, earphones half on, chatting to each other and occasionally breaking off to respond to incoming radio traffic. "These are the guys you talk to when you're flying," the sergeant said. He introduced Luke to the room. "This is Lieutenant Tuttle from the recon wing," he said. "This week's liaison."

Luke smiled, nodded. "It's nice to put faces on the voices I hear all the time," he said. None of the radio operators responded. He watched them for a minute, then he and the sergeant left. Walked down a hall. The sergeant pointed out the restroom and then a cafeteria the size of a coffee shop. The food line was closed, except for the coffee machine. "The food line closes mid-afternoon, the coffee machine goes twenty-four seven," the sergeant said. "You know you'll be working the night shift, right? When there's real activity." Luke nodded, and yes it made sense, though he hadn't really thought about it. He reminded himself to bring a snack, Maybe something from the club.

As they went down the long hall to the conference room they passed the *de rigueur* photo lineup of the chain of command—LBJ through McNamara through an assortment of generals none of whom meant anything to Luke. Next to last the general in command of Task Force Alpha. Then lastly a civilian. The sergeant watched Luke. "The civilian is the computer company project manager," he said. Luke found it strange that the man's photo was on the wall, and wondered the circumstances that deemed it appropriate.

Inside the conference room the sergeant said simply, "You'll finish your shift here every morning, with the general's brief. If there's an issue with the Fifty-third, this is where it'll come up."

A long table ran the length of the room, surrounded by chairs, a massive whiteboard and a map of Southeast Asia focused on the golden triangle. An American flag in the corner. And a row of chairs lining the wall facing the table for the hangers on. At the far end of the room a window gave onto a large computer room, its fluorescent lighting washing both rooms flat and surreal.

They stepped to the window. Metal computer cabinets lined the wall, most with magnetic-tape drive wheels turning randomly back and forth. Two enlisted men tended the machines, opening and closing cabinet doors, reading vital signs, for all the world like farmers tending cows at milking. An airman stopped one of the machines, opened the glass door and lifted out a reel. Carried it to another cabinet where he reversed the process, inserting the reel and giving it a twist. The whole process seemed natural to the room and totally foreign to anything having to do with convoys moving down the Ho Chi Minh Trail or Connies flying over Laos, or with Southeast Asia for that matter. Luke could barely make a connection.

A civilian stood at a table to the side, thoughtfully flipping through a large sheaf of what appeared to be technical plans. *Tech rep*, Luke thought to himself sourly. On training flights at the Cape, they had always been in the way, making sure their equipment was working right, yes, but always at inopportune times, or arguing with tech reps from other companies when there was blame to be apportioned for system failures. Recording their findings in little black CYA books they tucked in their chest pockets. Covering their asses.

This man was different. Comfortable in what he was doing, clearly fulfilling a position on a team, talking randomly with the airmen tending the machines. He stopped flipping pages to scan one in particular, then continued. Incongruously, he wore khakis and a tweed jacket. A button-down shirt. Must be cold in there, Luke thought. Harris tweed, he said to himself. Good taste. In Thailand. Tousled hair over his ears and nearly to his collar. The man stepped away from the table and Luke saw his shoes—Bass Weejuns, white adhesive tape wrapped around one of them, holding the sole to the upper. Luke laughed— the Colgate uniform. He stared. Started. As strange as it felt, he thought he recognized the man. Then knew that he did. It couldn't be but was. He looked at the man again. Broad face, wide-set eyes. Strong jaw. "I know him," he said to the sergeant. "I went to school with him."

"Mr. Truehorn," the sergeant said.

"Yeah. Yeah. That's right! Leo Truehorn," Luke exclaimed. "That's Leo, for god's sake. What's he doing here?" He went to the door to go into the computer room.

"Whoa, sir," the sergeant said, moving quickly to block his way. "You're not cleared to go in there, sir. Sorry. I'll get him," he added quickly, and went into the room.

How great! How cool! What a neat thing! Luke thought. Someone from college, someone from home, someone honed in philosophy and religion and narrow paths through deep snow. He remembered that Leo lived on the hill, in the dorm reserved for those few who didn't join a fraternity, by choice or rejection. The turkey coops. He remembered Leo's distinctive walk, hunched over and bobbing with each overly long stride. And the fact that he seemed always to be alone. He thought maybe they'd marched together in the civil rights demonstrations in Cazenovia and Syracuse just a few years before. He wasn't sure. Leo's exuberance came to mind.

Luke watched the sergeant talk to Leo. Leo looked at him, waved, and came out.

"I know you," Luke said as Leo came out the door. "I remember you from Colgate."

Leo laughed, threw his head back and enjoyed his humor. "You're kidding!" he exclaimed, quickly adding, "But I don't know you."

"I'm sure you don't. I lived down the hill. You were a year ahead of me. I just remember you around campus. Luke Tuttle."

Leo laughed. "I'll be damned. From Colgate. Not in all my time here have I run into anyone from back then."

"Me either," Luke said. "You're my first. Probably be my only."

Leo paused, looked Luke over. "I think I remember seeing you now. You were a Teke."

Luke nodded.

"I knew a lot of your brothers. Bill Stein. John Horowitz. Meb Sturtevant."

"Stein and I hung out together sometimes."

"That's great! Where is he now?"

"Graduate school. He was in the Peace Corps in Brazil. He didn't last long. He was sent home for organizing rent protests. Now he's getting his masters in urban planning at IIT in Chicago."

"And you?"

"I'm in the recon wing."

"The recon wing? You're with the recon wing? That's

great! That's fucking terrific! Someone from fucking Colgate in fucking Nakhon Phanom." He grabbed Luke's hand and forearm and pumped vigorously. "Come on. Let's go talk," he said, and led the way to the empty cafeteria and the coffee urn.

LUKE ASKED Leo what he did there. Leo slid his already half empty coffee cup back and forth on the table. The coffee sloshed and threatened to spill. "Computer ops. I keep things running."

"But how'd you wind up here?"

Leo recounted the steps from college, all logical, all seemingly a straight line. "Ain't a liberal arts education great?" he added.

"You learned Fortran, stuff like that?"

"I did. Pretty good for a psych major, huh? And somewhere along the line they decided I could run a team. Ain't that the shits? I couldn't get into a fuckin' fraternity and they think I've got people skills. And with this job I move to the head of the class."

"So when NKP goes down, that's you?"

"'Fraid so." He melodramatically hung his head. "In the beginning, we just couldn't keep things working. The tropics and all that shit. Heat and humidity. Dirt. This climate just isn't made for sophisticated electronics. I don't think anybody anticipated how it would invade everything, even inside this bunker. You can't imagine."

Luke recalculated his understanding of Leo. He had been slotting him into his campus role—loner, outsider, someone who didn't quite get it, or, to give him credit, marched to a different tune. Now the tables were reversed, and he felt like a neophyte looking into the real world. He

had been on the outside looking in all along and just realized it. He pulled out his cigarettes, offered one to Leo. Leo
shook his head and took out his own pack of Lucky Strikes.

"You've gotta be the only person in Southeast Asia that
smokes them," Luke said, looking at Leo's cigarettes.

Leo laughed.

"And when do you work? Maybe we can get together."

"I'm around nearly all the time. Just come find me."

"Well, how about tomorrow, in the morning? After staff.
A late breakfast. An early lunch."

Leo nodded. Grinned. And rubbed his hands together.

Luke went back to his office, amused and tickled. He
looking forward to settling in with someone with whom he
felt comfortable. He sat at his desk and watched the
command center, still trying to get a feel for the rhythm of
the place.

His office was sterile—desk, chair, a bookcase with one
blue, Air Force-issue, three-ring binder containing only a
map and guide to the base. Nothing else. He rummaged
through the desk. In one drawer, a wooden ruler and a
scramble of pencils and ballpoint pens scattered like empty
clothes hangers in a closet. A pack of pink *While You Were
Out* message pads, seal unbroken. In another a mass of loose
paperclips and their overturned carton. He righted the
carton and hunted down all the clips. In the center drawer, a
log book, mostly blank. On page one each liaison officer had
noted his arrival and then, seven days later, his departure.
He signed in. On another a graffiti-like phrase scrawled
across the top: *"Frodo lives in the mountains of Laos."* He
smiled. Remembered his own introduction to the hobbit,
"Frodo lives" scrawled a subway wall in New York, on a night
when he and Em were on their way to the village for dinner
at Em's favorite Italian restaurant. He remembered that he

had ordered spaghetti Bolognese for no other reason than familiarity, and Em had chosen spaghetti *al nero di sepia*, spaghetti in squid ink, which fascinated the hell out of Luke, thinking how far removed it was from the village favorite at Buck's diner in Mount Brookville, white on white, bits of cod in gravy on mashed potatoes. "Who's Frodo?" he had asked. Em didn't know. That was junior year. Senior year he read *The Hobbit* and *The Lord of the Rings*, finishing before November. And then Sholokhov's Don Cossacks, from Em's Russian lit class. He loved them all. As for his own course work—well, it was not his best semester.

And now he wished he'd brought a book. Then again he feared it would violate some tenet of office culture, which he suspected didn't include pleasure reading even when there was nothing going on. He wandered the command center, looked over the analysts' shoulders at their traffic. Introduced himself to each, made a stab at shop talk, moved on, sometimes came back. One man was friendly—tall, dark-haired, broad-faced, broad shouldered. A quick smile. Dennis. A big man, trim, but somehow awkward. Dartmouth, he said, when he and Luke compared notes. Luke's peer exactly, having graduated when Luke did. He was quite happy to explain the command center operation. He began at the beginning, pointing at the printer.

"It prints out every three minutes," he said. "I scan it for evidence of a convoy. Here," he said, turning his paper so Luke could see. The spread of x's was the same as what his men created on the Connie, convoys displayed as diagonal patterns over time and space. "If I have anything I take it back to the chief intelligence officer, back there," he said, pointing to the major sitting in the first ring of desks behind the drafting tables. "If he agrees, it gets posted on the map board. The other major calls it in to the command post." He nodded at the major sitting at a desk in the second row. "How does it compare to what you do?"

Luke momentarily raised his eyebrows. "Well, close," he said. "we record real-time. If we find something, I call it in to the airborne command post. At least that's how it was in the beginning, before you guys came on line. Now we just wait for you to go down, and when we take over, if we get anything, I call it in to your radio operators. My guys are your peers. And I guess I'm your two majors."

"That's it?" Dennis asked.

"Pretty much."

37

H is the graveyard shift, when desks and offices were empty and the cafeteria dark and a certain stark, middle-of-the-night nightmare loneliness took over the war room; shadows transformed far-off corners into dense deep jungle with soft movements as seen through theatrical gauze; fronds of unknown genus dipped, human figures appeared, the hard edges of man-made stuff moved. Incongruously he saw tiny drifts of snow behind the gauze as well, two, three inches high, a foot wide. He didn't question it. He watched the analysts at their tables, the two majors at the desks in the lowest row, all waiting for the soft movements to transpire into something threatening. When the tempo picked up he went onto the floor and wandered among the tables to see more closely what was happening, looking at first one table, then another, searching for the telltale parallel diagonal lines. In short order he found them, too quickly, it seemed to him, too many convoys of too many trucks, building as if he were watching traffic on an interstate, one convoy right after the other, nines and tens and elevens instead of fours or fives, seldom threes and twos. He struggled to get his head around what was happening. He'd spent hundreds of hours in the air, he'd seen the first truth, a sensor activating, he'd watched his men log the signals. That was real. That was basic. Fundamental. How could there be consistently activity more than he was used to seeing? He grew uneasy, though not in a way that anyone would notice—no theatrical body language for him. Something was at play, whatever it might be, and he wanted to understand.

Months ago, he'd had a conversation with Reilly about high numbers, not on his logs, but about what NKP was seeing, following a curios transmission with NKP about the high number of trucks in a certain convoy. That's all it was, a curiosity, like riding radio in a car and asking the driver about something he'd seen. Over there, what was that? That shadow moving in the woods. He couldn't remember the whys and wherefores of the discussion, only the moment when he and the man he was talking to at NKP agreed that NKP was seeing more trucks in a convoy than his own guys had seen. Who was it that night? John Constance? Rolphe? Maybe Tony Molino? And on the ground, who was it that he was talking with? Now he saw that that didn't matter. He'd been to the radio room and saw that the men there were as much a sidebar as the men of the Fifty-third in their Connies. He'd asked Colonel Reilly about the higher number, and Reilly went so far as to say, yes, such discrepancies had been noticed. He'd offered the fact that some—who, he never said—were wondering if the Connie's motors might be creating frequency interference that could be distorting the sensor relay to the ground, to TFA, but that he had no idea if such a thing was even possible. Luke didn't find the thought specious: on his road trip from Mount Brookville to West Texas for intelligence officer's school he'd had problems with his radio, not mechanical, but a constant, irritating noise almost like the rattle of machine gun fire coming from his speakers. He figured it was the firing of his spark plugs, and halfway there he'd stopped at a small town Western Auto in Alabama and bought some suppressors that he installed on the spot, hood up in the parking lot, and that took care of the problem. Never mind that a local cop pulled into the parking lot behind him and his red British import with New York plates and asked him what the fuck he was doing in his town and when was he leaving. Once he got to West Texas he brought his car in for something else, and the mechanic pulled the suppressors off the spark plugs and handed them to Luke in an old greasy brown paper bag with a look as if to say that he should know better. Not that the problem went away. It didn't. Luke just put up with the noise.

And now? Who knew? He remembered the ancient story that the southern colonists closed their bedroom windows at night to keep out the malaria that came with the night air. So, no, he didn't understand what was going on, but he was certain that something wasn't quite right.

It was busy for hours, a constant ebb and flow. Only towards morning did things grow quiet. Nothing happened for long stretches of time, and the tableau behind the gauze began to fade. The snow melted. The boredom was crippling. His mind wandered inevitably to thoughts of Lonnie, pleasurably, to things they'd done. Their intimacies. His penus began to swell and stiffen, and he felt like a seventh grader, caught at an awkward time, afraid the bulge in his pants would embarrass him. And just as inevitably, each time it happened, he slipped away to the men's bathroom, to a stall where he would quickly indulge himself, and return to his office satisfied and alert.

Not long after shift change in the morning Luke took a quick catnap before heading over to the conference room for the general's morning brief. He sat in the row next to the wall, next to Leo. The end of Luke's day, the beginning of Leo's.

The briefing was short and smooth. Once everyone was seated and attendance confirmed, the general's adjutant, a young major, came in and called the room to attention. Everyone stood and waited while the general—tall, trim, greying at the temples, strong chin, long face, aquiline nose —a man born a general—walked in.

"Seats," the adjutant called, and midst the noisy scratching of chairs, the briefing began. A young captain acted as emcee, calling up the status reports for each orbit, the number of trucks identified, the number destroyed or damaged. All noted on the white board. When the general didn't understand something, he'd say so. There was no faking of competence. "Help me with that," he would say, and wait patiently for an explanation. His humility was almost endearing.

The computer company's project manager sat next to the general, and they chatted *sotto voce* when issues or problems came up, conferring before the general commented. The project manager was true to the popularly known culture of his company, religiously dressed in a white shirt and dull, narrow tie, often making a wry comment about it. Ball point pens in a plastic protector in his breast pocket, random ink spots on his shirt. Luke snickered under his breath and Leo said, "Don't underestimate him. That's his front—playing the socially inept technician. He wants good evaluations for the company as much as the general wants a job when this thing is over."

Luke watched carefully for some sleight of hand that

accounted for how good the numbers looked, the high the number of trucks spotted, and, what he never had access to before, the percentage of kills per targeted convoy. These totals too seemed high.

The numbers pleased the general and he said so; the gathered staff preened in his attaboys, and Luke recalled the fighter pilot's bomb damage story, and the story of the errant rocket that blew something sky high. But he also recalled the stories they'd heard rumors about how body counts were tabulated after firefights, where it was said that company commanders would send a couple of men out to count VC casualties, and each man would make his own sweep through the field, and then the commander would total their results. After all, this was McNamara's war, and numbers were it and bodies were it. And trucks damaged or destroyed was it.

"Far be it for me," Luke whispered to Leo, "but if all this is true, how come the VC and NVN are so well-armed?" Asking the loaded question, hoping for a humorous view of the subject.

After everyone had left, Luke and Leo hung on, and Leo waited patiently for Luke to absorb what had happened.

"We never see any reports on trucks destroyed or damaged in Khorat. Or I don't, anyhow. They just seem so high," Luke said. "Is this typical?"

Leo nodded.

"It looks like we're doing pretty damn good."

Leo shrugged. "Here's one for you. So far we've claimed over fifteen thousand trucks destroyed or damaged. I've read the CIA reports and they say that there's only fifteen thousand trucks in all North Vietnam. Doesn't quite make sense, does it. Not when you add it all up. But it's all we're left with, isn't it? The numbers."

38

The officers' club was dark, a sealed cave, scarce a window, refrigerated much like the command center, with crudely milled teak walls and low ceilings. Luke and Leo sat at a corner table and ate fries and burgers and drank Coke and enjoyed the comfort of similar points of view, similar reactions to their recent experiences. Leo had been in country for over a year, and was looking at that much more. Early on he had lived with a *teelagh,* a mistress, in a bungalow up in the hills. She was Lao and worked at a massage parlor in downtown Nakhon Phanom and had offered to shack up with him the first night they met, when Leo came in for a massage. At first they rode back and forth from their bungalow to town on a local bus, chickens in cages on the roof, stares from everyone they met. Then he bought a motor scooter. "It was really pretty good," Leo said. "We got along, we each had our own lives. The sex was good. We settled in right away. I got freebie massages. I thought she was pretty mercenary at first. I figured she was just looking for a meal ticket and rights at the BX, and she was, but that was okay with me. We got along just fine. She had the softest, most beautiful voice, like a murmuring brook. She was always pleasant, and she didn't hesitate to laugh at me, only they were quiet titters, you know what I mean? Covering her mouth with her hand. Playing with the hair on my chest, laughing at the size of my feet. I came here, I must have weighed a hundred and seventy pounds, I'd put on probably twenty right after Colgate, and then I started eating off the economy and I dropped it all in two months."

"Eating what?"

Leo laughed. "Bugs."

"Bugs?"

Leo nodded, grinning. Luke was incredulous.

"Yeah, bugs. Pure protein. The best were the rice bugs. Most of the time Khet'd fry 'em up to eat with sticky rice. Khet. That was her name. The rice bugs were the bonanza, cause sometimes they already had rice in them."

"Yuck!"

"No, no, really. Don't knock it til you've tried it. They're good, frat boy. Don't be a pussy. Twenty pounds! It was great when we got rice bugs straight from a paddy. One afternoon, when we were on the bus going home, one of the passengers, Khet said he was a bug hunter, saw a rice bug at the edge of the road, right next to a paddy, and he started jumping up and down and getting all excited, and he got the driver to stop and he jumped off and half the bus followed him, running over and putting the bugs in their market bags..."

"And you ate them."

"I liked 'em."

"And now?

"After about six months Khet left. Her father was killed in a firefight between the Pathet Lao and the local police, so she said. She said he was just an innocent bystander, and it might be true, but from everything she said I thought he was probably Pathet Lao. Her mother said she needed her at home, so that was that. So I moved back on base and so far, I've only put five pounds back on." He surveyed the remnants of the meal, looked at Tuttle. "Sometimes I fry some bugs up in my room. You should come over. We could smoke some dope and you can try some bugs."

"I'm okay with the dope part," Luke said.

Leo laughed. "Pussy."

Three men came in through the door, still in flight suits, but of a different color than Air Force grey. Luke looked at them quizzically, wondering. Leo followed his glance. "Navy," he said. "They're the guys who drop your sensors into the jungle. They fly P-3s. Them and the Air Force F-4's, who shoot them in. Yet another cog in our smoothly running machine. I'm surprised you've never seen Navy flight crew before."

Luke shrugged.

39

On Luke's last day at NKP, at his last brief, one report stood out because of the high percentage of trucks destroyed. Seventy. For once the general seemed leery. He grilled the briefing officer on the provenance of the numbers. "Where'd they come from?" he asked, and the briefing officer named the fighter squadron at Khorat.

"You believe them?"

"They've been consistently reliable."

"Feedback from the airborne command post?"

"They agree, sir." He stood nearly at attention while the general thought about what he was looking at. Finally he nodded. "Okay," he said. "Let's go with it."

Luke whispered to Leo. "He *wants* to believe all this."

The men at the table turned to look, not because of their words—they weren't loud and probably no one could tell what Luke had said—but because he was talking at all. The general looked at Luke. "Ah," the general said. "Our man from the recon wing. Something you want to add, Lieutenant?"

"No, sir," Luke said. And of course, there was, but not by him.

The meeting concluded and the general and his staff left, leaving Luke and Leo sitting quietly as on the first day. After a few minutes, Leo said, "There's more, and if you were here every day, you'd think of it. You've been around long enough. You've seen how people move things down the road around here. Yeah, there's trucks. Toyotas. Datsuns. Some of the Mercedes doing long haul. Plus there's bicycles. Maybe not in Khorat, but up here they're everywhere. You should see how they load those things up. Christ, they even carry pigs. They put 'em in wicker baskets, and balance the baskets across their handlebars. They do it on motorbikes, too. But the point is, they carry damn near everything on their bikes. Baskets of veggies, engine parts." He paused. "Truck parts. Boxes and boxes of shit. A helluva lot of shit. It doesn't seem to matter how heavy some of it is, or how awkward, they find a way to strap it on. Think about it," Leo said. "Just think about it. They're like ants."

Luke laughed, recalling the Fachevsky ant incident. Considered the implications. "Have you ever suggested it here? That maybe it isn't all trucks. That maybe they're moving stuff down the Trail on bikes?"

"Are you shitting me? Really? Yeah, I've mentioned it at the lunch table, just talking, you know, with other grunts like you and me. Like we are right now. And they nod and they know it's true, just like you do. But here? In this conference room? There's no place to insert information like that. I'd be laughed out of the room."

"Where'd you get the idea?"

"Khet. Not directly, but yeah, from her. She knew what I did and what was going on out here. They all do. She knew the Navy and the Air Force put the sensors in. She knew we listened to them. She knew about the computers, too. She knew me. One night she asked me if we could hear bicycles. And I thought, what an odd question, but then I said I didn't think so."

"We've got road watch teams."

"Not enough. And who's gonna open his mouth and say this system doesn't work and we need to put a whole ton of men into Laos to watch the trail? That's career limiting." He paused, eyeing Luke. "There's something here that I don't think you've grasped. You know this is the most expensive thing in the Vietnam War, don't you? On a budget line, somewhere. All this..." he rolled his eyes and swung his head, as if to take in the whole of Task Force Alpha..."all of this, this place, the computer system, the sensors, you guys in your Connies, all this is costing well over a billion dollars, maybe two. No one's going to say this doesn't work."

The two of them fell silent, then Luke humphed. Looked at Leo. "Bicycles," he said.

Leo shrugged his eyebrows. "It wasn't long after that that she left."

40

They went downtown for lunch, to a patio bar overlooking the Mekong. Relaxed in the sun and looked across the sparkling, slow-moving sea of sparkling brown to the mountains. They drank too many Singhas and Luke felt his brain pushing against the inside of his skull, and he dreaded how he'd feel on his flight back to Khorat. Mid-afternoon they hailed a cab to go back to the base. As they settled into the backseat Leo changed his mind. "Wait," he said to the driver. He turned to Luke. "Have you seen the clock tower?"

"The what?"

"The Ho Chi Minh clock tower. You've got to see it. You can't come to NKP without seeing it. Kind of puts everything into perspective. See, the thing is, Uncle Ho lived here in the twenties. I'll bet you didn't know that. Hiding out from the French. They say he plotted his revolution here, how he was going to throw the fucking French out. There's all kind of Vietnamese around here, they came here to escape the French and to be with Ho. So this is like where it all started. Ironic, isn't it. Compare that to the circus out at

Task Force Alpha. You've got to be able to say you at least saw it."

The tower was on the edge of town, midst a jumble of corrugated-roof shops and garages and restaurants and an open-air market. Next to a busy street. Dignified, plain and humble, sixty-some feet tall. An open-sided covered space adjoined it, with benches, maybe for meetings. Or just sitting and eating and talking. At the moment they were alone. They walked around the tower while their driver waited patiently in the street. Thai writing adorned a space below the clock face.

"What's it say?" Luke asked.

"Don't have a clue. Probably thanks to the Thai who let Ho and a mess of Vietnamese live here. I really don't know."

"It doesn't look very old."

"It's not, I don't think. Early sixties, just a few years ago. Just before we came."

"Well that's ironic. Probably right around the time we were negotiating base leases."

They sat at one of the benches. Pickup trucks and motorcycles drove by in a constant stream. And dozens of bicycles.

Leo nodded at them, many overloaded with cargo—boxes, wicker baskets, plastic bags. "Beaucoup bicycles. Cool, huh?" he added, and smiled.

Luke nodded. There wasn't much more to say. He was tired, perhaps better said, resigned. *Mai pen rai*, he thought to himself. But not meaning 'It doesn't matter.' More like, 'Nothing makes any difference any more'.

Later that afternoon he packed. Went to the flight line to catch his flight back to Khorat. He stood in the shade of the Ops building, waiting. Armed Forces Radio was playing loudly inside, the Animals singing "We gotta get out of this place". The C-130 landed and taxied up and he boarded. The tune and the words reverberated in his head, all the way back to Khorat:

We gotta get out of this place
If it's the last thing we ever do
We gotta get out of this place
Girl, there's a better life for me and you.

41

Lonnie hired a young German boy, son of a diplomat, to paint a mural on the inside wall of their bungalow. She hadn't intended to fix up the bungalow in any way, but she saw the boy sketching by the pool at her apartment and, when she asked to see his work, which was mainly quick sketches of Thai in their daily lives, clerks in stores, vendors at their carts, *bonzes* walking along the streets, she was impressed. She asked if he could do a mural in her bungalow. In nearly flawless English the boy said yes, excited at the prospect. He painted a scene of the world just outside the bungalow, the *klong* and the children next door, two girls and their younger brother. He placed the boy in the center of the mural holding an immense balloon in front of his face that distorted his image like a fisheye lens. The girls were facing front and had rice powder on their faces, which made them look like ghosts. The German boy didn't prepare the wood, perhaps intentionally, perhaps happenstance, and the pigments soaked in and the mural was soft and dreamy, and came alive. She hoped Luke would like it.

She also figured out how to reach Luke by telephone. One day she called her father in Laos from his office, and then, after the call, on a whim she asked the operator for Lucas Tuttle, in the Five fifty-third, at Khorat Royal Thai Air Force Base. In a moment Luke was on the line.

"It's me," she said.

"What?" he said. "How did you?..." He had never used the phone for anything, let alone to call off base. As far as he knew, the phone was only for Squadron to call him.

"Aren't you proud of me? I'm on the phone in my father's office. I just figured that if I'm on a US government phone system, probably it goes all over Southeast Asia, so I asked the operator for you, in the Fifty-third at Khorat Royal Thai Air Force Base and here you are. And here I am."

It felt good to hear her voice and sense her smile. Still, there was not much of substance to say and the conversation soon devolved into mush, and they both became uncomfortable. Last thing, Lonnie told him about hiring the German boy to paint the mural, and that she was excited for him to see it. "It's magical," she said, "really magical the way the colors are soft and almost surreal. The whole thing looks like it's a place out of time, out of the past. You're going to love it."

AND HE DID. Standing in front of the painting, taking it in.

"Our home," Lonnie said.

He agreed, sensing the bungalow no longer as just a place to be alone, less a covert getaway or a love nest, and now the catalyst of their maturing relationship. At least he hoped so. No doubt next the mattress would come off the floor, then maybe a small refrigerator. Certainly some dishes. He looked at Lonnie in a new light, not just as a creature of passion, more as a comfortable mate. He had been thinking she might be the one, and now he was convinced. It was good to be with her, and with her came a sense of security that brought him great relief.

Weatherwise, the first trip to the bungalow had been a gift, though he hadn't known it at the time—the vicissitudes of Thailand's weather were beyond him. It had been warm and pleasant, the bungalow like a prize-winner's visit to the Caribbean in April or mid-fall, or maybe the Mediterranean, places of the rich if not famous. Light breezes had lifted the leaves of trees and bushes, tracked across the *klong* in gentle ripples. Not so this time. Heavy, stifling heat and humidity stripped away all but the search for a breath of air. Their slightest movement brought sweat and discomfort. They wanted not to move. They stood staring at each other, mutually agreeing without a word that they did not want to do a thing. Luke unbuttoned his shirt and held back the mosquito netting and they flopped onto the mattress. Took off shoes and sandals. Shirt and blouse. Pants and skirt. Down to their skivvies for reprieve from the cloying heat. They lay back onto the mattress. Smells made their way. Garlic being cooked in the bungalow next door. A touch of the smell of mildew. The tropics. Life went on, people ate, moved around. Children played. They did not talk, but just lay staring up through the netting to the dark of the roof, the pattern of rafters against boards. For how long? They didn't know. In time what they had been before faded away, the cool of air-conditioning forgotten. Hot became the norm, and it was all right as long as they didn't move too quickly. They turned to each other, looked in each other's faces. Luke ran his finger along Lonnie's upper lip. "Your sweating," he said.

"Glistening," she said. "Ladies don't sweat and they don't perspire. They glisten."

They laughed and kissed and Lonnie turned her back to him. Luke ran his hand along her arm, to her waist and hip and she cooed, lightly. He moved closer and they were baptized in their shared perspiration.

THE FIVE-DAY BREAK PASSED QUICKLY. The heat broke, the nights became more gentle, the humidity a balm, the days again tourist-like, a vacation without responsibilities. They went to the *wats,* the floating market. They saw a crowd in the stands at the Royal Sports Club and joined them to watch a game of rugby, Thai versus a *farung* team, and were amazed that there enough Thai big enough to compete. But they knew nothing of rugby and soon left. Walked through Lumpini Park and took a *tuk-tuk* back to their bungalow, where their conversation was easy and pleasant and they knew it was good to be together.

The last day Luke stayed as late as he could. Again there was a conversation about how long it would be before he could make it back. "I've got a three-day break in a couple of weeks," he said.

Lonnie was crestfallen. "Really?" she said. "There's no way you can make it sooner? Even if it's just for an overnight?"

Luke shook his head. "It'd be a squeeze," he said. "I don't know if I can take the chance." He looked at her. "You could come up, you know."

"To Khorat?"

"Sure. Hire a limo. Take the train. I'll help."

"It's not the money. I'm just not comfortable with the idea. Going to the base like some camp follower."

"We don't have to go on base. We'll stay in town. Take the train. First class. I'll meet you at the station."

"I'm not so sure I want to see your world," she said. "The Air Force, the whole military thing." She paused, serious expression on her face. He recognized it from Pattaya when the B-52s flew overhead, and from the night at Nick's Number One with Saint and Vicki.

"You see it now," he said. "I'm here. You know what my life is."

"No, I don't see it at all, and I'm just fine with that. I don't have any trouble keeping it out of my mind."

"Listen," he said. "Come on up to Khorat and we'll just hang out around town. I'll get you a room at the Sripatana. You'll like it, I promise. See what life's like in the provinces. You can stay a couple of days, more if you like."

"We'll see," she said.

"But you'll come, right?" he said. "Just let me know the train."

42

10 October. Green. On at 2000. Three positions. Rickey made beef stroganoff again, this time with water buffalo from the butcher shop downtown. The sweetness of the meat and the sauce was nearly too much. Minimal activity.

17 October. Blue. Takeoff at 0600. Late in the morning Gropper called him forward to watch and listen to another Search and Rescue.

"Down there," Woody said, pointing to the left.

Luke looked out the a/c's window, and caught sight of the flashing blades of a Jolly Green. The helicopter was hovering close to the jungle canopy; pink smoke was seeping up through the trees.

"How long's it been going on?" Luke said.

"Maybe a half hour." Gropper said. It felt odd to be so close to another life and death situation and yet so divorced from it, like watching the TV news at home. After a few more minutes the Jolly Green lifted off and Luke went back to his area.

20 October. Yellow. Takeoff 1600. Rickey took them on

and they worked three positions. Moderate activity, a few strikes. It looked like they got some of the trucks but it was hard to tell. Their relief aborted about twenty minutes from changeover and they stayed an additional three hours. By the time they touched down they were exhausted.

25 October. A letter from home. Fergie Gunn had been killed at Pleiku. "I can't stand it!" his mother wrote. He imagined her saying just that, all despair and frustration. During college two of his Mount Brookville friends had died in car accidents, speeding on the road between Mount Brookville and Brookville, riding the crown, and now Fergie. "I can't stand it." she had said each time. And now. He imagined Fergie jumping out of a helicopter into a hot LZ, carrying an M-16. And his photograph in his dress greens atop his family's upright piano, next to the line of photographs of the World War Two Gunns. Lace curtains lifting softly in the breeze through the open window. He wondered how Fergie's death would affect the feeling in the village about the war, if at all. He suspected that Fergie's parents, even Walt, wouldn't want to believe that Fergie had died for no good reason. If they weren't before, they would be all for the war now. He wondered if the plaque at the community hall could be expanded. He thought it was full; probably no one had thought about the wars to come. He couldn't remember if there were any names from the Korean War.

43

Pink. A new orbit, off the coast of North Vietnam, far from TFA, off the coastal plains, where straight roads paralleled the shoreline and led south into the DMZ. The weather was calm, the flight out smooth. Sensors had been planted along the roads a few days before, and reports back were that they activated sporadically, and not in any order, and no one had yet made any sense of them. It was dark by the time they arrived, and almost immediately Luke began pacing the aisle, watching each position, anxious to make sense of what was out there. He went to the map to locate the sensors. He wanted a convoy, something big, moving massive quantities into the NVN warehouse. That's what everyone said was happening, the rumors, *Time, Pacific Edition*. The buildup in the DMZ for the big push. But for the moment, nothing.

He went forward and looked out the galley porthole at the coast of North Vietnam, black on black in the distance. Went to the flight deck to talk to Woody and Gropper.

"Anything?" Woody asked.

"Not yet."

"Total blackout," Woody added, nodding toward North Vietnam.

Luke returned aft, sat for a moment at the galley table. Waited. After a time, how long he couldn't say, McAuley came to get him. "It's picking up," he said.

Saint was resetting a sensor and could barely keep up. He turned his log for Luke to see. Held his hand up in a gesture of confusion, shaking his head. The sensor was the fourth in a string of five. The first three were activating sporadically and in sequence, but the fourth was constant, activating immediately each time Saint reset it. The fifth wasn't activating at all.

Luke looked at the map and tried to figure out what was happening. Saint's five sensors paralleled a coastal road, and nothing hinted as to what might be going on. He pulled down the jump seat next to Rickey.

Rickey was watching Saint's fourth sensor on his own screen. They looked at the map. "Whattaya think?" Luke asked. Rickey shook his head. "Maybe we ask Moonbeam to send a Forward Air Controller out," Rickey said. Never before had they done that. Never before had there been reason, or frankly, the authority. Luke imagined a FAC flying over the road, sliding his window back, looking, perhaps taking ground fire, and seeing nothing. He couldn't imagine a more dangerous job in the Air Force—low and slow and unarmed. He looked at the map again, noted that John Constance was covering a nearby string and went over to look.

"Here, Lieutenant," John said. His log was the opposite of Lawrence's, a blob of activations, then a few activations trailing off, like a balloon trailing a string. Luke suspected only a bird's eye view of the activity would tell them what was going on. He walked back to his position, leaned over.

"Okay, call the airborne command post," he said to Rickey. "Ask them to send a FAC out. Tell them we have a ton of unidentifiable activity."

He waited for a response, watching Rickey talk, pause, talk again. Rickey looked at Luke, nodded his head.

"What'd they say?"

Rickey shook his head. "He wants more."

"Tell him it's a lot. We don't know what it is, but it's a lot." He looked again at both Saint's and John Constance's logs. Checked the map. John leaned back in his chair and looked at the map. "Is that a river?" he asked, pointing to the area around where his and Saint's sensors were located. There was a line indicating what could have been a watercourse, but it wasn't clear. A drainage ditch, maybe. Maybe a brook. Maybe a river. They had no idea. "Between Saint's and my strings. What is it?"

Luke shook his head.

"How big is it?"

"I can't tell."

"Okay," John said. "Near the coast. Let's figure it's a stream of substance. So, you've got Saint's sensors, leading down, maybe to a bridge. And here, down river, on the other side, we've got mine."

Luke looked at the map again. "Seems possible," he said. "There's something going on between the two strings." He leaned over to Rickey. "Ask the airborne command post what they know about the area," he said.

In a moment Rickey came back. "We knocked a bridge out this afternoon. Over the river. It's a river."

John Constance pulled an earphone away to listen. He made a fist, shook it. "Yes!" he said. "That's it!"

"Tell them we think there's something going on," Luke

said to Rickey, "like maybe they're ferrying stuff across, something like that. Maybe that will warrant a FAC."

Rickey got back on his radio, talked, and in a moment smiled and nodded yes. They waited. Luke stood by the officer's position, looking periodically at the sensor lights flashing on John's position. Abruptly his sensors went dead. "FAC must've arrived," he said to Rickey.

Rickey called. "The command post says the FAC doesn't see anything."

"Dial up the conversation between the FAC and the command post," Luke said. "I want to hear." He slipped his earphones on and listened. The FAC was silent. Five minutes. More. Traffic was picking up again, again looking like mirror images of two balloons on strings.

The FAC came back on. He was ecstatic. Luke could hear the wind blowing over his open mic. "This is Bird Dog Three Two," the FAC said. "We've got 'em!" he said. "They're ferrying stuff across the river. They're all over the place. The place is swarming. Get me some ordnance pronto!"

"Roger, that," the command post said.

Luke grinned at Rickey, stepped over to John and poked him in the arm. "We've got 'em!" he said. "We caught 'em out in the open with their pants down! They're all over the place, right at the river!"

The command post came back on. "Bird dog, I've got ordnance coming your way."

The radios went silent. Luke waited, excited, his heart thumping, hoping for the best, fearing the worst. This was Vietnam, after all. Nothing worked out the way it was supposed to. He stood in the aisle, absent-mindedly watching Rickey. He breathed slowly and evenly to keep himself calm.

The FAC came back on. "Holy shit!" he said. "Holy fucking shit. I've got secondaries all over the place. It's like nuclear fission down there. Four, maybe five. No, six. Seven. I've got to get out of the way, some of this shit is blowing sky high, it's going off right under me. And more. It's unbelievable. It's huge. It's as bright as mid-day down there. I've got boats trying to get away and men jumping in the water and piles of shit on fire. Men scrambling everywhere. I can't count it all. It's unbelievable! Sorry 'bout that, Vietnam, you little motherfuckers!"

"Roger, Bird Dog, this is Moonbeam, can you go up river and see if there's anything up there?"

In another moment, the FAC was back. "Roger, Moonbeam, they're up here, too. This is where they're putting in. They're running away but the shit is everywhere, piled on the shore, piled on boats at the edge of the river. Get me some more ordnance!"

"Roger, roger Bird Dog. On the way!"

Again Luke and his crew waited, long, interminable minutes, trying to imagine the scene below. The FAC came back on. "We got these guys, too!" he said ecstatically. "We got 'em!" With his mic open he began to count the explosions aloud. "Seven, eight, nine, ten, eleven, no, a dozen secondaries. Unbelievable, it really is! I've never seen anything like it! You pass the word! This is fantastic! You tell 'em! This is fantastic!"

Luke's crew was laughing. They'd all been listening. Now they were sharing a relief born of months of deprivation. John Constance and Saint, still at their positions, gave up trying to keep up with their sensor activity and sat back and watched their boards flood with the lights of the activating sensors. Those close to the bombing went dead, blasted into oblivion. Luke, standing next to his position, put his hand out to Rickey, and they shook and smiled.

The pilot's intercom flashed. Rickey responded, then handed his headset to Luke. "Yessir?" Luke said."

"Lieutenant," Woody said, "the horizon is lighting up over there. Do you know what it is?"

"Yes, sir, it's us!" Luke said. "We caught 'em in the open. I'm coming up to see."

He hurried to the flight deck, suffused with a feeling of success, months of useless flying flushed away by spectacular results. He looked out the cockpit. As far away as they were, the explosions were lighting up a portion of the night sky, irregular domes of light on the distant horizon. Woody slapped him on the back. "Well done, Tuttle," he said. "Well done!"

At zero four hundred they left orbit and headed back to Khorat. The explosions had died, and only the glow of burning stores remained. No one tried to nap, truly they couldn't; their adrenalin was continuing to pump. They sat in their seats, grinning like a high school football team coming home after a victory following seasons of drought. It was a good feeling, honest and true, all their own, and no one could take it away from them.

44

Two days later Lonnie arrived. Luke was still floating on his crew's success over the river, and felt complete, at least for the moment. He was sitting on the edge of his bed, waiting until it was time to go, having been long ready.

"Prom tonight?" Gropper asked.

Luke laughed.

The phone rang. Wing. "Lieutenant Tuttle, Colonel Reilly wants to see you."

His mood collapsed. Not now, he thought. Not now. He can't. He just can't. He hastily changed into uniform, his summer tans, his 1505s, muttering under his breath, tension rising. Hopped onto his bicycle and pedaled furiously over to Wing. Not now, not now, not now, he kept saying to himself.

Reilly heard him coming down the hall and stepped out to greet him. All smiles, all warmth and pleasure. "All hail the conquering hero," he said, and clapped Luke on the shoulder. "That was terrific, Tuttle. Really terrific. That was the best mission we've ever had, I'm not kidding you. Truly the best."

The praise filled Luke's head, pushed out antsy worry about getting to the train station on time. For the moment.

"TFA has had some great days," Reilly said, "where we got transshipment points and storage depots, but this was the best day for us, the best day for all of us. We're gonna write you up."

"And my crew?" Luke said.

"And your crew. Anyone in particular?"

"John Constance."

"Our philosopher king?"

"Yessir."

"I just wanted you to know," Reilly said.

45

And now the train slowed to a stop and the passengers began disembarking. He scanned the gathering crowd, anxious, harboring still the idea that Lonnie might not show. This day of clear skies the rich azure blue of fall, the air full of the exotic scent of Khorat. He saw her step down far down the platform and waved. He knew he was all smiles, a shit eating grin that he couldn't help. Lonnie returned his wave, but it seemed to him that she was studied and mannerly, going through the motions like a queen acknowledging a crowd, without enthusiasm. It put him on guard. He suspected what might be on her mind, considering their last conversation. He hoped he was wrong. He would be careful. Still, he couldn't help himself. She was here and there wasn't another thing in the world he wanted. She wore a sleeveless sheath belted at the waist, light blue raw silk that lay soft on her form. His imagination took off; he couldn't wait. He kissed her lightly.

"No PDAs," she whispered.

He wondered where that came from, a thought so unlike their time in Bangkok. "What's that about?" he asked.

"What's what about?" she said. She smiled almost politely and he knew she knew perfectly well that she was being cool and stand-offish, that she was striking a pose. That she wouldn't admit it didn't bode well. He took her overnight bag and led the way through the station to the street, where he hailed a *samlahr* to the Sripatana.

She kept to herself all the way to the hotel, despite the tableau unfolding around them, the central market, the throngs in the streets, the small-town compared to the big city. The *samlahr* rolled up to the front door of the hotel; Luke couldn't hold off any longer. "What is it?" he said.

"What's what?" she said again.

Shit, he said to himself. And to her, "Your stand-offishness."

"I'm not being standoffish." she said.

There was no point. He checked her into the hotel and they took her bag to her room. Top floor. Drapes open, bright sunlight beyond. The view stretched for miles across the Khorat Plateau, the horizon disappearing in distant haze. She stood at the window. "What's that?" she asked, nodding into the middle distance. "It's the air base," he answered, cursing the fact that he hadn't asked about the view, hadn't even thought about it when he reserved the room. A flight of F-4s were taking off, two, then two. The aircraft were mere dots, yet even with a window and distance between them they could hear the boom of their after-burners.

Lonnie shuddered.

"What are they?" she said.

"Aircraft."

She looked at him, tight lipped, eyes hard. He hadn't seen the look before and it was disconcerting, even hateful.

It didn't fit. "Don't play games," she said. "I know they're not B-52s, I've seen those. What are they?"

"F-4s."

"What do they do?"

"They're fighter-bombers."

"Meaning they're on their way to Vietnam."

He nodded. "Probably. Maybe Laos." He kicked himself as soon as he said it. This was not a time for accuracy.

"What?" she said. She turned toward him, again with the hateful look.

He grimaced.

"What's that for?" she said.

"I'm thinking maybe you were right; this wasn't such a great idea after all."

"I'm here, aren't I?" she said.

He chose not to say anything. Knowing there was nothing more he could say that could change or put a better light on reality. And all he wanted was a moment of closeness, a moment when they would put their arms around each other and he would feel needed and wanted and they would be together. He could see no way to get there from here. "I don't know what you expect me to say," he said finally. "Why don't we just go for a walk. Khorat's really an interesting place. It's not Bangkok, more folksy. You might enjoy it."

A row of *samlahrs* was parked outside the front door, backed up to the sidewalk, drivers lolling on the passenger seats of their vehicles, chatting while they waited for fares. They watched Luke and Lonnie exit the hotel, expectant.

"Ride or walk?" Luke said.

"Walk," she said.

They went a short way up Suranari Road and turned

onto the first *soi* they came to. After a few paces the road changed from paved to dirt, rutted and randomly puddled, as if they had just exited through the back of a Potemkin village. The sidewalks disappeared. A young boy sat beside a puddle bestride a broken crate, stirring the water with a stick, his feet in the water, his legs streaked with mud. His tee shirt ragged and large, the stretched-out neck falling off his shoulder. He expressed a look of surprise at Luke and Lonnie. When Lonnie nodded and smiled, he lit up. She responded in kind.

"You made his day," Luke said. She smiled again, happy with the idea.

There was construction everywhere, forms for new sidewalks, foundation work in the fields beyond. Heaps of rock pushed aside, mounds of dirt. At the moment, everything was at a standstill, not a worker in sight. Ahead of them another young boy was tending a racehorse grazing on the grass at the side of the road, holding a rope tied to the horse's halter. He watched them approach, face expressionless. Again Lonnie smiled, and the boy returned the smile. Lonnie slipped her hand around Luke's arm. "This is better," she said. "I like this."

He hoped her mood was turning, the intellectual cloud of her objections moving on, freeing her to be with him. After a moment, she said, "We could live here."

"What?"

"I've thought about it. We could. We could live in Thailand."

They were walking beside a patched concrete wall surrounding an old *wat*. A light breeze rattled the leaves of nearby trees. He thought for a moment. "What would we be doing, living here the couple of months before I leave?

"More than that. You could leave the service now and we could live here for good."

"What're you thinking? I'd be AWOL. I'd be a deserter. We couldn't disappear into the crowd. We'd stick out like sore thumbs. Two *farung* on a back *soi* somewhere, anywhere. They'd have me in a moment. Do you have any idea what that would mean?"

"What?"

"It means that when they caught me, I'd be dead."

"But couldn't you disappear?"

"*Farung?*

"Stop making such a big thing about it."

"It is a big thing.

"Stop!" she said. "You're not being positive about this, you're just tearing down everything I suggest."

"But it's true. We're big in every way. There's no way we can disappear here. Not anywhere in Thailand. And the farther away we get, Malaya or whatever, the more we'd stand out, because we'd be the only ones." He watched to see if she was listening, if she understood what it meant.

She stared at him, silent. "You hate the war," she said. "Just as much as I do. You've said so." There was a glimmer of possibilities in her eyes.

"It wouldn't be easy," he said. "Okay, so maybe in the beginning we could get away with it. For a while. I can't believe we'd be able to for very long. And it's like I said, if I got caught—no, <u>when</u> I get caught—that would be it. You'd go on your merry way, but I would be fucked. They would chew me up and spit out my bones and I wouldn't see the light of day in my lifetime. And that's if I was lucky."

"And I'd just move on? That's what you think of me?"

"I'm just being realistic. The truth of the matter is that I can't just walk away. Not so long ago they shot deserters.

Maybe they don't do that anymore, but I'd spend the rest of my life in Leavenworth, and maybe, if I was lucky, they'd let you visit me now and then."

"What about Cambodia?" Lonnie said. "They could never reach us there. Do we even have relations with Cambodia, any American government officials on the ground?"

"I don't know. I don't even know if we work through another embassy. But I'm certain there would be a way the military would go looking for me. And if they didn't, if we stayed there, we could never go home."

"Does that matter?"

"I'm not sure I could do it," Luke said. "I don't think I could give up home."

"You would if you cared enough."

"I have the greatest respect for the draft dodgers who give everything up for what they believe," he said. "I don't think I'm that big a person."

Lonnie stepped in front of Luke, turned to face him. "We could live there. In Phnom Penh. Surely we could."

"And do what? Live on what? You turning tricks? 'Cuz I don't have a skill. I don't even know the language. I can't even speak Thai, let alone Cambodian."

"Couldn't you be a farmer? Like you are now?"

Luke imagined himself slogging through a rice paddy planting seedlings and laughed.

"Don't laugh at me," Lonnie said.

"I'm not. I'm just imagining myself as a rice farmer. I know nothing, absolutely nothing, about growing rice."

"No, cows. Milk. That's what you do, or did. They drink milk in this part of the world. We buy it. It comes from that place near Saraburi..."

"The Thai-Danish dairy."

"Yes, that place. You could do that, couldn't you?"

Her idea was so beyond the Pale he didn't know how to explain it without sounding condescending and tutorial. The idea of building a dairy in a tropic country, the land he'd have to buy or rent, the equipment he'd need. Refrigeration. The diseases dairy cows might get. Buying the damn cows, getting them from where? It was ridiculously impractical. And money to get started? He couldn't even begin to get his head around the idea, it was too overwhelming, made more so by the magnitude of the idea of deserting. And in the end, he just couldn't give up the idea of going home, some day. He looked at Lonnie, reminded himself that he loved her, but the idea, the mere idea. He simply didn't want to.

At that moment a strange, incongruous noise fell on their ears, washing into their consciousness. Quiet at first, but quickly building. The noise became a torrent, unlike anything either of them had ever heard before. A roar. Demanding attention, sparking a feeling of flight. For a moment Luke wondered what was going on. They were standing next to a small grove of trees and the foliage confused the noise and blocked the view and for a minute Luke couldn't tell where it was coming from and what it was, only that it was loud and growing louder. Then it dawned on him. Aircraft. Lonnie looked at him, questioning. The sound grew and Luke knew it was heading their way and coming full bore, louder and louder. They looked up and an F-4 hurtled towards them not three hundred feet off the ground. The noise became deafening, driving out everything, became the sole center of the world, like a nearby crack of lightning sucking up the air they breathed, stopping time. The F-4 flew into full view, free of the blocking trees, and Luke saw that it was doing a one-hundred mission roll. Lonnie grabbed his arm. The F-4 was above them, so close he could see where the camouflage paint had worn down to metal, he felt helpless in the face of such raw, unbridled power, he didn't want it there, he didn't want it factoring into this day, he wanted it gone, and then it was, continuing its roll as it spun past their horizon and out of sight. A stunning, hollow silence returned.

"What was that?" Lonnie asked, her voice stressed, her face tense with fear.

"An F-4," Luke said.

"Why? What was he doing here? Are they going to bomb someone? Here?"

Luke paused, not wanting to say anything more, wanting the moment to be gone. "He was doing a hundred-mission roll," he said, hoping that would downplay its presence, turn it into something non-threatening. "They do that when they're done. It means he's going home."

"Some kind of victory lap?" she said. "Like cars on a race track?" Her voice was still stressed, creeping towards anger.

"No, that's not it," he said. "It's a survival roll. He's done. He made it."

She shook her head. "I don't care. A hundred times he's dropped his bombs? I can't even stand the thought." She looked at Luke. "Just take me back to the hotel," she said. "Take me back! I want to go back to Bangkok!"

"Now? You just got here."

"Yes, now. The next train out. I can't do this. I can't do this anymore. I tried but I can't." She gave him a compli-cated look of distress and resolve devoid of affection. "Just get me out of here," she said.

. . .

THEY DIDN'T MANAGE the next train out, and she didn't want
to take the one at midnight. Morning would have to do.
They agreed at least to meet that night for dinner. Luke
walked her to her room. She opened the door and stood on
the sill, still clearly resolved. Luke saw there was nothing he
could say, and knew that she didn't want him in her room.
He left, and went back to the base.

In early evening, he returned. He called her on the hotel
phone and they met in the hotel restaurant, a plain and
simple space presented as Danish modern—walls decorated
with sterile, manufactured art, plain chairs and tables, a
single orchid on each table, not even a linen tablecloth.
Nothing to distract, adding to his feeling that the world was
emptying. They ate in silence and looked like an old couple
of many years that had exhausted everything there was to
say. Lonnie spoke of the weather, made observations about
the other diners, mostly Thai. It fell flat. Finally he said, "I
saw a future for us. I thought we were pretty special."

"I think we're too different," Lonnie said. "Another time.
Another place. But not now. It wasn't apparent at first, but
now it is."

At the doorway to her room he pulled her close, and for
a moment he was ecstatic when she acquiesced. But then he
sensed that she had gone as cold as a dead fish. They went
into the room and he eased her onto the bed. Realized that
she was going to let him fuck her, but that she was just
playing along, an emotional bystander, letting him know
that it was truly over. She lay there while he unzipped,
undid his belt and dropped his pants. He pushed inside her
but she didn't move. He climaxed and felt like he had just
fucked a soft mannequin. He was embarrassed. He dressed
and searched for words. She said nothing, only looked at
him, her face a blank slate. He left.

He went to the front of the hotel. The row of *samlahrs* waiting for fares had shrunk. He'd never hired one to go all the way back to the base, always it had been a car. He wasn't even sure how far it was, but he knew it would take a while to get there, and that was what he wanted, a long moment to lose himself in the passing night. He nodded to a driver and told him where he wanted to go. They agreed on a price and he climbed aboard. He settled into a corner of the seat.

The *samlahr* started slowly, the driver standing alternately on each pedal, his calves stressing, using his full body weight to gain momentum, shifting back and forth, finally building up enough speed to sit down and settle into a rhythm. The tires *shushed* on the pavement. Luke slowed down, thinking of ways to reach Lonnie, remind her of what they had had. Perhaps, he thought, once the memory of the F-4's hundred-mission roll had faded, she would remember. Perhaps, when she went back to their bungalow, she would remember the good things and want him again.

The *shush* of the tires and the clank of the pedals and the creak of metal faded into the background. Luke watched the world pass by, sizeable newish houses on pilings, Japanese sedans parked beneath. Electric light pouring out open windows. They passed the last street lights and darkness creeped closer. They reached open landscape; lights from occasional houses in the distance peeked through the trees. The temperature fell and he shivered. Snow began to fall, light, silent, cushioning the sound of the tires. He wrapped his arms around himself, trying to keep warm and fend off his overwhelming loneliness, his fear that somehow something warm was gone forever and all that was left was cold, isolating desolation. The smells of Thailand were gone, blanketed in snow. The snow began falling more heavily, and the lights of the base, once apparent in the distance, faded. He could barely make out the white-white-green, white-white-green of the rotating beacon atop the Khorat tower. The snow began piling in the corners of his mind and there was no comfort in it, it was like the isolation and loneliness of his uncle's farm; soon he would be buried and he would be no more.

46

E ngine start in the soft light of dawn, the western sky a dark formless mass. Taxiing for takeoff on runway 24, pausing to be cleared onto the run-up pad.

Ground control: "Batcat Six-five, be advised there is a large cell five miles off the end of 24 heading your way. It's moving fast. Hold your position."

Gropper confirmed the observation on the Connie's radar. He had noted the front at pre-brief, communicated his surprise at seeing a rain storm amid December's cool days to Major Morgan. Now Major Morgan looked at his watch, fidgeted. Rubbed his knuckles back and forth across his mouth, fiddled with the lay of his mustaches. Looked out the window at the growing darkness in the western sky. Gropper feared what might be bothering him—a delay that would disrupt Colonel Crawford's record of on-time take-offs, and a black mark on his own. He settled back in his seat, waiting for the thunderstorm to move through. Five minutes, ten at the most. Not much more. Surely that could sustain any criticism.

Raindrops the size of lima beans began beating harm-
lessly against the windshield and the fuselage, and he felt
snug, like finding cover in a hut in the woods. He loved
moments like this, when everything was full stop and there
was nothing to do but sit in the cockpit and wait. He
indulged the moment and closed his eyes. It was crew day,
the day Woody's men were available to sub on other crews,
and he'd been in a rush since the call in the wee hours. It
had all been a drag until the moment he saw Saint
Lawrence board the crew bus, and he realized there'd be
someone on this flight he knew.

Morgan called the tower. "Request takeoff clearance."

What the fuck? Gropper said to himself and sat forward.

He'd been through lines of fierce weather with Woody
and it was something to be avoided, something he didn't
wanted to repeat, least of all if he didn't have to. "What the
fuck are you doing?" he said to Morgan.

"*We* are going to take off on time," Morgan replied with
feigned authority. He set the brakes and advanced the throttles. "Engineer's throttles," he said to the flight engineer.
"Run-up check list."

"Are you shitting me?" Gropper said. Meanwhile the
flight engineer began working quickly through his checklist.
He returned the throttles to Morgan and Morgan headed for
the runway.

"Jesus!" Gropper said. He turned to the weather radar
again. Watched the cell moving quickly towards their position. *Maybe,* he thought, *maybe we can get around it.*

"Ready for takeoff?" Morgan asked.

"Fuck, no. You have got to be shitting me," Gropper said
again, looking out the window at a landscape haunted by
black skies. "Are you looking out your goddam window?" he
said.

Morgan ignored him. His lips were tight, his look determined. He turned on the intercom. "Crew, this is the aircraft commander. This is going to be a normal takeoff as per squadron regulations. Fasten seat belts. Be advised there's a cell off the end of the runway and it's going be a little bumpy on takeoff."

Gropper looked again at the weather radar. "Jesus, look at that," he said. "And it's moving fast. We wait just a minute it'll be gone!"

They began takeoff roll.

I could abort this mother, Gropper thought. Pull the feather buttons, turn off the ignition switches. He knew he could, but he couldn't bring himself to do it, he couldn't imagine the repercussions. "Jesus!" he said, louder than before, wanting to get through to Morgan, knowing full well and fearing that he wouldn't listen. <u>What</u> an <u>ass</u>hole, he screamed to himself. And then: It's hopeless. He worked to keep the fear in his gut under control.

They accelerated down the runway and reached the point where there wasn't enough room to stop. That's it, Gropper thought. That's it. All that's left is hope.

They took off into a ferocious headwind. Then, in a minute, a tailwind hit, and they started losing what little altitude they had gained. The stall warning went off; Morgan started pulling back on the wheel.

"For God's sake!" Gropper shouted, "Don't you know anything?" He leaned into his column, pushing hard to counteract Morgan. "We need speed," he shouted; at the same time Morgan shouted "Get your hands off the column!"

The right wing dipped and Gropper slammed his foot onto the left rudder to counter the rotation, but it was too late. Just like that it was over. The Connie rolled onto its back and began falling like a rock, breaking through the storm at 200 feet. From nowhere Gropper heard Country Joe and the Fish,

> *And it's one, two, three, what are we fighting for*
> *Don't ask me I don't give a damn, next stop is Vietnam*
> *And it's five, six, seven, open up the pearly gates*
> *Ain't no time to wonder why, whoopee we're all gonna die.....*

47

Luke and his crew searched through the wreckage, grey human forms appearing and disappearing in mists that swirled like smoke through the ruins of the downed Connie. Grey the day, grey the wreckage, grey the sodden ground into which the wreckage seemed slowly to be sinking, as if the marrow had been sucked from the earth and only a begging vacuum remained. The air reeked of spilled fuel. They treaded carefully, kicking over unrecognizable pieces of metal, looking for documents, maps, pilots' briefcases, navigators' briefcases, intelligence officer's briefcase, the code paddle.

The Connie had crashed upside down, and most of the fuselage had collapsed. Some structure remained in the intelligence compartment, and consoles hung like stalactites from what was now a ceiling. Melted plastic hung like jungle vines. Luke pushed them out of his way. He picked his way slowly to what had been the intelligence officer's position. Rainwater dripped off the ripped skin and fractured ribs of the fuselage, fell on the back of his neck, slid down the inside of his fatigues like cold blood. He cringed.

Nothing was where habit told him it should be. He bumped into the intelligence officer's console, banging his head on the display screen. He swore that he saw a sensor number glowing in the dim light, as if current still flowed through the electronics like a last spark of life. Logic told him it could not be, but he was certain he did, and it felt as if he had stumbled onto a hidden truth...that their electronic wall, the sensors and radios, the screens and computers and printers that spewed data at TFA, had a life of their own that had nothing to do with life itself and the reality of supplies and troops moving down the Ho Chi Minh Trail, with A1E Sandies and A-26 bombers and F-4 fighters and B-52 bombers dropping ordnance, with build-ups in the south and with men's lives lost in a Connie that didn't need to be taking off into a storm in the pre-dawn darkness. This so-called war would suffer the same ignominious end as the crashed Connie, and like the Connie it would glow with a hideous life of its own forever.

He slipped on a splotch of blood become a puddle in the rain. A rivulet formed and flowed beneath a piece of fuselage. He didn't connect it to anything; he couldn't. He didn't want to. Where had Saint been sitting? Maybe in the intelligence center, maybe forward in one of the passenger seats. Gropper he knew. He'd leave the cockpit search to someone else.

Four Thai workmen had been killed that morning as well as they walked on the road near the end of the runway, hit by wreckage. He wondered where their bodies had been found; all the bodies had been removed by the time he and his crew arrived for cleanup. At least they didn't have to cope with that. Still he harbored a fear that he would come upon Saint's remains hanging upside down in a chair, eyes open and staring at him, accusing him somehow of allowing all this to happen. And he would be right; it was his fault. He should have done something. He could have.

The wreckage felt small and insignificant, hardly big enough to account for seventeen men. Two maintenance men poked around the crumpled engines. He wondered what they were looking for. The Connie's distinctive tail section survived, right-side up, a dozen feet away from the rest of the fuselage, the three vertical stabilizers overlooking the wreckage like Shakespearean witches.

He stepped over a strip of metal and torn fabric, pushed aside a section of formica countertop with his foot, unwilling to dig down with his hands. So much was unidentifiable. He came across the intelligence officer's briefcase. He didn't know the man. An FNG, a fucking new guy, here barely a month. He dug through the briefcase—pieces of paper, *Stars and Stripes*. The security code paddle. He retrieved the paddle, relieved to have found it. Done here, he thought, wishing he could leave but knowing he couldn't, not yet, not until he and his men had combed through everything.

Molino approached, stepping through the debris. He kept his balance by grabbing onto an electronics rack now stripped of its equipment. "Lieutenant," he said. "Smoke break?"

God, yes, Luke thought, get me out of here. Molino led the way to the tail section. He caught his foot on more debris and nearly fell. Molino grabbed him, held on. "You all right, Lieutenant?" he asked. He paused. "Really?"

Luke nodded.

Rain still fell in dribs and drabs, from clouds that hung low like fog. There was a smell of ozone. He felt empty, his insides evacuated. He couldn't tell where he ended and the rainy mists began. He feared he might simply slip away into the ether, and wanted desperately for some outside force to surround and protect him. It was all too much, too sad. This war, Lonnie, now Gropper and Saint. He felt extraordinarily alone and isolated. Yet he knew that if he tried to talk about it he would lose control and the dam would burst and he would collapse into tears and he wouldn't be able to stop, and he couldn't do that, he just couldn't. He just couldn't.

He and Molino lit up, took deep drags, let the smoke fill them.

"Were you and Lieutenant Gropper buddies?" Molino asked.

"Yeah, sort of," Luke said. "We did some things together. We were roommates and we talked."

THE PHONE in their room rang. He rolled over in his bed, answered it. "Lieutenant Tuttle," he said.

"Duty officer," the voice on the other end of the line said. "Lieutenant Gropper, please."

Luke looked at Gropper's sleeping hulk, his head buried in his bed clothes. "Whatsup?" Luke said.

"He needs to cover Major Morgan's crew today. Pickup at zero one hundred."

"Right, zero one hundred. I'll tell him, He's right here."

He hung up, got out of bed and went over to Gropper and shook him. "You get that?"

"Yeah, zero one hundred. Who with?"

"Colonel Morgan."

"Oh, Jesus. That asshole."

"Sorry 'bout that, Vietnam."

"Yeah. No shit."

Luke was wide awake now, and watched Gropper pick up his toilet kit and head for the latrine. In a few minutes, he returned, still seemingly half asleep. He pulled on his flight suit, picked up his jacket and web belt and headed out of the room. He stopped at the door, hand poised over the light switch. "You still awake?" he asked.

Luke grunted.

"I had a dream last night. I've never dreamed about you before, but I dreamed we were swimming together in the North Atlantic. No one else, just you and me. Don't ask me how I knew it was the North Atlantic, it just was, and I knew it. We couldn't see the shore, but it didn't matter. We didn't talk, we weren't talking. We were just swimming. The sun was shining. And we were happy. And it felt like we were going to swim forever." He paused, turned out the light, and left, quietly closing the door behind him.

48

December 24, 1968. Tuesday. Christmas Eve. Two more missions and done, home in a week. Part of Luke feared he wouldn't make it, something would go wrong and he'd buy the farm somewhere between now and then. Short-timer jitters. Something stupid and wildly unpredictable and therefore something he couldn't guard against. Not really, but yes, really. He knew the idea was pathetic, full of all the superstitions of flying, the omens and crashes that came in threes, there, down deep, in his gut. Why not? An accident in a bus or a taxi. Riding his bike to squadron. In a *tuk-tuk* in Bangkok, never mind that he couldn't conjure any part of his trip home that required a ride in a *tuk-tuk*. Why would he take a motorized *samlahr* anywhere? Absurd, yes, but wasn't everything? Wasn't everything ridiculous? Hadn't everything lost all sense and meaning? Wasn't everything a waste?

Mostly he was marking time, willing the minutes to pass until the moment he'd leave. Sitting on the portico, drinking beer. Tracking the sun across the vibrant blue sky of the Khorat plateau, watching shadows move across the portico and lawn. Staring so closely at the setting sun that he could see the earth move beneath it. How small it felt; how small he felt. Watching the hootch girls at their work. And the crews coming and going. Everyone was a short-timer; every day someone said good bye. Sporting the open-ended Thai lei around their necks, given by their hootch girls, a token of farewell and good luck. Acting a little strange, each with their own brand of jitters. They were all emotionally crippled, though so many of them didn't know it; it would be years before they healed, and only then, like bobbing to the surface of a pond, would they realize there was a large, beautiful, vibrant world out there that they had long ago lost.

There wasn't even anger. Not yet. That would come when they got home, those who could afford to, those that got out. That, and the bitterness. It wouldn't be because he and any of the others were spat upon. That never happened, not to him, nor to any of his fellow crew members. He didn't doubt that it happened to some; just not to him. No, it would be the careerists that would set him off, those who made decisions always for selfish reasons, never with an eye to consequences, never with an eye to their fellow men. Those who had lived closely with other men and never realized the significance. And the fear mongers, who whipped up crowds for their own purposes, and were always dumbfounded when people responded with brutality and ugliness. And the sad ones, who could not accept that their loved ones had died for no good reason, and could never question nor say no to this, nor any war.

A vision came to him of late fall on the farm, corn harvested, so many stalks remaining. Broken down, worn-out, unable even to sway in the wind. And come winter, the odd stalk poking up forlornly through the vast expanse of drifted snow. And in the spring, plowed under. His cycle of life.

He went to the refrigerator, found a mango, flipped a quarter into the change basket. Stood at the edge of the sidewalk and ate, dripping onto the grass. Thought of Lonnie. It pained him. He didn't want to think of her, but she popped into his mind as inexorably as the rising tide. He went to bed early, slept facing the wall, haunted by Gropper's bed lying empty across from him. Soon base housing would assign someone to take his place; he hoped he'd be gone by then, so he wouldn't have to expend the energy necessary to make conversation to someone new.

He woke in early morning darkness, moved by rote, shit, shower, shave, alone in the latrine. His movements echoed off the hard tile, shower water gurgling in the drain. Insects of unknown name circled the light bulbs over the mirrors. He donned his flight suit, picked up his gear. Breakfasted at the club alone and in silence. Sat in a beach chair waiting for the crew bus. Others came by. Woody. Captain Marcetti, Bronfmann's replacement, a caricature of a navigator. Tall, thinning hair, heavyset, paunch straining against his flight suit. A cigar stuffed in the corner of his mouth that he never lit. Lieutenant Davis, another FNG, this mission's substitute for Gropper.

Quiet ruled on the crew bus. Everything moved in slow motion, as if underwater, the air dense, movements tedious. They gathered in Wing, took their seats like cows filing into the barn from the field, automatically going to their accustomed stanchions. Davis fumbled to find an appropriate seat. Reilly waited patiently on the dais, resting his pointer over his shoulder.

Molino sat behind Luke and whispered over his shoulder, "Ask him when we're going back to Pink."

Reilly overheard. "Pink is no more," he said. "We're not going back. Sorry 'bout that."

"Really?" Luke said.

"Not enough convoys to warrant the mission."

"But we caught them out in the open."

"As I understand it," Reilly said, "TFA made the argument that our mission is to find convoys on the Ho Chi Minh Trail, not transshipment points going into the DMZ. Someone else is supposed to handle that. Your mission was a blip. They want us back on their orbits."

"Were there no others? No others as successful as us?"

Reilly shook his head.

Luke nodded, Molino sat back. *Maj pen rai.* Soon they'd all be gone.

He didn't realize it was Christmas Eve day until they'd boarded and he'd finished pre-flight. He was sitting at his position, reading, when he heard voices singing carols. He put his book down and followed the sound forward to the cockpit where Tanaka and John Constance were in the aircraft commander's and co-pilot's seats, singing along to Armed Forces Network on the cockpit radio. Bing Crosby, *White Christmas.* Outside, brown and dry to the horizon, the sky clear. A light breeze blew dust devils across the tarmac. He went back to his seat.

The mission was a yawn. He opened three positions, but there was nothing. A few hundred activations, most seemingly spurious. Rickey made spaghetti again. Luke ate last and lingered at the galley table watching the western sun track across the galley walls. He returned to his position for changeover and the flight home. The enlisted men cleaned their positions, stripped the masking tape off the panels, swept the Connie fore and aft. Luke dozed and was awakened on final approach by the smell of charcoal rising from the kilns of Khorat. After touch down and while the plane was still taxiing John Constance and Tanaka dragged the jugs and trash and gun box to the aft galley. That wasn't the way it was supposed to be, but who cared. They popped the hatch. John Constance stood in the open doorway, holding onto the door frame. Tanaka sat on the gun box. They watched the flight line pass. Luke joined them. Strangely, looking forward, he glimpsed himself still sitting at his position, still with his earphones on, still dutifully watching his screens. Twilight crept throughout the plane, obscuring details. Luke saw snow building in the deepest recesses of the plane, soon to spill into the open. John Constance lit a joint, passed it to Tanaka, who dragged and passed it to Luke. He toked and was a million miles away. Their smoke wafted out the open hatch. One more mission to go, but he felt like he would be flying forever, doing useless work for people who couldn't care less, certainly wouldn't care about the Vietnam War. Forever and forever and forever Vietnam. He wouldn't have a choice. The very thought exhausted him. There was only existence, flat, empty, devoid of sense, a cold wind blowing through. All of it would come falling back on him, like a dormant disease awakened, the feeling of having been abandoned, that they were all mere ciphers. He shivered, knew finally that looking for, expecting something or someone to care about—or care about him, really care, help him through the pain—was dead. Somewhere, sometime, somehow, a cocoon of numbness had encapsulated him, he knew not how, not even that it was there, and it protected him from anything more, like the snow, cold, deep, drifting, soon to bury them all.

www.ingramcontent.com/pod-product-compliance
Lightning Source LLC
Chambersburg PA
CBHW070626260626
47161CB00007B/2596

* 9 7 9 8 9 8 8 3 1 5 9 0 2 *